HORNS & HEAT

HORNS TRILOGY | BOOK ONE

R. N. ARCADIA

To everyone who questions who is looking back in the mirror
and doubting your worth.
You are more than your weight, and you deserve love no
matter what your body size is.
Fuck societal expectations of beauty.

Ritualistic Suicide; non-binary side characters; death & trauma of a loved one; big, *scary* demons; bullying (not by MCs); low self-esteem/body image issues, two-peens, breakup trauma; depression; anxiety; metabolic disorder.

A protective demon cinnamon roll, and all the 18+ spice!

If there were any content warnings I missed, it wasn't intentional.

BECS

YOU ARE
BEAUTIFUL

ONE

BECS

"Lock your doors and windows or they'll sneak in and bargain for your soul!" The news anchor howled as I did some unassuming task.

I rolled my eyes, huffing out a laugh. Apparently, demons were running loose. All around the globe was slowly becoming infected with creatures ready to take your soul.

I thought it was another fucking hoax put together as another 'the apocalypse is coming!' propaganda move by religious zealots, but what did I know? I've never come across one that I know of. Would I even care if I did?

Probably not.

Demons would make life more interesting, that was for sure. What would a demon want with little ol' *me?*

As I mindlessly picked out work clothes for the following day, my mind pictured several scenarios of a horned demon climbing in my window on the top floor of my apartment complex. *And falling.* Who knew, maybe a demon would fly off into the sunset afterwards?

I giggled, grabbing work pants and laying them on my pink velvet chair in front of my vanity.

As funny as something like that would be in my mundane life, it did make me wonder. Did the demons look scary like in some movies, or were they hot? Or both? Maybe they were sad and lonely, like me, too.

Pushing my wavy brown hair out of my face, I stared at my reflection. A battle I often lost was one with the mirror. I was no one special, certainly not worthy to be the main character in anyone's story—not even my own... Certainly not this math-nerd cosplayer.

Who writes about that stuff?

Geek-slash-introvert aside, I was a product of society and low standards, and a health condition that made it hard to lose weight. Curvy people like me were judged whether we had confidence or not. Personally, I found the whole societal construct around weight equating worth to be stupid.

My opinion was also slightly biased, thanks to my douchebag ex-boyfriend. I mean, can you blame me for being bitter when he cheated on me supposedly because of my weight?

A bleak outlook on life wasn't great but as a twenty-six-year-old, recently graduated student with my master's in mathematics, I had nothing to show for it.

Like so many others, I got a degree only to end up working in a completely different field.

I know, I was disappointed, too.

Student loans and credit card debt, what *fun.*

Said no one ever.

My current job was a miserable receptionist office job at one of the skyscrapers in downtown Atlanta. The boss was a tool bag and so was his snobby assistant.

Working, and going home every day—exciting, right?

Well, there were some exciting things such as designing my own cosplays for cosplay conventions. It gave me reasons to look forward to something not so monotonous. Cosplays and conventions helped with my creativity and confidence. Boring in everyday life, but fuck, *I was a kickass cosplayer.* I had one friend, Figgy, that I knew who also enjoyed conventions, but unfortunately, they didn't live near me, so I only ever saw them when any conventions occurred.

Either way, pretending to be anyone else was a welcome change.

I lived alone in the city, while my family and siblings lived out of state. Not that I minded much as I tended to bicker with my oldest sibling and be lectured by my mother. We were close, but not too close because I enjoyed my much needed distance and space.

With a flick of the lights in my apartment, I was soon shrouded in darkness. Alone, just as I liked being. No one could hurt me if I was alone.

Huffing a long, steady sigh of what my life had become, I flopped onto my bed, staring up to watch the shadows dance along the ceiling.

My gaze turned to the side where the window was. *What if something changed?*

If only I could morph into a dragon cosplay and fly away to something bigger and better. Be anyone else, rather than this body I was given.

No one else had hypothyroidism in the family. The knowledge of being the odd one out plagued me.

But oh well. I'd worry about life tomorrow.

My problems weren't going anywhere. I *should* take charge of my life.

Tomorrow.

BECS

$(x-$

$y^2 = z$

$\frac{d}{dy} = \lim_{\infty} \frac{dx+2}{dy-1}$

$+a)$

$\sin x$

$e = \cos x + tg y$

$(y-1)$

$\sin a = b^3$

YOU ARE
BEAUTIFUL

TWO

BECS

There was a phrase I came up with for Friday's. Instead of TGIF, it was TFIO.

Thank fuck, it's over.

Unfortunately, the day was only beginning as I grabbed a coffee from a cafe on my way to work. The stifling Atlanta air permeated my nostrils. I sipped my iced latte, my shoulders relaxing slightly as the caffeine took hold of my system and pushed my way through the small groups of people on the street taking shelter in the fans scattered on the cafe's outdoor patio.

As I made my way to the office, the buildings were looming all around as the storm clouds rolled in above, the scent of the city morphing into rain.

I walked through the glass double doors towards my destination at the front desk in the lobby. I began to organize between my to-do files and my completed pile. I logged in and checked my email, finding twenty unread emails on scheduling appointments. Definitely a busy morning ahead, that was for sure.

I was an hour into scheduling all the meetings in

various calendars when my boss walked in with his assistant in tow. He wore a beige suit, looking like the total tool he was.

His assistant, Katherine, wore way too much makeup, hair extensions, and long ass nails that were freshly manicured. A sneeze from her strong—*but not in a good way*—perfume lingered in my nose. She was full of herself and the biggest bitch. Because she had a smaller stature, she automatically proclaimed herself as better than me. She made sure to remind me constantly as if we were in middle school.

Although her name was Katherine, she didn't like it shortened to Kat or Kathy as it pissed her off.

She was part of the reason I hated eating at work as she always had a comment to make.

Should you be eating that?

Did you eat all the donuts again?

Don't hog all the carbs.

Or, my favorite one, when she turned down her nose at the last Christmas party over freshly baked chouquettes because she was dieting. *"None for me thanks but offer it to Rebecca—she'll eat everything."*

Had I not been at work, she would have *caught these hands*. Good thing I'm a professional and not a toddler.

Shaking the memories from my mind, Katherine gave me an unimpressed look as my boss, David, greeted me. "Good morning, Rebecca. Please hold all my calls until noon, and buzz me down when the merger clients arrive at eleven a.m. Remember to smile when they arrive, because if all goes well, then the meeting next week with Toom, their investors and ours, the merger will be successful. A profitable window of opportunity. We will be the *new Toom*. Production won't manage itself."

"Yes, sir," I said, and he nodded, walking off with his scowling bitch behind him.

Katherine rolled her eyes at me before they left. I offered no smile in return, just a deadpan expression to match her shitty attitude. *Toom, what a weird name.*

The phones began ringing off the hook fifteen minutes later, and that kept me busy until eleven a.m. when a small group of men walked in.

They looked like they belonged in Men in Black; typical eye candy. A Black male with piercing blue eyes strutted up to my desk first, and we greeted each other with an equally matched smile.

"I'm here to see David Smith."

"Of course, he'll be right with you. Can I offer you any refreshments or answer any questions?" I sounded so hospitable and professional. *Customer service voice —activated.*

"No, but thank you. It's nice to see a genuine, smiling face. We'll wait for him," the gentleman answered, and I gave him another friendly, customer-service smile. It was my default work-mode, despite what David said.

I clicked the button on the phone that fast-alerted my boss instead of me physically calling him.

Sure enough, he showed up two minutes later with Katherine, and they led the men out of our large glassed lobby area.

About an hour later, I saw the group leave, and they all smiled at me as if I did something spectacular.

Weird.

"See you next week," Mr. Sexy Secret Agent said.

I nodded with a smile, telling them to have a good weekend.

It seemed like the meeting went according to plan if

they were returning the following week. David came up to the desk five minutes later with Katherine in tow, *of course.*

"There's sandwiches in the cafeteria, Rebecca, and thank you for doing such a good job up here, welcoming the guests who enter."

I nodded, feeling slightly awkward. It was my job, after all, but the compliment felt weird and out of the norm.

"Thank you," was all I could think to say.

I ignored Katherine's look and her spiteful tone as they walked away. "Oh, David, don't you know? Rebecca is watching what she eats."

"Very well, then," he responded back before they both disappeared towards one of the breakrooms.

I entwined my fingers, squeezing hard before my mouth got me into trouble.

I swear if I ran into that bitch outside of work, I would have some words *and* some hands for her!

Another grumble slipped from me, silencing the phones, and I clocked out for lunch. I ended up just walking for exercise, because leave it to Katherine to get under my skin.

With another heavy sigh, my thirty minutes blinked by, and I was back at my station, finishing the day up.

Thank fuck, it's over.

The rain poured as lightning flashed overhead. The smell of rain gave me a sense of relief as I made my way to my gray car, half-wet. I cranked the engine, relaxing into the seats before driving to the mall for some needed retail therapy.

It was my favorite store *and only plus-sized store* due to the confidence boost I always received, but plus-sizing aside, the workers were great, too. It always uplifted my mood, as the workers were plus-sized themselves and it broke the weird taboo people held on *fat* people. We existed and we were *not* fucking lazy.

A sales associate stopped me as I was browsing absent-mindedly.

"Is there anything I can help you find?" A sweet voice lulled me out of the storm cloud that matched the weather outside.

I blinked at her, realizing she was talking to me. Distracted by her gorgeous dark purple hair, a thought crossed my mind.

"Yes, actually." I went on, "Do you have anything that says, *this is my sexy at-home outfit for feeling confident?*"

She tapped her chin, thinking and looking around before pausing and inclining her head with a cheeky all-knowing grin.

"Yes, a couple of things right over here meet those requirements. We just restocked these, too." She led me over towards sexier fits.

Maybe, I should just abort that silly mission? Tell her I changed my mind?

She grabbed a lingerie piece that had lacey parts along with some sheer mixed in. It was all black and *very* alluring. It sure as hell wasn't my go-to of an oversized t-shirt.

"There's also this if you're *really* feeling some type of way," she indicated towards a black sexy bedroom outfit. There were matching garters and bustiers with the whole works. It was intriguing, but I hesitated as I always did. The voices of the past and present nagged at me.

I didn't realize they made clothes like that in your size.

It must take a lot of confidence to wear something like that on your figure.

Your tummy is showing.

"I'm not sure if I could pull that off," I admitted quietly

as the gorgeous lady took a step back with an odd look on her face. I grabbed my arm, positioning it over my stomach awkwardly, feeling exposed.

"I know we're supposed to lie to customers for the sales, but honey, you could pull this look and that one. *I mean that.*" She indicated to the two things she showed me and gave me a serious look. She wasn't joking.

I sighed in defeat, not quite believing her but gave in. "Do you have these in a 16 or 18? My bra size is 38 DDD."

The lady grinned. "Coming right up. I'll have it waiting at the front for you. Please, keep looking around while I do so and feel free to ask for recommendations—I'm great with styling!"

She walked away as I kept looking, finding a few comfortable shirts with funny slogans on them, and a couple of new pieces to try something new. I was feeling inspired.

I eventually checked out, paid with my credit card, and left with the large bags, happily satisfied after thanking the woman for her help.

I grabbed a soft, salty pretzel on my way out of the mall for a treat. A scowl covered my face as Katherine's voice popped into my head. *"Wow, Rebecca, another carb? I thought you were watching what you eat?"*

Fuck, I'd kill for one of those demons to eat that condescending bitch. In fact, I'd probably sell my soul then buy some popcorn and a fucking Dr. Pepper to watch that shit happen.

With a small smile at the thought, I drove to my apartment twenty minutes outside the inner city. After belting out off-key songs on the radio as my sister, Penny, would do, I was already feeling a lot better than when I left work.

I made it to my third-floor apartment, quickly putting away the items, minus the negligee I laid on my vanity. I sat on the edge of my bed, eyeing the lace from afar. The thought that I should have put it back at the store plagued me. I couldn't stop thinking that it would look terrible on me; that I was so hideous that I shouldn't even try wearing it. My head was spinning with traitorous thoughts.

I nibbled on my fingernail, my leg shaking erratically.

"Get it together, Becs!" I shouted, shooting up from my place on the bed. "It's literally a piece of fucking lace, it should not have this much control over your goddamn mind!"

I smacked the lace like a pissed off cat and stormed into the bathroom, slamming the door behind me. I stared at myself in the mirror, trying to talk myself out of the downward spiral I was heading into.

"Jesus, Becs!" I screamed, racking my hands down my face. Huffing, I walked over to the shower, turning it on, rocking back and forth.

I tried to wrack my brain for a happy song to sing, hoping it would help the spiral. *I got a pocket, got a pocketful of sunshine* started echoing in my brain. I groaned; of course, it would be the quintessential 2000's happy song to get stuck in my brain. *Whatever.*

I took a deep breath, wrapped the towel around my body, and felt slightly better.

Padding back into my bedroom, I grabbed the lace from my vanity and put it on before the spiral could start again.

Adjusting myself in it, it covered my large breasts perfectly. *At least I wouldn't poke my eyeballs out.*

I hopped around, struggling to pull on the matching lace underwear and getting them to sit perfectly.

I hung up the wet towel, braiding my long hair and then finally opted to look at my reflection.

"Well, shit. Not bad, Becs."

I turned to the side. Then the other and did a little turn-around to see my ass. A curvy cutie was what I was. *A little fupa never hurt anyone.*

With something so seemingly simple, too. I was certainly feeling myself in the sexy bedroom wear. It was a confidence booster, after all, even if I didn't have anyone to wear it for. There was nothing wrong with dressing for yourself.

I put on my current favorite playlist on my phone and danced my way into the kitchen, deciding to make a salad for a late eight p.m. dinner. While wiggling my hips, the more I moved around and wore the thing, the better I felt. The lacey babydoll was growing on me. A small part of me felt stupid, but for the majority, it was just what I needed to drown out all the unnecessary noise in my head.

I sat at the small table I had in my kitchen to eat. The kitchen was opened to the living room; the couch could be seen from where I sat. I was still proud of that thrift find. A flat screen was mounted to the wall from a Black Friday sale two years ago. The only thing I really spent money on were clothes and cosplays, the rest I bargained for.

My student loans would be paid off within the next decade—well, *hopefully anyway.*

Whoever said college and grad school was the way to prove yourself was a money-grabbing idiot. *Which, in turn, made me an idiot.* What sane person pays over fifty grand for a piece of paper that says, *"Yes, I went and learned this thing, and I know something."*

Grad school is just that, with the added pizzazz of, *"I can do the thing even better now!"*

Sighing to myself in contentment, I finished dinner and turned the music off. Another few hours passed as I binge-watched a new Asian drama show before calling it a night.

The bachelorette life sure was fun. I had been living it for three years. After a while, I just didn't bother with trying; what was the point? My confidence was also a fickle thing after the breakup.

I realized people went through their lives, then they'd get complacent in relationships and forget about themselves, living for someone else. Then, shit happens, and people grow apart; you're left in the dust or cheated on. I tried the dating game and those stupid dating apps, and...*gross*.

Don't get me wrong, I wouldn't turn down a hookup just to scratch an itch, and hell, I did indulge one time, but that was the most boring sex I *ever* had. A vow to myself was made after, I'd rather masturbate and have multiple orgasms than none from some douchebag who doesn't know where the clit was. *Fucking Christ.*

Despite my nightly ritual of having an orgasm before bed—because fuck, life was too short to not have an orgasm at least once a day—I decided to pass it up. I was too tired.

Sleep found me fast, and I ended up having a sexy dream about a dark-haired stranger, and by luck, the stranger looked in my direction.

The things we did after that... Well, multiple orgasms from both parties were had.

BECS

YOU ARE
BEAUTIFUL

THREE

BECS

The sound of my floorboards creaking woke me up at 6:66 am.

I cocked my head, rubbing my eyes. *"What the—"* I looked back at the clock, my vision no longer blurry. 3:33 a.m. showed back in bright red numbers.

I fell back in bed, my eyebrows wrinkling. I could have sworn I saw 6:66. I pulled the covers over my shoulders, as a crisp cool breeze wafted over me. A shiver raked my body, sending goosebumps crawling down my legs and arms. My eyebrows wrinkled again as a realization washed over me. *I never opened a window last night.*

A soft creak echoed through my bedroom. More awake and aware with sleep a distant friend, in its place there was an awareness of something—*or someone*—in my room.

My heart began to race as I raised my head and saw a huge shadow standing at the edge of my bed. I sat up, immediately slamming my body into my headboard. The shadow —no, the giant fucking *monster*—moved into the moonlight illuminating its features.

Before me stood a seven-foot-tall form with a tail that

swished back and forth, spiraled horns that protruded through dark, black hair, and pale blue eyes that glinted in the moonlight. I sat stunned as both the monster and I stared at one another, until a strange scent wafted through my bedroom. I blinked a few times to make sure I still wasn't asleep.

It was the tail swishing from side-to-side that made reality seep into me.

What the hell was even happening?

What was that scent?

"Do you normally stand in a stranger's room, watching them sleep like a weirdo?"

I couldn't think of anything else to say, and I wasn't scared per se, just confused.

A deep, masculine voice came out of the creature. Dare I say it—he sounded sexy.

"No... I'm not surprised by a beauty like you having the sexual energy that lured me here."

Ignoring his statement, I asked another smart question. "Are you sure you have the right place?"

Realizing again what he had said, I felt myself warming up at the words *sexual energy*. I didn't realize sexual energy was a thing? *Who knew?*

The tall ass creature leaned forward, placing his hands on the edge of the bed, and I could make out more features. Tail—confirmed. Horns—check. Definitely male, too, by the way the hips formed a V with ungodly muscles, but who was I to say? Can't forget the strange, unnamable, tantalizing scent consuming my sense of smell, either.

It was certainly not a creature, but a half-giant, human-like demon.

Maybe this was one of the demons the news kept talking about?

He had thick muscular thighs—from what I could see—and more corded muscles up his arms, wearing absolutely *no* shirt; *like who does that?* There was what appeared to be medium-length dark hair, and his skin looked to be bronze in color. He was also buck-ass naked.

The more I tried to focus my eyes, I couldn't quite tell, but his low tone erupted through me and my daydreaming.

"Yes. Although, I'm certainly not complaining. Do you normally wear that kind of thing to bed?" He indicated his head towards me.

I looked down at myself, "N-No."

A wave of insecurity passed over me.

He already saw me; it wouldn't matter now. *Also, let this demon look. HE* came in here; if he didn't like what he saw—he could leave.

Oh hell, what was I even thinking?

I took hold of the comforter, almost deciding to bring it up to cover myself, but he interrupted me. "You do not need to hide yourself from me. I'm not here to kill you or harm you, unlike my other brethren."

I raised my eyebrow, considering him as he kept his blazing blues locked on me.

"I've heard the reports... What kind of...*demon* are you? I'm assuming that's what you are, right?"

I felt dumb even asking, but he didn't comment on it being dumb either when he responded.

"I'm a sex demon."

A...what?

He was still leaning forward on the bed, and it made me realize he looked less like a giant and more *human,* minus the horns and tail. A cosplay came into mind over the thought. *Okay, I suppose I'm awake and not dreaming.*

The worry drained from me as intrigue sparked instead

as I took him in again. My eyes had adjusted more, and it was like the more I saw, the more I *liked*.

Was I ill? Maybe I was still dreaming within a dream? I had watched Inception last week... That's what this was. *A demon inception.*

He realized I was doing as much. "It's beyond flattering how you aren't screaming and running from me in terror. Perhaps it's your energy... *That* is delightful." He took a deep breath, inhaling, and closing his eyes.

There was something sexy about the way he did it that another wave of heat washed over me, pooling at my spine and lady bits in satisfaction.

I don't remember it being this hot in my room... Did this guy touch my thermostat?!

He was a demon, maybe he was used to a furnace? *Or Hell. It was Hell, right?*

"Not sure what that means, but if you aren't here to kill me, then what?" I dared to ask the obvious.

His lips turned up with secret intrigue as he opened his eyes again.

"I'm here to worship, never to hurt. And I'm one that asks for permission before doing so."

My brain malfunctioned immediately. *Uh, what?*

Was this dude serious? *With me?* I was having a stroke, which was the only plausible explanation. This was unreal.

Wake up, Becca! Dreaming of dark-haired strangers and demons—you might be losing it.

Also, just what kind of weird energy did I give off? *Did being horny and lonely come with a scent?*

If so, that was fucking embarrassing.

I had never heard anyone say anything like that to me *ever*. My inner heat stayed, desire overtaking me next.

Calm down, girl, don't get crazy.

I mentally cursed my vagina for being slutty and taking over.

"I've...never been worshipped before," I admitted quietly, looking away in shame.

When I turned my eyes back to him, I found his claws fisted in my sheets, showing restraint.

While my brain was loading, a husky edge to his tone echoed, "I'll be more than happy to demonstrate for you. That is why I'm here, after all."

I wanted to understand him better then, a different perspective, too. I couldn't see *why* of all the people in this city, he was in *my* room.

"Help me understand why you're here in my room. What does it all mean? How does... *this* work?"

We shared a gaze before he answered. *With the way he looked at me, I couldn't tear my eyes away.*

"I was nearby." He pointed his thumb toward the window as the curtain moved with the breeze. "I caught your scent...your sexual energy. It's what lures me, you know, with what I am. Yours was radiating so much, I *couldn't* ignore it. Think of it as a *calling* or *summoning*. Now, here *we* are."

Still not entirely sure I understood, my eyes found his form again in the dark.

"If you decide to grant me permission to touch you, I will spend the remainder of the night worshipping you as the goddess you are. No strings attached if you want. Since you treated me surprisingly well at my entrance, you can keep your soul."

He said it as if it were a normal transaction...

"S-Soul?!" I pulled the covers up over myself then as if it would help.

"Yes. *Soul*. But I promise, it wouldn't be in vain, nor

would it be so terrible. Despite what horror stories you've probably heard, I am not like everyone else. Cliché as it sounds, I'm sure, I don't get pleasure from taking unwilling souls. It's more like an exchange than dragging you to Hell. It doesn't work like that. I'd be yours and you'd be mine."

Somehow, in my lizard brain, it sounded strangely romantic. An exchange of souls, hmm? Why did that bring the warm fuzzies to my lonely heart?

"That sounds fair. Thank you. I agree to tonight... But I want to apologize first."

He stood up to his full height then, crossing his arms, seeming conflicted.

"Whatever for?"

Let's get this insecure shit over with.

I sighed in defeat and began my spiel. "I'm the woman that gets overlooked. No one finds curves like mine sexy or desirable. Unless it's a joke. It's why I bought this silly thing," I said as I relaxed my hold on the covers and indicated at the bedtime sexy wear.

I began to ramble then. "I felt different when I put this on. The people at work are assholes, and I'm a loner. Needing to feel less insecure, I went shopping. I...haven't been touched by someone in a long time. Other than myself, of course. I'm afraid you'll find me disappointing to waste a night with."

He seemed troubled still, almost fidgety, before he yanked the covers away from me completely.

I stared at him, shocked.

You okay, dude? Was it something I said?

"The *only* thing that would disappoint me is if you turned me away. Humans are assholes to begin with."

You got that right, buddy.

"*I'm not human,* and I would never dream of making

you feel that way. If after tonight you decided to continue forward and share souls, *I'd like to fix things.* For tonight, it's all about *your* pleasure. No strings attached as I said. You need to give me full permission but before anything else... What is your name?"

I barely hesitated or thought about it—I knew for certain what I wanted.

Goddamn it all, I'm a sinner.

"Rebecca, but call me Bec, or Becs. I give you full permission to touch and worship as you please... Shall I call you by anything?" I asked him, adjusting my legs in front of me, which he paid special attention to, as need drove me forward.

I heard a small noise of approval as he gripped the sheet and pulled it, bringing me closer to him at the edge of the bed.

Not being able to help myself, I wondered how he'd be able to lay in my bed and how far his legs would hang off. *Thinking of the real questions here.*

He was a giant.

Good thing I had nine-foot-tall walls. Poor demon-guy.

Once I was at the edge of the bed, I looked up at him, wondering if he knew about human anatomy better than our human counterparts as he answered.

"Belke is my name, but you can call me whatever you'd like. I give you full permission to touch me as you please, Rebecca. But, before you do, I need to do something first."

I tilted my head as he kneeled, retracting all his claws. I realized this was a sweet gesture so he wouldn't hurt me.

He placed his large hands on my thighs, making me feel small and causing wetness to gather at the apex of my thighs.

"What do you need to do, Belke?" I asked, not recognizing the tone of voice I gave. I couldn't deny my desire after being demon-handled.

"*This.*"

And before I could think, I was on my back, spread wide for him, as he leaned in and inhaled the scent of my pussy. His nose was all up in my business, *literally*.

I wasn't sure what to think as he kissed the outside of my underwear, and I knew immediately I was *hot and ready*.

He used his sharp teeth to tug them down a bit before using his rough-but-gentle hands to take the rest off. The way he squeezed my thighs caused all my senses to narrow in on where he touched *and* where I was throbbing.

This was going to be an interesting few hours.

Belke

FOUR

BELKE

I kneeled before my prize and kissed up her luscious inner thighs. Each side—*slowly*. Her curves were a thing of dreams.

At her confession, of what was no doubt horrid, I internally made a promise that those people who put those thoughts in her head about herself would *pay*. It was the least they deserved for making the beautiful woman before me believe she was anything but.

I shifted her legs over my shoulders, groaning in approval when I met the moisture of her *lips*.

Fuck.

She tasted like the sexual energy I smelled.

Fucking worth it.

I heard her gasp, arching herself up, giving me *more* of her.

I was harder than a sinner on Sunday.

Flicking and teasing her sweet bundle of nerves with my tongue, I felt her hand intertwine into my dark locks.

Little did she know, it was one of my favorite things to have done. It drove me wild, having hands in my hair.

I heard her soft sighs, and I made it my personal mission to hear more from her.

Managing a small peek upward, I realized she was using her other hand, grabbing her breast. *Mmm.*

I focused back in; tonight, I'd take her to new depths.

Slyly, I moved my left hand up under her sexy negligee firmly rubbing up on her soft skin to touch where her hand was outside the fabric.

Breath quickening, I could feel her body build up. Both of her hands gripped and held firmly on me. The energy of her release was building up before the fall of a roller coaster ride drop.

Seconds later, she was shaking in quiet cries.

I'd have to teach her how to scream, then.

She shook still as I flicked her with my tongue on her already sensitive clit.

"Thank you for knowing where the clit is. I'm glad you aren't human."

Surprised by her words, yet still flattered, I began to chuckle.

What an interesting human woman.

"Never been told that before, but I'll take the compliment," I said, sitting on my knees as she sat up, smiling.

"Good, as you should."

The edges of my mouth curled, and she began to move toward me, pushing me toward the floor.

"Since you did what *you* needed to do... *My turn.*"

I felt overjoyed as she climbed over me until she was saddled at my hips.

My horns disappeared as did my tail; Rebecca's hands ran up my bare chest.

"What are *you* going to do to *me?*" I asked, amused to find her smirking like a feline. A purr of appreciation rumbled quietly through my chest. I arched my hips up slightly so that when I did, she could feel my cock pressed up against her ass.

Biting her lip, she reached around, rubbing me.

"Perhaps, I'll take you for a spin," she said. Her gaze turned wicked while my eyes closed in bliss at my lover touching me with eagerness rather than fright.

"I'm in no position to refuse," I whispered, feigning helplessness.

Seeming pleased, she shifted herself down on me, rubbing against me with her wet pussy. Here, *I* was supposed to be doing the seducing, yet I was the one being taken advantage of—or letting her, rather. Demons are curious and inquisitive creatures, like humans, so I wanted to see the depths she'd be willing to go, since I had invaded her space and sleep.

This woman was full of surprises and deliciousness. Good on me for catching the scent of her sexual frustration —her energy. My radar was always on point.

I was interested in seeing more of what she was capable of.

Rebecca moved further down on my naked form, pausing once she straddled at my knees.

"What... am I supposed to do with *that?*"

I sat up on my elbows amused and appreciated her kind words. My form was created for desire, so my cock was ribbed for her pleasure with a barbell at the base for *mine.*

"I can give you some pointers..." I told her as she looked at me in wonder, then up towards my face.

"Are you *trying* to kill me?" She released a squeaking noise that made me laugh in amusement while I decided to baby-step her, sitting up.

"I assure you that it will work out. I'll help. Does my size deter you?"

I had her speechless then as I kept my small smile and maneuvered out from under her and reached for both of her hands.

"Do not be afraid of me. You will adjust, and we'll take it slow until you feel comfortable enough. Okay?" My tone was tender as she stood with me, and I found her even more charming up close.

Her eyes were bright despite the darkness of the room and lighting from the window I came through. The moonlight was just enough that I could see the details of beautiful mixtures of earth colors in her eyes, and I could see faint freckles on her face. My eyes worked differently than her human ones, so I could see details in darkness and dim lighting. Her scent was sweet, and I could smell the fruitiness of her shampoo.

Not being able to help myself, I leaned down, obsessed with her smells, tipping her chin up toward me and capturing her lips that were full and aching to be kissed.

I could tell she hadn't been kissed in a long time, because it took her a minute to adjust to my mouth's movements. But then she matched my need and desperation to have her, slipping her tongue into my mouth. I didn't want to alarm her with my split demon tongue, so I made sure it was more human-like at the start of our interaction.

Having my tail appear again, it brushed against her leg, rubbing slightly. My tail was an extension of me, one that I could make and mold into whatever I chose.

It caused her to giggle as she broke our kiss.

After looking down at where my hairless, smooth tail was on her leg, she smiled before focusing back on my heated gaze. Her reactions were not only humbling, but I was *ready and waiting* for this delightful woman. I only hoped for her soul to be the icing on the cake.

"You're handsome up close, you know," she told me honestly.

Leaning in, I stole a kiss before moving my face away to respond. "You are beautiful, and I want to be buried deep inside you."

I felt her shiver against me as I leaned closer, kissing her cheek then her neck. I placed my hands on her delectable hips, holding her in place as she leaned her head back to give me better access as I trailed my kisses down her shoulder and chest, towards the top part of her breasts. A soft breath escaped her, and I knew she was enjoying the beginning of my worship.

Part of me cursed the universe that such a human never experienced the worship I was offering, and it made me hate humans even more, minus the one I was devouring.

I kneeled, kissing down the center of her. I pulled her closer as I did so and used one hand to cup her shapely ass, and the other went under her negligee.

"You are all woman and the object of all my desires and affection... Will you let me see all of you?"

I looked up as I lifted the garment slightly, kissing her belly and appreciating its soft plushness. She ran a hand through my hair, sighing.

"Perhaps in due time... What was that about being buried deep?" Her voice was wet with seduction as my cock twitched in response.

I smirked up at her and lightly nibbled on her stomach when she caught my gaze, tugging at her own lower lip in anticipation.

I gently nudged her back towards the bed until she laid

back and I crawled over her, positioning my cock at her entrance.

"How long has it been for you?" I asked, feeling curious.

"Long enough that I know it will hurt with your size, so go slow initially. I will tell you when to speed up."

I gave her a satisfied look, capturing her lips. "Works for me. If something's too much, please tell me immediately."

She nodded while I slowly parted her thighs further, positioning myself better at the edge of her bed before easing my cock into her tightness.

Good thing she was already wet and ready. I was throbbing and aching, but I took my time with her because I didn't want to hurt her more than necessary.

I watched her carefully as she gasped between the recesses of pain and pleasure.

Slowly, I inched my way inside her, and I could feel her stretching where she was tight. To contain myself, I bit my lower lip and held back a moan that was desperately wanting to escape my mouth.

Looking down at our bodies, I slowly kept at it before pulling out slightly, then leisurely going back inside her warmth.

Tight and incredible, goddamn.

I was doing everything I could not to take her hard and fast—*no, I'd work my way to it and get her enticed enough to continue with me after tonight. Or so I hoped.* I was after her soul, not just that pleasurable body that was made just for me.

After a couple of minutes, she began to relax more, until she adjusted to me better. Then, the magic words hit, "Alright, fire away, *big boy*. You can speed it up."

Speechless, I found her words pleasurable to hear, undoing any other restraint.

"Be careful what you wish for, Rebecca... Again, if things get to be too much, please tell me."

"Okay."

I increased my pace slightly, gazing down at her as my tail lightly touched her face then made its way down her body. She held back her noises of pleasure, biting her lip.

Immediately, I bent down to tug on her lip, too.

"Don't withhold from me. I want to *hear* you. Whether they are soft sighs or loud cries."

She tugged on my lip in turn as I thrusted a little harder. I heard her gasp while I ran my hands up her body under the garment, squeezing lightly as I made my way up to her breasts.

I positioned my hands, feeling frustrated over the fabric being in my way, and ripped what she wore.

She was surprised, her breath hitching softly, but I didn't give her time to think about the torn garment before my lips and tongue were descending upon the sight of such voluptuous breasts. I lightly used my teeth, and my large hand slipped down to her clit, happy to hear her cry out finally. I focused in until she almost came, and I paused.

"Why'd you stop?" she asked, seeming surprised as I smirked.

I effortlessly pulled her up, turning us so that I was pinned under her so she could straddle me again.

Rebecca huffed out a breath, slowly finding her rhythm atop of me.

I nearly came from the sight of it, of *her*. She was built like a goddess, and I savored every curve.

Moving with her, my hands were on her hips as we watched each other. When she moved faster, taking control, she reached for my hands, moving one back to her clit and the other to her breast. A woman who knew what she wanted and what gave her pleasure—I adored it.

I could feel my own pleasure build, growing as I squeezed and toyed with her, until I finally sat up. The rush of orgasmic energy was all-consuming.

Kissing her fiercely, I felt her orgasm build again by the way her inner walls clenched around me, and this time, I wasn't planning on stopping. I moved my hand to cup the back of her head and the other to hold her backside, pressing tightly against me.

She gave me lovely, light breaths, moaning softly with her arms around my neck and in my hair, driving me over the edge completely.

When we rode our wave of ecstasy, she cried out into my ear as I moaned lowly into hers, holding her head to rest against mine.

We pulsed together, and I felt a strange sort of energy shift, somehow knowing that she was and would always be mine. Not only a sexual connection, but something else entirely.

I kissed her at once as we continued to hold each other in post-sex bliss.

"Belke," she whispered, and my skin tingled slightly at the sound of my name upon her sweet lips.

"How much more stamina and time do you have?" she asked, leaning back slightly looking into my soul.

"For *you*, until the sun comes up, so another hour and a half," I said gently.

"*Good.*" Her words were like silk as I had her turned over on her back as I smirked, leaning down.

"Very well."

BECS

YOU ARE
BEAUTIFUL

FIVE

BECS

When I say, *holy shit,* I mean *hot damn.* Belke fucked me into next week a day early!

He fucked me on a level that my brain stopped working. And it didn't even dawn on me until the sun came up and I cried out in release that *I just fucked a demon. Wowzah.*

It was some good shit!

Before he left, I lay on my side wrapped in my sheet in some sort of sexual bliss. *Is that the proper term for sex with a demon?*

"So, how do I get in touch, if I decide to..." He stood nearby, pulling up his pants I didn't know he had with him with a small smirk on his face.

"I will find *you*. How would you rate your experience this evening?" he asked me coyly.

"Ten out of ten, would fuck again, Bels," I hummed in approval.

He gave me a smug and satisfied look as if I rated his customer service five stars for his demon job promotion of pleasure.

"Bels is what you came up with, hm?"

"Yep!" I gave him a teasing look as his lips curled.

"I like it, and also likewise, *Becs*."

Nearly swooning over the sexy demon in my room, I gave him another look.

"You owe me a new slip. I just bought this less than twelve hours ago."

The morning light came in through the window, and I could see how beautiful he was. Bronze skin with black and gray horns, and beautiful, haunting blue eyes. His dark hair was a mess from our sexcapade, but he had a strong jawline and lickable skin. Perhaps I'd wake up at any moment and realize I fantasized the whole night. It was too good to be true to think otherwise.

I'd happily sell my soul for more of *him*.

There wasn't much of one there anyway.

"Perhaps," he went on, giving me a side glance, "It looks better on the floor anyways."

I felt myself blushing at his words. After such a mind-blowing night, insecurity hit me again. Was I good enough for this hot demon?

We shared a gaze, and I decided to ask the obvious, future disappointment weighing on me. "I won't see you again, will I?"

I'm sure I sounded sad and desperate, but if he just told me up front, then I'd get over it and be thankful for the experience anyway. I'd deal with the self-esteem issues later.

Belke turned around, walking slowly towards me until he was beside the bed where I sat.

"Do you want to see me again?" he asked softly, drinking me in.

Some emotion flashed over his face, so fleeting that I couldn't quite decipher it. He almost looked like he was sad to see what I'd say back, like he wanted to see me again. But I didn't trust myself enough to believe that.

"Yes," I said without hesitation, looking up at him as his expression became sweet. I relaxed instantly at his blue eyes, taking me in like I was someone cherished.

Before he could disappear forever though, I added, "Thank you, Belke, for making me feel less like a monster and more human."

He leaned down, kissing me gently and catching my gaze. "We will see each other again, Rebecca. This, I assure you. I told you, after all, I'm here to worship, not to hurt."

I gave him my own thoughtful look and a smile of understanding at how much I appreciated him and his words. It quieted my anxiety if only for a little while.

He pets my head once, a slight smirk of his own before disappearing into the morning sun right before my eyes as if I really did dream him up.

I stared at where he was before looking towards the window, missing, and craving his touch already. His hands were crafted for pleasure and care, a touch I didn't know could exist.

One thing was for sure; I knew having demons loose in the city would be interesting...

Totally worth it.

I ended up sleeping late into the afternoon, feeling sore but secretly delighting in the tender ache between my legs.

Instead of complaining about walking funny, I was giddy and content.

After bathing again, I ended up lounging around for the

rest of the weekend. I did, however, find a cosplay convention to attend in two months, which I bought my tickets for the entire weekend. Dragon Con.

Making a list, I debated on doing a gender-bend cosplay or being more creative with things.

Part of me thought it would be hilarious to do a demon cosplay. So, I grinned like a child, looking for inspiration until I went to bed, grumbling that I had to work the next day.

Who likes Mondays—not me! There weren't enough iced lattes for it, honestly.

Work shit aside, and the busy week that no doubt lay ahead, I felt like a million bucks after a few hours with Belke. It made me wonder how long it would be until I saw him again.

BECS

YOU ARE
BEAUTIFUL

SIX

BECS

The following Monday and Tuesday, so many people were in and out of the building at work. There were also renovations, interviews, and final contracts signed.

My boss and Katherine were up my ass constantly. She must not have gotten laid, because she was a Grande bitch with extra bark whip and no bite foam. She even went so far as to ask what I was so happy about.

Without faltering or faking it, I told her with a genuine smile how I had a fantastic weekend. It led to a scoff of disbelief, *of course*.

I ignored her though; she wouldn't kill my vibes or the demon cloud I was still sailing on.

Tuesday afternoon, I was informed by David of how Wednesday was an important day, and I got a pre-lecture on putting more effort into my appearance by both my asshole boss and his all bark, cold-foam assistant.

I had to dig deep in my closet for a look that night. The choice was between a dress or a suit.

I refused to get belittled by Katherine, so I played it safe with a black suit that made me look profesh and cool. I added a bright red blouse and would do my makeup with bright red lips, because red lips were always a statement piece. Simple, but effective.

I even pulled out my black heels that I hardly wore, unless I was making a statement or wanting to make an impression. Smiling to myself, I ate soup and made sure I bathed and smelled fabulous for the next day, braiding my hair to sleep in.

My hair mostly cooperated the next morning as I took out my braids and added some texturizer for the waves.

I checked the mirror before leaving the apartment, feeling satisfied with my look. *Win, win, Becs!*

I grabbed my necessary cold brew per usual, then began preparations for our important guests that would arrive in a couple of hours. The whole building was full of tension and chaos.

Ensuring things were in order, I double-checked cleanliness and made sure things were as hospitable as possible. I didn't have too many scheduling requests, thankfully, as I'd caught up the previous day so I could assist with greeting the guests, not being behind the desk.

Ten a.m. arrived quickly.

The three of us—me, David, and Katherine—stood in front of the reception area as people, both familiar and not, entered the building, looking sharply dressed.

Katherine stood beside me wearing a dress that showed off her assets. She wore heels that would break my neck and a dress that made her look like a weird peach. *Maybe she was a demon, too.* My boss stood on the other side of her as a selfish part of me hoped she'd fall.

The previous hunks from the week before greeted us, followed by a newer group that included more than men. I tried to bite down my insecurities to focus on the task at hand.

We exchanged pleasantries and welcoming smiles until the last person stepped forward.

A hell of a handsome man, I'd say. He was so distracting that I missed his name. Was I a cat in heat because I wanted to rub up against him? Probably.

I sighed silently as I took him in. A little taller than six feet, combed-back dark hair with bright brown and blue eyes that I found to be fascinating as he was...absolutely making me drool. Figuratively speaking, as today was not the day to embarrass myself.

I tried *not* to stare, but as he shook my boss's hand, then Katherine's—who gave him a cutesy look that made me want to hip check her—but no, his gaze was locked on *me*. It should have bothered me, but I basked in it. I couldn't describe why my insecurities faded into the background as I held my breath with him standing before me, looking like something out of a dream.

Wait a minute, I did have that one dream of a dark-haired stranger... *Shit.*

Why am I like this?

He gave me a professional handshake, interrupting my dreadful thoughts. His smile was lovely, and I was melting internally.

"This is our receptionist, Rebecca," David spoke then, reminding me to snap out of whatever fantasy my brain came up with. *I'm at work; focusing on being professional, I told myself.*

"It's a pleasure to meet you, *Rebecca*." The way my name rolled off his tongue had my toes curling.

He didn't greet anyone else, except me. I didn't know

what it was, but the touch from his handshake felt familiar. *Probably from my dream.*

Don't even get me started on how sexy he sounded overall—*I was dead on the spot.*

"It's nice to make your acquaintance," I said, meaning every delicious word.

As we looked at one another, his thumb lightly rubbed the top of my hand. It was brief and sweet, but it was enough for me to realize what he was doing as he let go.

He stepped away as Katherine gave me the dirtiest look. I gave away nothing, not even a gloat, as David began leading the group away. The stranger's touch lingered as if he were still touching my hand.

The man himself smiled at me again before other employees joined, walking away from me and my receptionist's area.

Sitting back down, I glanced around before I started fanning myself.

Two people flirting with me in the span of one week; was the universe playing games with me?

Whatever was in the cards, I hoped it wouldn't stop as my life was usually so boring and dull, so the excitement brought red to my cheeks in giddiness. *Confidence, who?*

Thankfully, I didn't see anyone else before my lunch break as I walked to the café for more caffeine and a pastry. I sat in a high top table seat by the window, watching people walk by.

Part of me began to wonder what exactly was going on within the company. The people that came in looked far more important than my boss. I was a receptionist, so I certainly wasn't told anything other than if it was an important meeting. I got a lecture on what I wore instead.

I didn't dress down or anything, I just wasn't on a

notable code that Katherine was on. She was stylish and fancy, while I wasn't. Not that it mattered or should've mattered to me. I didn't care about being fancy or trendy. I was uneventful in comparison, until it came to cosplaying as I made sure I shined *somewhere*. My insecurities didn't make sense to anyone but me. It wasn't always about weight but not being good enough for anyone to stick around.

Regardless, I hoped the pretty man would be around more often. Eye candy aside, I wondered what his position was.

Smiling to myself at the thought, I finished my snack and drink, making my way back to the skyscraper where my lonely desk was waiting.

Settling back into the day, I was busy the rest of the afternoon answering calls. I did feel eyes on me at one point, hoping it was the handsome man, but I didn't look to find out.

The day ended and I made my way to my car, driving home.

I wasn't sure what awaited me the next day, but I hoped to see the dark-haired stranger again.

BECS

YOU ARE
BEAUTIFUL

SEVEN

BECS

I didn't see the dark-haired gentlemen or any of the others the rest of the week, but I did find out more of what was going on that Friday afternoon in the breakroom.

Katherine wouldn't shut up about how our company was merging with another big corporation. There would be a lot of changes, job losses and promotions as well as new departments and areas to meet the company's production needs.

Of course, Katherine caught me and had to say shit. "Hope you don't lose your job, Rebecca. I'm sure the front desk would miss you drooling on it."

Were we still in high school? Like, what the fuck?

I gave her a fake smile as she laughed with others.

"Likewise, *Kat*," I crooned, and her face changed immediately as I nonchalantly walked out of there, feeling evil and magnificent.

Once I got home, I realized there was a text from Figgy. They asked if I was going to the upcoming Dragon Con, and if I wanted to get drinks in an hour since they were in town visiting some family. I decided to go and put on my favorite jeans and a cute top with my wedges.

I took a taxi back into the city. Figgy had come out recently as queer and nonbinary, which was certainly fine by me. Figgy was awesome in my book, so I'd respect them, not that it was hard to do. Figgy was a good friend and they deserved it.

I saw them once I arrived at a local bar downtown, and Figgy's face lit up. Their hair was medium length and blonde, and they were dressed casually. I hugged Fig as we went inside.

"It's so good to see you, Becs. It's been over six months!"

"I know, Figs, *I know*. It's good to see a friendly face amongst the sea of bitches."

Figgy laughed as we were seated in a corner by the window of the bar and grill place Figgy chose for our meetup.

"Tell me about it. What's been going on? Have you figured out ideas for the convention coming up yet?"

A server came over to take our order, and we both ordered a tasty-sounding ale that was blueberry and vanilla flavored.

"I have some ideas. Nothing really new is happening here. Same shit, every damn day. Living my best loner life as I plot and plan for the Con."

Our drinks came out right on queue with bits of foam spilling over the edges. It smelled amazing as we clinked a toast to being reunited at long last before chugging it.

"I'm sorry, Bec. Normally, I'd say the same, but I started seeing this girl recently and she's a fucking delight."

"Oh, Figs!" I squealed in delight, hugging them tight.

They beamed, clearly ecstatic to share the news with me.

"I'm so happy for you. Tell me more!" I added sincerely, taking a drink while listening in.

"Thank you. Like I said, she's great; we met at a smaller convention months back between our last visit," Figgy paused and finished their drink. "You look great, too, by the way. Have you lost weight? Or did you meet someone, too? There's something different about you…"

Fig seemed most interested in my response as they leaned on the table, suspicious and waiting. I held back my knowing smirk. Damn, guess I'd have to spill the tea, or beer rather.

"So, you heard about demons running about this city, right?"

They nodded in agreement as they ordered another round. "It's not just here, it's in other cities, too. I see the news, Becs."

"Crazy, right?" I drawled out the words in length, and they agreed, raising their eyebrows.

"Are you drunk already?"

I shook my head. "No, silly, *listen*. One of them came to visit me about a week ago."

Fig smacked the table, grabbing the newly filled drink. "What?! No way!"

I gave them an awkward look and a nod in confirmation.

"Yes, way! And hell be damning was he h-o-t. *Lordt*. I don't think I've ever been fucked like the way he fucked me. *Goddamn*."

Figgy's mouth dropped, blinking at what I said. "Rebecca! What the hell?! *You're crazy!* I'm also somewhat intrigued. Was he…*big? Was there a tail? Horns?* Give me the deets!"

I belt out a laugh, taking a long drink. "Yes, to the crazy.

Uh, well, he was *made for pleasure.* You know, like the condoms, right?"

Figgy shook their head. "Ribbed for her pleasure, you mean?"

I smacked the table and pointed at them, "Yes! There were all those things. I've been thinking about dick all week... *So worth it.* I wish he'd show up tonight, honestly."

They wiggled their nose as I burst into laughter with them, clinking our glasses again before taking another long drink.

"Well, good on you! You'll have to keep me updated! If you find any she-demons that don't mind non-binary, queer peeps, send them over to me?"

I give them a thumbs up, chugging back my drink.

Laughing loudly, I tell them, "You're just as bad as *me,* Figgy! Also, what about your lady? Or are you into polyamory now?"

Figgy shrugged. "Nah, it would only be to satisfy my curiosity, nothing *crazy.*"

I gave them a look, and they wiggled their brows.

"It was so much fun, however unconventional. I'm curious, though, if demons have human forms, too. If they look as good as they do in full-demon-mode. I can only imagine the perfection if they could take on human appearances."

Figgy considered me as I sighed sadly. "I'm almost jealous I didn't run into one."

More drinks arrived as I felt the booze full force. After we thanked the server, I responded back after she walked away.

"Apparently, there's bad and good ones, I suppose?"

"Oh? Really?" Figgy was all in on the tea.

"I haven't met a bad one yet, so I can't really answer the specifics. The one that came to me though was certainly eager to please." I fanned myself dramatically, and we snickered.

"Oh, how I've missed you, Becs. You keep your demon. For the Con, I decided to do some anime characters this go-around, since I did the Boy-Lolita theme last time."

With a smile, I commented before chugging my booze, "It was adorable, everyone loved it! You do great cosplays!"

"It was, wasn't it?"

I gave Figgy a "Hell yeah" in response.

"And what about yours? You looked amazing as Wonder Woman last year!"

"Thanks," I said sheepishly, remembering how hot I felt in it.

Figgy sighed. "I need you to have cosplay confidence 24/7. You look great and should believe in yourself more, Becs. Fuck what those bitches, or anyone else for that matter, thinks and says!"

It was my turn to sigh, finishing the drink. "I know, and I wish. The job isn't a dream one, but it gets things done."

They grumbled, finishing their drink, too. "Uh-huh, just like that promotion you were supposed to get two years ago... Let's drink one more and head upstairs to the dancey-fun."

I gave them finger guns in agreement, remembering that I was supposed to be promoted if a more suitable position opened that meshed with my math degree.

We idly talked, drinking our last drink as I came loose on the dance floor upstairs under the flashing lights and modern tunes.

Giggling, but enjoying ourselves, Figgy and I danced around for hours. It wasn't a fancy dance club, and people weren't grinding up all over each other. It was fun and lighthearted, but after a few drinks, what did I know about *anything?*

I was unsure of what time I made it back to my place alone in the back of a taxicab, but I stumbled out and up towards my apartment.

Why did I think the third floor was the place to live again?

Damn stairs.

BECS

YOU ARE
BEAUTIFUL

EIGHT

BECS

I woke up the following Saturday afternoon, feeling like a goat smacked me in the head.

Figgy and I ended up drinking more throughout the night, but it was fine. I didn't do that type of thing often. So, I may have gotten a little drunk. *Sue me!*

Actually, don't—*can't afford that shit.*

I took some medicine for my growing migraine and showered before putting on a comfy t-shirt that had Dungeons and Dragons on it. I flopped on the couch shortly after, dozing off.

It was dark in the living room when I awoke later to a tail rubbing my leg. I yelped, sitting up and turning on the light beside me on the end table quickly. The light revealed a demon lounging at my feet.

"Fuck, you scared me for real that time!"

I leaned back against the couch as the tail rubbed my leg in apology. *Assuming a tail can do such things.*

"Sorry," he whispered sleepily.

"I'm surprised to see you," I said, my insecurity rising to the surface while catching his yawn.

"I was here yesterday, but you weren't…"

Damn.

I cursed not only internally, but outwardly.

His lips curled, seeming smug. "Miss me?"

"Yes." I wasn't going to hide it. Initial shock wearing off, the reality was that I was absolutely thrilled to see him.

"I brought you something, for tearing up your other one." He casually held up a familiar lacey garment draped on his finger.

Scooting towards him, I waited until we were skin-to-skin before I put my head in my hand, leaning it on the back of the couch. His gaze lingered as I thanked him.

"I'll try not to rip *this* one."

I hid my smirk, watching him tilt his head to meet my inquisitive look. "So, how does *this* work, then? Do you make house calls and leave every time? Or?"

House calls, really, Becs?

I realized how sleazy I worded it, but he seemed to pay no mind. "What do *you* want?"

He mimicked me, leaning his pretty horned head into his hand. Somehow, I found the gesture *adorable.*

"I don't know how this demon thing works or how long it will last. I'm not used to anyone being around *or wanting to be.*"

"It can be whatever *we* want," he said simply, his voice soft and sweet, reaching over to tuck hair behind my ear. "You're beautiful and perfect: of course, I want to be around you."

I shivered over his words, feeling yellow butterflies floating around in my belly.

"What else do you want, Bels?" I asked in return, maneuvering myself to straddle him, to which his blue-eyed gaze followed me and his large hands settled on my hips.

Placing my hands on either side of him on the couch, he moved his head to watch me as I leaned close, my hips on full display.

Sometimes you just have to air your shit out.

His look was full of desire as I arched myself into him. I knew exactly what I was doing, and he knew it, too. Belke didn't move to stop me, in fact, he tugged on his lip, enjoying the view, apparently.

"I can think of many things that would satisfy my needs. Most of them involve the position we're in." His words made goosebumps rise across my skin as I held my breath.

"Let's get to it then. We can figure out the rest later because *I* also have needs. One of them involves you being *deep inside me.*" I lowered my voice at the last part, and he grunted his approval, shifting himself to free the monster cock in his pants.

Biting my lip, he set me on him as if I weighed nothing. Before I could even think about it or protest, I adjusted with a gasp until he was stuffing me full of him.

I let my held breath loose, and his arms went around me and into my hair holding me to him while searching for my lips.

I moaned against his heat-filled kisses and motioned my hips, beginning to find a suitable pace that turned into greediness.

"Fuck," he whispered in my ear as he nibbled on my earlobe, tugging and moving his lips down to my neck where he bit down semi-hard and sucked.

A moan unleashed from deep within as he gently massaged my breast under my shirt.

"Bels," I said in calling after he lifted the shirt, moving his lips and tantalizing tongue where his hand was.

Nibbling on the top of my breast, I exhaled with pleasure, leaning into his touch.

"You have the most beautiful breasts, and perfect body, made just for me," he whispered above them, trailing burning kisses upward while taking my shirt off at the same time.

Tossing the shirt, he found my lips again and I cupped the back of his head, holding him close, my fingers entwining in his soft hair. I ignored my dark inner voice saying that he was lying because he was horny, but his next words distracted and quieted any inner thoughts trying to stop me from enjoying the demon on my couch who chose to show up.

"I'm going to fuck you all night," he said in quiet determination, holding the back of my head too as we both increased our pacing.

"Don't threaten me with a good time, Bels," I said breathlessly, feeling the pressure build within me and a finger right on my sweet spot. It wasn't long until I moaned louder than I intended, clutching him to me as I fell down into euphoria.

He held me in turn, grunting out with his own release.

Catching our breaths, I made sure I had his gaze and attention, asking, "What do I have to do to keep you around?"

God, I hope I didn't sound too desperate and whiney.

"Everything you've done so far has been sufficient—consider me *kept*. You are perfect for me, Becs."

"Don't you need my soul?" I searched his gaze, ignoring the embarrassing sweetness.

"Let me worry about your soul, Rebecca. Let me keep it, and you, safe."

I moved back slightly, giving him a meaningful look from his sweet words that made my heart ache.

"Tell me how this works then," I urged on.

"It's as I said before. I am yours and you are mine. If you'll have me."

"Sounds like a fair trade," I said, running my hands through his hair.

He leaned in, reminding me of a cat or a dog that pressed their faces closer.

"Then, that's all there is to it. You don't need to do anything other than to be *you* and all that you are."

"Yeah? What am I?" I asked in challenge, curious of his answer.

"*Delicious,*" he said, capturing my lips immediately.

He lifted me up with him while he stood and had my legs wrapped around him tight. His lips were eager as he slipped his tongue inside my mouth, and I ran a daring hand up one of his horns.

His tail caressed my back and side as he walked us to the bedroom where he sat on the bed, still holding me tight before breaking the kiss.

"Careful, if you keep touching my horns, I'll have to *double* penetrate you."

I paused, tilting my head when a mischievous look appeared on his lovely demon face.

"My tail can not only disappear, *reappear,* but I can make it into a second cock. *I can fuck you in both ends.* For you, it'll be pleasurable. For me, *heaven on earth.* I mean that in the best of ways."

His tail wasn't a tail then, but another cock pressed up against my ass cheek.

"Oh." I reached to touch it, and it did feel like a real cock, not like the monster that was just inside me, but more human sized. *I was* both nervous and intrigued at the thought of double penetration.

Alright, Becs, where'd this inner freak come from?

"It's weird, but that's the cutest thing I've ever heard. A demon that said *heaven,*" I admitted with a cheeky grin.

He seemed amused, caressing my hair. "Do you trust me?"

I bit my lip, knowing what he was asking and nodding my head *yes* anyway.

I felt him harden against me as he set me on him again effortlessly, and we both breathed out in pleasured relief.

"Lean forward slightly and open your mouth."

I slowly opened my mouth, obeying and leaning forward, arching my ass upward.

I kept my devilish look at bay as I saw a tail connected penis coming towards me.

Not paying attention to the magical dick, we locked gazes as he watched me lick it when it got closer until slipping inside. He moaned, thrusting up into me, pumping steadily. At the same time, I still licked and teased dick number *two*.

Belke's eyes closed, and I realized I was doing some crazy shit, yet it was the sexiest thing I'd ever done.

I guessed I was certified now.

He held me steady, fucking me *and* my mouth.

"You feel unlike anything else," he whispered, and I found him so fascinating, so otherworldly.

A non-human guy with two dicks...who would've thought?

I got lost in the moment until he moved dick two out of my mouth and positioned it near my ass, smearing saliva with the tip.

"I'll change the sizing for you until you get used to it. It is self-lubricating."

Confused on what he meant, his lips captured mine blissfully as he somehow slipped inside, but the cock felt smaller in my ass, almost as if it were a finger.

So, that's what he meant.

Double penetration was a new and exhilarating experience. I cried out in a new wave of pain and pleasure, never having been fucked in the ass before.

I didn't realize I could make the noises I did as the dick sizing increased in real time.

"The increase is to prep you to take my size without hurting you. Like fingers stretching your rim." He sighed softly.

"F-fuck m-me, Bell-key."

His lips devoured me as I cried out at my finish, my dripping pussy, clenching him hard along with my ass.

I'm pretty sure my eyes rolled back into oblivion.

It was a spiritual experience, and I couldn't think afterward.

I spaced out of my own existence until I heard his groan and our heavy breathing. I took initiative on kissing him and pushing him gently back onto the bed.

"I need a quick break after that, *goddamn.*"

He gave me a hearty low laugh, slipping out of both holes. I crawled up over him until I found myself at my pillows.

"Thank you for trusting me, Becs."

I lay on my stomach, my head turned to the side, as he laid on his side to my right.

"I'm sorry I wasn't here last night, and I will be angry at myself for at least two weeks. How dare I miss that lovely dick of yours. *That tongue, too.*"

He gave me a look that made me decide my break would be over soon.

That whore vagina of mine would fall out before she learned to take a break. Sheesh.

"The night is still young, Becs," he purred, scooting closer as his horns and tail disappeared.

"You aren't wrong there, Belke, and by all means, remind me of what I missed last night," I countered back, rolling onto my side.

With a wicked grin, I was on my back as he kissed and groped down my body until he arrived at the center of me.

Boy, was I reminded alright.

BECS

YOU ARE
BEAUTIFUL

NINE

"Becs," a voice lulled me awake slowly on Sunday afternoon.

A smooth touch rubbed down my leg and side. Soft and gentle. Awareness overtook me that it wasn't his hands due to him holding me.

A small smile slipped onto my face as I yawned and stretched, not wanting to be a person. Eventually, I opened my eyes, seeing two blue gems staring back.

As my eyes adjusted, he appeared relaxed and content, too. Like a cat or dog with his tail movements. What a cinnamon roll. I was clearly not awake enough to decide if Belke was more cat or dog-like, demoness aside. The great debate.

What made me fully aware was that I couldn't see his horns. His tail was still rubbing me like a third hand while he held my hands tucked in-between us near our chests.

I found it to be...so fucking cute.

"I'm surprised you're still here since you left last time," I told him quietly, kissing his hand mindlessly as if the situation happened every day.

My insecurities still called to me, but I'd noticed lately how quiet they were becoming as Belke's sweet words often took over me rather than my own inner demons and lack of self-confidence.

"You weren't *mine* then."

I searched his pale blue gaze, feeling myself melt at the big demon mush beside me. What did *mine* even mean? I still *felt* like me, so I assumed my soul was still intact. I don't know much about demons except fire, brimstone, and damnation. *Supposedly.*

"And now?" I couldn't look away from those pools of blue, those eyes that could probably destroy worlds.

A strange emotion occurred then. We were both fascinated and smitten with each other's company; energy, too. I was probably more smitten. I lived a lonely single life, what could I say? The company was...nice as fuck.

I felt him squeeze my hand briefly, leaning his head closer. "You're going to have to try *very* hard to get rid of me now."

"Really?" My tone was almost silent in disbelief.

"Yes," he answered in a whisper, too, capturing my waiting lips.

As if that's all I needed was a kiss awake, my lady bits alerted me immediately that she was ready, salivating. His touch became electrifying as I released his hands and pulled him closer, those arms wrapping around me as if I'd dissolve away.

Belke was already erect and ready, too. The realization caused me to smirk between kisses as he rolled with me over so that I was on top of him. Adjusting to straddle him, his gaze lingered, taking me in fully as his human-appearing hands began to wander in long strides across my sides. The tail, also, *poofed.*

"I want to have breakfast with you after this," he suggested.

I nodded, saying nothing and leaning down for a smooch before placing his cock inside. I took the lazy Sunday afternoon approach and rode him slowly.

Our morning round was sweet, slow, and sensual, which wasn't a bad change of pace. It was more intimate, and we held each other as lovers did when we came together at our finish.

I knew we weren't, but I also knew it would be an honor to someday be loved by him. Not that I knew him well enough, but he treated me better than any exes and bullies ever did—that was saying a lot. He was a thing of dreams, or nightmares, rather. Hell on earth, I supposed.

I was sure I'd find out how things would turn out between us.

People—*beings*—always revealed themselves.

Later, I made us breakfast and sat at my little mostly-unused two-person dining table. I normally sat on the couch since it was just me most of the time.

Before cooking, we managed some semblance of clothes which for me was a baggy t-shirt and for him, pants.

The interaction was endearing to me, simply because of how it all looked. A large demon at my table with a tail, horns, sitting there eating breakfast as if it were the most normal thing to do. And me, well, I was a curvy cutie with a fupa, but even next to this demon, he made me feel small.

A giggle slipped out as I watched him, highly amused by my life circumstances in the present moment.

He caught my humored look between bites of food. "What?"

I took a bite of scrambled eggs and hashbrowns, "Nothing."

He gave me a look that said he didn't believe it, and I just winked.

"Do you do *normal* things like this a lot?" I found myself asking.

"What did you think I did? Summon hellfire and portals to hell?"

I shrugged. It was possible.

"How am I supposed to know? You're the first demon I've met... I'm curious," I stated, wondering if I sounded like a stereotypical *human* to him.

He seemed entertained more than anything as he answered me. "I know we're *different*. You know with the tail, wings, and horns... But we do mediocre things, too, like grocery shop and pay taxes. *Shocker, I know.*"

I beamed, appreciating his response. His lips curled up before he took another bite of food before finishing his plate.

"You have wings?" I searched my memory, trying to recall anything of the sort, but turned up empty. It must have been too dark that first night.

Belke nodded, and I finished eating also.

"Why do you hide them away?" I was inquisitive today, what can I say? I'm curious about my hot, demon boyfriend. Regardless, I couldn't help my attraction to him.

"They're rather large..."

You *are rather large, Sir*.

"Can I see?" I asked in quiet intrigue.

He gave me a considerate look before glancing around the room, contemplating.

"I can make it work. Since, I can stand at full height here... Yes, I'll show you if you want to see *me*."

With how he said it, it made me believe that in a way it was him baring his soul to me. I wasn't sure on the meaning or if there *was* any deeper meaning, but I was soothed that he feels comfortable enough to at least show me.

"I do want to see you," I went on quietly, standing up with him, appreciating his bronze skin in the lighting and the way his hair fell, a few strands in his face. He may have appeared somewhat large and scary in the dark, but the light reveals so much more than meets the eye.

There was a decent amount of space in the path between the doorway to my bedroom and the living room, dining, and kitchen since that part was one long rectangle all open and connected.

Belke moved towards my doorway to the bedroom, turning around to face me. As I blinked, large dark-feathered wings appeared. They were semi-tucked in behind him, partially going into my bedroom, because of the space we were in.

I gathered that he felt shy and exposed. Still keeping my curious mind at work, I inched closer in silent fascination.

He was watching me carefully, trying to gauge my reactions as I half-circled around him from his left side then to his right. I wasn't paying attention when I moved past him except the feeling of his eyes following me.

Taking him in was a feat. Belke was fucking *breathtaking*. His wings stretched out wide, dark, and lovely. They were longer than his total height at the very least. I wanted to weep at how unreal, otherworldly, and spectacular he was. He looked more like a fallen angel than a demon, but what did I know?

Wondering what real life was, I asked him in a hushed whisper, "May I touch them? Is that okay?"

Feeling like I was at an art exhibit staring at a masterpiece, I stood at his right side, finding his sweet, but intense eyes locked on me.

"Yes..." Belke's tone was low and curious. A part of me wondered if I was doing something sacred. Was touching wings not a normal thing, I wondered?

Slow and careful, I stretched my fingers, starting at the base of the wing at his shoulder blade. My eyes moved from his stare, and I basked in how soft and light they were on my fingers. I continued to trail my fingers further back, wanting to bury my face into his feathers like someone would do to a soft cat after a long day for refuge or de-stressing. I didn't though because my gut instinct told me that I wouldn't want someone I barely knew burying their face in *my* feathers like a soft, fluffy pillow *or cat*.

Belke went still, and I questioned if I had hurt him because he seemed as if he were in pain almost. With how tense the air became and somewhat stiff under my fingers, I turned and looked to find him with his eyes closed.

"Am I hurting you?" I asked with uncertainty after I moved away from his soft wing, feeling guilty that I hurt him. I placed my hand on his arm, concerned.

"No."

It was so hard to tell by his response as his voice sounded strained. I didn't quite believe that anything *wasn't* wrong.

"What's wrong?" I was afraid of the answer, to be honest, because I was over the moon.

"Nothing is *wrong*," he went on quietly.

With how fragile he sounded, I wanted to hug him.

"Then, what is it?" I moved my hand away from his arm, uncertain if I should be touching him at all.

He opened his eyes, reaching for the hand I had moved.

"It feels lovely...when *you* touch them."

Oh.

It was *pleasure*, not pain. I see.

He looked like he was in pain, though, so how was I supposed to know?

I sighed in relief, relaxing.

"I thought you were in pain, Bels... You scared me."

He leaned to kiss my forehead.

"My wings never get touched. Your touch feels incredible. I was overwhelmed, *not in pain.*"

I melted on the spot as he took my hands, kissing them.

A smile crept onto my face. "I didn't realize. Do you... not let many see them, or..."

Considering me, he was quiet, serious even. *"No."*

A moment of silence passed between us as I appreciated that he was sharing a part of himself with me. It meant a lot and I wasn't sure what it meant in the grand scheme of things, but regardless, I was positively content.

"Because I'm a sex demon, contracts, souls, and deals are already an ordeal... I only show either the horns and tail, or one instead of both. Unless I'm around my own kind, the wings stay hidden always. Also, because of their size, it would scare any normal person."

I smirked, tipping my chin up. *Normal.* That word always humored me. What the hell was normal nowadays?

"Good thing I'm not *normal,* then."

He seemed satisfied with my answer, continuing to share. "Not all demons are like me, just so you know. Sex demons are important, too, and can be given important things to do that aren't sex related—I'm sure that sounds very strange. There is rank, variety, shapes, sizes, colors—just like humans when you truly think about it. I hold my wings sacred—it's a deeper extension of me. My tail and horns are also, so I have to be comfortable for anyone to even touch those too. I feel...energy, as I've said before, so I can sense both the positive and negative, as well as neutral."

I nodded, taking in the information, feeling happy that he trusted me with it. A big, scary, *but sexy*, demon, feeling safe with little ole' *me*.

The universe is full of surprises.

"I'm flattered that you feel comfortable with me, Bels. I'm not sure I understand what you mean about energy, it sounds very science-y. Are you an atom demon?" I tried to crack a joke, but he closed his eyes briefly before making an odd noise which caused me to tilt my head to the side.

"I love when you call me that."

Goddamn, was he sexy. I swallowed down my inner creeping heat.

Belke's eyes opened, and it was my turn to kiss his hands.

It dawned on me how he kept his sharp demon claws from shredding my skin and how, more often than not, they were retracted. It made me appreciate his thoughtfulness to not cause harm to me.

Absolutely swooning over it.

"So, you don't mind *my* touch then?"

His eyes flickered their intended desire when he leaned down to kiss me sweetly in response.

"No. In fact, I encourage it. Please, continue, if you wish."

I held my breath, releasing it slowly. "I didn't realize demons could be so *cat-like,* human-like even, or be big, mushy cinnamon rolls."

His low, amused laugh prickled my skin. "Not all, but some, I'm sure. Especially *this* mushy *one*."

"Did I take your soul?" I asked him with my own smug look, happy that he's in sync with my not-so-funny-to-anyone-other-than-me humor.

Without hesitation, he replied, "*Yes*. Although, now I'm wondering... How am I cat-like?"

"Your tail, for one, and your actions. It's possibly one of my favorite things about you, so far," I admitted honestly, and his smirking face remained amused.

Belke gave me a low humming noise, playing coy. "Nothing else?" he asked suggestively, and I gave him an obvious look that there's more to like.

Releasing his hands, I moved closer, cupping my hand where he was already hard.

"There's also this, big guy." My tone was low as I gave him a stare that held all my seductive intent.

Heat filled those lingering eyes, pulling me toward his needy lips.

"Someday soon, I will have you in my full form in a space that would allow me to spread wide comfortably; then you would feel the deepest reaches of our souls. Yours *and* mine."

His words were so heartfelt, I nearly combusted. The heat... The *passion* from his words. Belke was so sweet with me, it made me want to cry.

"I don't know what to do with myself when you say the prettiest things. Are you sure you're not a wicked demon?" I sighed, questioning my entire existence on why he was so seemingly nice to me.

"We have demons like that, too, of course. However, let me demonstrate *my* wickedness for you."

With that toe-curling response, I was more than happy to receive it as his lips captured mine and large hands squeezed my ass, cupping it after and bringing me closer against him.

Moaning in response, I spent the following hours in *wicked,* sexual bliss.

I could definitely get used to this.

BECS

YOU ARE
BEAUTIFUL

Belke left sometime late into the night, kissing me goodbye, but not before whispering sweetly in my ear of his promise of seeing me again Friday. Drifting on the edges of sleep, I pouted at the cold empty spot next to me, missing that demon warmth of hellfire before falling back asleep and waking up hours later for work.

It was to be warm that day, so I wore my cute sandals and a black dress with my hair half-up and down. My makeup was light, and I was sore.

Delightfully, of course. *It was my reward for being fucked into next week.* Literally.

I had weekends to look forward to now, and someone who liked hanging out with me, *even if it was just sexually.* No complaints here—minus the lack of coffee. *Fucking Monday's.*

While I waited in line to order my iced latte at the café by work, I turned and saw a familiar dark-haired man dressed in a black suit, looking all official and sinful.

What was his name again? Gosh, I was the worst with names.

The new boss was probably the only one who could ever distract me from Belke. I wondered what Belke would say? When I turned and suddenly caught the man's gaze in turn, he offered me a smile. His smile felt familiar in the depths of my mind.

"Good morning," I said, trying to sound friendly, *not gawking*, and like I wasn't a grump without my coffee.

"Good morning, Rebecca." I turned shy under his brown-blue gaze. *What an interesting color combination for eyes.*

Thankfully, the universe was in my favor as I stepped up and ordered. I went with a salted caramel flavor with *three* shots of espresso this time—*you know, for good measure.*

The guy behind me stepped up, offering to pay.

"Oh, you don't have to do all of that," I tried to tell him, and the poor barista looked uncomfortable at the interaction.

"I insist," he went on.

"Alright," I told him, sighing in defeat, extending my hands up to showcase my point.

The guy ordered black coffee with cream and sugar, paying for us both. I felt awkward since he seemed like an important *higher up* in the company. My confidence gained from Belke was waning in front of this guy.

"I guess that means I owe you one," I said as we walked over to the waiting area for drink pickup. "Lunch on me one day this week?" I added it as an invitation, hoping I wasn't pushing my luck.

He didn't even consider or think about it before responding, "Not necessary at all, but I won't decline the company of a beautiful woman."

Oh, my.

I turned my head away, my cheeks reddening. My entire nervous system malfunctioned. *Was this guy serious?* No, he couldn't be. *Could he?*

Soon, I heard my drink order being called. Once I retrieved it, he appeared next to me taking his order that came up at the same time.

"Thank you again," I told him as we walked out towards our office building.

"Anytime, *Rebecca.*"

Why did he have to say my name so sexy? Ugh.

Poor Belke had competition, I think.

I hid my smile, walking through the front doors while sipping on my tasty choice for coffee. A groan of inappropriate approval slipped out, and I saw the male pause in my periphery.

Pretending not to notice his reaction, I made my way towards my desk, waving towards him as I presumed he walked towards wherever his office was.

I took a seat, organizing my area before checking my emails and diving into the hundred emails I had waiting. With the merger though, *I wasn't surprised by the upcoming busy work.*

That day flew by and so did the next. I didn't see the dark-haired gentleman until I ran into him at the café on Thursday morning.

I wasn't as awkward, in theory. He paid for our drinks *again*, and I convinced him to go out for lunch—*my treat*—later that day. He agreed and I hoped I wasn't crossing any work boundaries. The more he showed me with his dazzling smile, my confidence began to rework. Although, he probably didn't have many work friends with the big merger, but what did I know?

The morning blew by before I knew it, and he showed

up at noon at my desk. I couldn't deny the flutter within me that he didn't bail, like everyone else did. Perhaps, the guy wasn't bad at all. *Hopefully.*

With a smile, I grabbed my bag and brought him to a healthier place three blocks away and we sat near a window since the weather wasn't as gloomy.

Awkwardness filled me, but I decided small talk was safest. "How is the merge going so far?"

He didn't seem to mind my small talk as he answered. "Good at the moment, I think. My specific department is growing, but it's still a process. New company. New people. The others are working on what we had previously and what we're working with now–merge-wise that is. Of course, these things take time."

Again, asking smart questions, "Should I be worried about my job?"

He looked surprised as if that were the last thing on his mind. "You? Not at all. You're perfect."

I sighed in relief, trying to ignore his words as his expression lightened.

"Work changes aside, how long have you been employed at the front desk before this merge?"

"A couple of years. I had just graduated and was looking for employment."

He nodded, seeming interested in what I had to say as he continued. "Congratulations. What was your degree in?"

"Math. I have my master's degree in it. I'm good with numbers and analytics."

Seemingly impressed with my response, he tilted his head, "Really? Why are you at the front desk, and not in the finance department?"

I shrugged as our food arrived. "I was told there wasn't a

position available at the time but that I could work recep-tion until there was…"

He didn't seem to like my answer but ate in silence, appearing lost in thought.

I made no move to continue the conversation either as I ate, unsure if I said too much or the wrong thing. I stole a glance from him when I was half-way finished with my salad to find him already staring at me, still contemplating whatever it was.

Before I could ask, he went first. "In your time there, have you ever felt alienated, harassed, or belittled by coworkers? I ask off the record and if I should keep an eye for anyone in particular since your company is newer to me. Unfortunately, I do not know all the staff, and I know there's always office talk and politics."

Wow, direct, isn't he?

As much as I'd love to throw those bitches under a bus… I could handle myself.

"Every job has their grievances, as I'm sure you know. Not sure on the grand scale since I'm in my front-center spot to the main door of the building. Regardless, normal stuff, it's nothing I can't handle," I said coolly, continuing to eat while avoiding his all-too-aware gaze.

I thought I saw his jaw clench out of the corner of my eye but couldn't be too sure. "Very well. With this merger, and since it's a larger corporation, please come to me if you have any problems. We have a strict policy against harass-ment, especially when it's unwarranted."

I slowly glanced up at him, offering a polite smile. "Of course."

The guy was smart, I'd give him that, but *I wasn't no snitch.* We handle our problems or we don't—simple.

Shortly after, we finished our fancy salads, and I

handed my card over to the wait staff to pay, to which he looked conflicted over. He didn't make a move to contradict me, yet I had the feeling he wanted to intervene.

Damn men and their impressions.

"My apologies for asking this now, but what shall I call you?" *Again, with my dumbass questions, but I can't fucking remember his name to save my life.*

"Call me, Zavier."

Hmm, okay, mister sexy man.

"Thank you," I said once I received the check and signed it. Before I wrote the tip, *Zavier* placed a ten on the table.

"I'll cover the tip."

I didn't want to argue, so I nodded, standing up and putting my wallet in my bag.

"Thank you for lunch, Rebecca."

"Thank you for the coffees this week, Zavier."

He cleared his throat, seeming slightly tense but it quickly dissipated.

We walked back to the office in comfortable silence. Normally, I'd feel awkward with it, but with him, I didn't mind the least bit. At least I got his name this time *and remembered it.*

Once in the building, I gave him a smile that he returned as he headed towards the elevator in the distance while I went to my area.

With a heavy sigh, I went to work with busy back-to-back calls the rest of the afternoon.

Friday came and went, and TFIO.

Work had certainly been interesting after Zavier's arrival. I wondered if anything would change?

BECS

YOU ARE
BEAUTIFUL

ELEVEN

BECS

After grocery shopping, I hauled those pesky bags up to the third floor, *in three trips,* while hating my life because of it. My sisters would be disappointed in me for not getting it in one single trip.

As I was putting all I bought away, a familiar demon appeared in my periphery, leaning on the front door with his arms crossed, watching me. *My demon puppy-cat.*

I gave him a quick, warm smile with the turn of my head.

"Hello, you," I greeted while putting veggies away.

"Hello yourself." He seemed casual and comfortable wearing his typical black pants and a black shirt. No tail or wings, but his horns weren't hidden.

I recalled what he said before about showing various parts of himself or lack thereof. Feeling special about it all over again, I kept my small smile as he continued watching me thoughtfully. My mind drifted over the fact that my inner demons were quieter with Belke around as he often showed me that *I am* good enough. It was certainly refreshing as his unknown scent washed, reminding me that he was still around and very much real—*not a dream*—even if he was otherworldly.

"Are you hungry?" I asked, leaning on the counter near where he stood.

"Not for *food*."

I snuck a sly glance, seeing those blue eyes light up with heat.

"I'll order takeout then. While we wait, you can have what *you* are hungry for. Although, I supposed I could indulge too," I told him in a coy, yet teasing manner.

Belke gave me a knowing look as I went into the bedroom and undressed completely. I sat on the edge of the bed, calling my favorite Asian takeout place that delivered.

As the line rang, I caught Belke walking over with purpose before kneeling in front of me. I stared at him as he quickly spread my legs at the same time someone answered.

Really, Bels? Right *now?*

Before my thoughts could continue, I bit my lip, holding back any noise when his tongue descended to my clit, licking and teasing.

I quickly rambled off various food items over the phone. The person on the other end was in the middle of repeating everything I said, and I moved my phone away from my face to sigh out and run my hands through his hair.

"Yes, that's correct," I told the person on the phone before I gave myself away.

I rattled off my credit card number I had memorized, confirming the delivery address.

Belke was certainly enjoying himself as I struggled to form words. If I didn't get off the damn phone soon, I'd be doomed to moaning in the person's ear. The person then confirmed and said it'd be an hour.

"S-sound great, t-thank you." I hung up immediately, tossing the phone somewhere on the bed.

"You are *terrible*," I barely got the words out before moaning while he licked me harder, my thighs squeezing his skull.

Okay, Bels, I got you.

Feeling mischievous myself, I ran my hands sensually over his surprisingly smooth and thick horns.

He grunted in response, squeezing my thighs in return. My center was wet and full of his touch. My legs twitched, and the familiar rise of orgasm began deep within. Keeping his head in place at my entrance, I began to fuck his face in desperation. My mouth went slack with a finishing cry out as I shook under his hold, his hands gripped tight to my thighs. Bels groaned when I came, licking up my sensitive clit.

In a hazy bliss, I fell back toward the bed while releasing my tangled hold in his dark hair.

"*That* was the sexiest thing *ever*. Also, now it's *my* turn," he said, suddenly flipping me over to my stomach, and I gasped. Still feeling sensitive post-orgasm, he eased his ribbed-for-my-pleasure demon cock inside me as I adjusted myself, both of us groaning.

Two easy pumps and he pulled out before a familiar tail-cock ran along my spine in warning.

"Open that pretty mouth of yours," he instructed in a husky, low voice that made my toes curl.

A cock came into view, not sure which one initially, and I did as he requested, taking it into my mouth. Awareness came to me as I half-hung off the bed, his hands gripped tight on my hips.

"*Fuck*, Becs," he managed to breathe out in a satisfied manner, making delicious noises. Another cock eased back into my pussy as I licked and teased him, noticing how his tail-cock went into a tip, curling around my tongue in sync. I could feel the girth increasing slightly as I took dick-number-two into my mouth deeper. There were small grooves and ridges that I knew would feel amazing.

At the same time, something wet glided over my back entrance, prepping me.

Belke began to increase his pacing, harder too, and I soon found it difficult to focus on the task in front of me.

He took note as I released noises I didn't think I was capable of making. Once my ass was prepped enough, he slid a finger in, slowly adding another once I stretched to him.

"You ready to take my cock in this sweet ass?"

"Y-Yes, please," I moaned my plea as he dominated my pussy.

"Tell me if I hurt you, okay?"

"O-okay," I nodded, not knowing which way was up and down as I dove into sensation as the tapered tip of dick-two teased my other entrance before sliding in slowly.

I cried out immediately, not being able to help myself, but *fuck*, did it feel amazing.

"How's that, little one?" he grunted while I felt him penetrate me deep in both holes.

My eyes rolled back when a large hand gripped the base of my neck in such a way that made otherworldly sounds come from my lips. A second orgasm creeped up and slammed into me. My vision faded as I cried out his nickname.

"Bels!"

"Right there with you," he whispered in turn.

He shuddered and stuffed both holes full of him, and by God's green earth, did I descend and fall right into Hell.

Sweet mercy.

His arms circled around me, squeezing slightly as I broke back into the barriers of reality after being fucked silly.

"I feel better," he said against my skin, trailing kisses across each shoulder blade while pulling out of me.

"Rough week? Also, I'm right there with you. I feel reborn," I concurred.

Demon dicks, five stars.

"You have no idea how right you are, Becs."

I moved, rolling onto my back to find his arms on either side with eyes locked on me. Leaning closer, he stole a kiss before I could even think.

Once we caught our breaths, his nose rubbed up against mine.

"What do you do during the week anyway?" I found myself asking.

"Demon shit. Which is human shit like sleeping, working, you know—everyday things."

I smirked, nuzzling my nose in return. "Trouble in paradise?"

"My brethren don't know how to behave up here or party with the humans properly. There's chaos everywhere. Your people may wage wars, but there's trouble stirring with mine, too. I have to keep an eye on things and monitor movements."

He sounded more stressed out with his job than mine.

"I'm sorry. Now that I know you aren't avoiding me during the week... You're actually busy doing what you need to."

He pulled back to look deep into my eyes with a frown. "You thought I was avoiding you?"

"I'm one measly human. You could have other clients to attend to—*I don't know the rules here.*"

He sighed, shaking his head in response while moving his big warm hands to cup my breasts that fit the mold perfectly.

Basking in his warmth and having him pressed to me, he ran his nose along my neck. "I've told you before, but you have fantastic breasts and the curves to go with it. Your ass is *glorious.*"

My lips curled in flattery as he massaged both breasts in a way that had my cunt ready and throbbing.

"You are not just any human, *you are mine. I would spend every moment with you if I could.* Weekends are easier to steal time away from responsibilities and share in these precious moments with you."

And there I go, turning into another puddle.

"So mushy. *My horny demon,*" I chirped, holding back a moan.

Belke simpered, nuzzling his face in-between my breasts. He peppered gentle kisses, trailing down my stomach before moving back up to my chest.

Turned on by his sweetness, I arched under his body, spreading my legs in invitation.

"We have fifteen minutes before our food arrives," he said in a low, needy tone before I could wonder where this sex demon got his sex drive. The depths of Hell more than likely.

I arched up my hips in turn, showing that I was more than happy to go along with whatever he had in mind until then. He nibbled on my chest, running his hand down between my soaked legs.

"So creamy with us both," he whispered before claiming

my mouth and plunging into my depths as I held him close to me.

As soon as I had my earth-shattering orgasm, a knock sounded at my front door.

Belke used his fingers to push his release back inside me with a pleased smirk.

"Easy, demon boy. Let me answer the door," I huffed out before he smiled big.

"Can't let it slide out of you now, can I?"

I managed to get up, grabbing my black robe and tying it around me as I walked away from Belke's coy look.

Sheesh, there's no shame in that demon body.

I opened the door, took the food, and shut it behind me quickly afterward. Good thing I tipped over the phone.

"Help yourself, Bels. We had our main course, let's enjoy course number two," I offered, bringing the food to the coffee table in front of the couch.

I turned on the TV, sitting on the floor and opening the bag. Belke sat behind me with his thick, muscled thighs on either side of me, making me feel small.

It was so stinking cute.

"I won't be offended if you don't eat anything you don't like."

"I'm not a picky eater, Becs."

I took a quick bite of the chow lo mein, handing it over my shoulder to him. I slurped the noodles while he took the chow lo mein, and I opened the edamame container and began eating those.

Sharing the rest of the food, we watched The Wedding Singer, which was one of my favorites. As corny as it was, I adored Adam Sandler movies.

I leaned against the couch and him as we both watched.

Throughout the movie, I laid my head against his knee. I could feel his hand in my hair, stroking and playing with it.

Big cat.

Full and happy, both inside and out, the movie ended.

"I liked that movie," he said casually, and I turned my head slightly to answer, "Yeah?"

"Yes."

Somehow, knowing that, it made me happy, too.

"I'm glad; it's my favorite. I like cheesy, Adam Sandler movies, or any romantic comedy."

"We should watch all of them, then," he suggested.

I took a sip of water before turning around to lean on his thighs.

"I'd like that."

He leaned closer after my answer, pecking my lips tenderly.

"Question for you, though."

Concerned curiosity crossed his face as Belke leaned back.

When I formed the words to my question, he ran a hand through my hair, asking, "What is it?"

"Have you ever been to a cosplay convention?" *Not a weird question to ask a demon, right?*

He shook his head. "I've heard of them but never went."

I sighed in relief that I didn't have to explain them.

"It's one of my favorite things to do, and it's something I'm good at... Do you want to go with me to Dragon Con?"

He took my hands into his. "I'd love to. What do you have in mind?"

Unashamedly grinning in response, Belke returned his own look of amusement at my plotting look.

"I have a few things in mind. For the Saturday part,

would you be willing to show up as yourself and I'll cosplay as *your sex demon?*"

A quiet look of shock grew over him. "You want... to cosplay as *me?*"

Without wavering and almost sure he'd never been asked that before, I replied, "Yes."

"That's... I've never...been asked that before. I'm beyond flattered, Rebecca. *I* don't mind. I bet you'd look fantastic. I can picture it now. A beautiful demoness." He moved his hands away and made a rectangular shape with his hands, framing my face in it as he leaned back.

A giggle slipped out of me as I hugged his leg.

"We'd look adorable, and I want to mess with people and make them believe you're in cosplay too. *A demon in disguise.*"

Wiggling my eyebrows, his laughter tickled my ears as I joined him.

"Deal. Sounds like a date."

"I'll buy your ticket, if you book the room?" I offered, extremely thrilled to corrupt him to *my dark side.*

"Works for me. My curiosity is peaked. What other ideas do you have?"

"I have a go-to student outfit I wear. But I was also thinking of doing a gender-bend of Howl from Howl's Moving Castle."

He made a humming noise, tapping his fingers against his thigh then. "I may need you to put on this *student* outfit for me before then. For research purposes, of course."

"*You* can see it at the convention. Keep the mystery and intrigue, Bels. Also, I think there's an anime that involved a student outfit like character and a demon boyfriend or something if you wanted to remain as yourself or... something else." I paused, realizing I didn't even ask him the obvious. "Do you have a human form?"

"I do." His eyes were glittering, and my eyebrow rose.

"Oh? Well, don't keep a lady waiting. Why haven't you shown me?" I was half-pouting, half-curious about it.

If he were anything like his demon form, I could only guess how otherworldly his human form was. A real heart snatcher.

He leaned forward, bringing his face closer to mine and I took notice of his lovely lips. *"Keep the mystery and intrigue, Becs."*

I narrowed my eyes as he stole my lips briefly, leaning back with a satisfied look. I didn't push him further on it.

With a sigh and my hands up in defeat, "Fine, you win. *This time.*"

"I always win."

My eyebrow went up again and I climbed into his lap. "Oh really?"

One of his hands went to my hips, and the other to cup my cheek.

"Yes. I win because I have *you.*"

Plotting to be sassy and get him back, I paused, unsure of what to say to his unexpected and sweet response, so I kissed him.

"And I have you," I whispered, and he claimed my lips again.

"We're both winners, Becs."

I stole a glance, feeling his heat radiating from him as I brought my arms around his neck.

"Indeed, Bels. *We are.*"

BECS

YOU ARE
BEAUTIFUL

TWELVE

BECS

The next few weeks went by. Belke visited every weekend, sex included. Zavier began to run into me more during the weekdays, making sure to say good morning most mornings he was in. A couple of times a week we'd run into each other at the regular coffee spot; slowly but surely, I began to find the big boss less intimidating. His smile was easy to fall into, along with his friendly and welcoming demeanor. Part of me wondered if he was just being friendly because he felt bad or pitied me. I didn't see him with any other women, and he didn't have a ring, but one couldn't assume either. I was more appreciated by the new boss than anyone else in the fucking company—both as a human being and as an employee. It was a start, I supposed.

Good thing he's not my boss or it might be weird to ogle him just like Katherine.

Speaking of, the woman herself walked by with yet another dirty look, as per usual. She interrupted my constant Belke daydreaming—*rude*. My current boss still dismissed me; *nothing new*. My only excitement was Fridays and weekends when I was reunited with Belke, along with working on my upcoming Dragon Con cosplay design every moment I could.

It was coming along if I do say so myself.

The hardest part was trying to get the colors right for Belke's skin tone, along with all the materials to create a tail and horns. I made it work though. It didn't feel right to make wings, so I kept that for my own arsenal of Belke-secrets-not-meant-for-everyone.

Belke was already willing to be seen as himself at the convention, which I'm sure would be a different experience for him. Although, it was more socially acceptable to be a demon in that scenario, minus the outbreak reports still happening on *demons*. Dragon Con was a safer bet though.

The closer it got to the convention, the more excited I became as the final product was coming through. I was always giddy before an event. Especially now that it was less than two weeks out. *Holy crap!*

On a Monday morning, I grabbed a caramel latte before I was stuck at the front desk until lunch.

I went about my morning, as per usual, until Katherine showed up.

Great.

She was scowling when she appeared at the front of my desk.

"David wants to see you immediately. I'm here to cover the front desk."

She wore heels higher than the building itself and a silver dress that was probably too fancy, but who was I to question *her majesty?* I exhaled heavily, standing up to let her take over. I couldn't remember the last time I was called to David's office.

I walked briskly over to the elevator, waiting for it to arrive after pressing the button. Looking down at my outfit I chose that day, I was suddenly glad I went with heels—not as high as Katherine's, but it was enough. My dark purple pantsuit looked good, and it made me feel slightly more confident.

Distracted and wondering about the sudden visit without an email notice first, I didn't remember getting inside the elevator until the ping for the twentieth floor echoed.

Shaking myself loose of distractions, I was confident of not losing my job as I hadn't done anything wrong. *Oh no, what if I was one of those people getting laid off since the merge?*

Shit!

My nerves were shot by the time I stood outside David's door, knocking. I heard his voice telling me to enter a moment later, enough to make my heart skip a beat. *Fucking palpitations.*

Opening the door, I caught him leaning against the large window behind his desk. David donned a pale gray suit, matching the cold, undecorated vibes of his office. He had his large gray desk with his chair and messy stacks of papers, and his laptop just sitting idly. There was a wall of shelves with random crap on it, yet somehow organized. The only thing messy was his desk. No decorations other than a basic bitch painting that you'd see at hospital to give off faux peace vibes.

I held my breath as I stared at the two visitor chairs that were also gray.

"Please sit, Rebecca."

So, I did.

"Am I in trouble?" I dared to ask, my voice shaky with concern as I fought the growing uncomfortable feeling in my stomach.

"No. At least, I hope not."

I tilted my head in question as he turned and stared at me from his window view of another skyscraper across the street. The view wasn't too bad altogether, but that was biased since I got a view from the front desk every weekday.

"Do you like it here, Rebecca? You aren't thinking of leaving, are you?"

I couldn't help but stare at him from his odd, out of the blue questions.

"Yes, of course... No, sir."

He moved toward his desk chair, tapping on the back of it as if he didn't believe me.

"Then, why would he want to see *you* of all people?"

I blinked at him, clearly missing something.

"I'm sorry, I don't understand?" *I seriously don't.*

"Zavier wants you in his office in ten minutes. He never sees anyone or wants people to meet in his office and when he does, *it's not good.* I thought maybe you had done something to offend him, so when I asked, he wouldn't give me an answer. So, for all our sakes, I hope you didn't offend him. I don't think he likes some of the employees here, especially *us.*"

You, maybe. But I didn't *say* that. I didn't catch the fakeness from Zavier like I did everyone else.

"Alright then... Well, I don't want to keep him waiting. Where can I find him?" I sprung to my feet as he nodded in dismissal and waved me off.

What a douche nozzle.

"Fiftieth floor at the end of the hall. Good luck, you'll certainly need it and make us look good."

"Of course," I said flatly, leaving at once.

I rolled my eyes and flipped him off after the wooden shut behind me.

Storming toward the elevator, I pushed the button for the fiftieth floor once it opened to let me in, and I tried to steady my nerves.

I didn't *think* I was in trouble, but after listening to David, now I wasn't so sure. Not that his comments were welcomed either, *but whatever, I was used to it.*

I spaced out, leaning against the corner until the ping for my destination came.

Here goes nothing.

I stepped out of the elevator and began my long walk to the end of the hallway.

To be honest, I'd never been to any floor other than to David's office and the conference room on the fifteenth floor.

Taking deep breaths as I neared his office at the end of the hallway, I saw the nameplate.

Zavier Bel.

I blinked several times. My heart rate increased along with a rush of realizations.

No, he didn't.

I don't know why, but I began to feel unsettled. I swallowed down the rising emotions and knocked.

I heard him tell me to come in, and I found his friendly face behind his desk in his chair, waiting. He closed his laptop as I entered. Zavier had a large dark wooden desk with bookshelves lining the wall behind him and to his right was a more spectacular view of downtown. Already the atmosphere was warmer and inviting than David's. The walls were a forest green matching the visitor chairs in front of his desk. There were more shelves along the other wall to my right with various objects on them and leafy office plants.

Semi-shocked by what I was seeing, I took the room in

as I shut the door quietly behind me, letting the distraction of looking around stifle my rising emotions of just *who* was sitting in front of me.

"Please sit, Rebecca." Even still as he said my name with a certain tone, it sounded and felt like silk wrapping around me.

I began to piece things together in my mind as I sat down across from him. *How the hell did I not notice this shit before?*

Blue-brown eyes observed me silently as I crossed my legs, placing my hands on my knee to stifle the shaking. The more I thought about it, the more I was certain it was him in his human form. I began to feel like a fool, a blind, *lustful* idiot. *The spelling was the same, a shortened version.* He paid attention to *me* and was nicer than everyone. Lunch dates and coffee surprises. I should've fucking *known*.

Then, I remembered something Belke had told me from the beginning, *"I'll help."*

For fuck's sake.

"Thank you for coming on such short notice. I would have called you up here personally, but I had to go through the proper channels first..."

Whatever that means. Not ominous at all.

"Am I in trouble, *Mr. Bel*?" I spoke in a way to let him know indirectly that I knew. In case the small percent chance proved me wrong.

Yet, my mathematical brain told me that I was spot on, especially when he froze after I spoke.

I may be a dumbass with most things, *but my intuition was never wrong about shit.*

"No, why would you think that?" He cleared his throat, adjusting his coat.

Real smooth, Belke. I know it's you.

I moved my hands from my knee, placing them on the armchair in a tight grip as my temper rose.

"David suspected and warned me, since people who come in here are always in trouble... So, you tell me Belke."

I gave him a serious look. Depending on how he answered, it would change how I let him have it and how I would leave his office.

He sighed, closing his eyes briefly. *Busted.*

"Becs—"

I glanced up, gripping the armchair and uncrossing my legs.

"Did you get this job *before* or *after* that Friday night?" I cut him off, biting back my hurt tone of being made the biggest fool.

He splayed his hands on his desk as if he were grounding himself for *my attack.* He fucking knew this whole time.

"It was around the same time I first appeared to you. I hadn't met you in this form yet."

I scoffed, wondering what his game was. Dark thoughts from the past were rising to the surface.

Was he pretending with me? A joke for everyone to laugh at? Why the special attention in both forms, not bothering to tell me it was him?

Perhaps I shouldn't have let it go weeks ago when I asked about his human form.

The mystery was over.

I rose promptly.

"Becca—" He tried to rise and stop me, but I held my finger up, shaking my head that gave him pause.

Interjecting and fully upset, I went on, "If I wasn't such a lonely woman before you came to me, would you have even given me a second glance, walking into this place amongst all these *other high-end pretty people?"*

I knew I sounded insecure and stupid then, but I couldn't help but feel that if he didn't meet me as he did, he'd never give me the time of day. *If I hadn't had that sexual dream that elicited that sexual energy.*

Zavier–*Belke* winced at my statement, standing up with his palms still on the desk.

"Of course, I would. *You know I would."*

Scoffing at his words, I continued on, "Do I? Do I *really?* You know what this place is like and who I have to deal with. You could have told me at *any time* or when I asked about your human form *weeks ago!* You aren't playing games with me, are you? You didn't do this for a laugh? Or some sort of sick, twisted demon thing like the others that are running amok all over the world? The ones where you prey on people like me, *who have nothing to offer or give."*

God, I'm so fucking stupid.

Tears filled my eyes, blurring my vision as I took steps towards the door.

"Hells, no. *Becs, just let me explain."*

An onslaught of an emotional breakdown was headed toward me fast. I held my hand up to stop him from speaking as I quickly left.

This was not the place for an emotional outburst.

I walked briskly down the hallway, hearing his office door being thrown open.

"Rebecca!"

Keeping my pace to the elevator, I flipped him off as I hit the button down, getting impatient as I blinked back my tears. Zavier was marching towards me.

Hurry up, you stupid ass elevator. I need to let it out in peace.

Thankfully, it did.

I kept my eyes on him, closing the door in his face before he got there.

You're worthless. Of course, he wouldn't like you. In Katherine's voice, ringing through my head. *Eating your feelings again, Rebecca?*

Worth. Less.

As I went down all the floors, I frantically typed an email that I was leaving for the day due to not feeling well. David probably thought the worst, but he emailed me back the moment I got to the first floor with the elevator ping.

Holding my breath and tears at bay for a while longer, I'm surprised by my restraint not to cry at work.

I marched over to the desk, grabbing my bag as I told her I was leaving for the day. I ignored Katherine's scowl and grumble as she dialed David to no doubt complain, but I frankly didn't give a single fuck.

"She's probably being let go, David, I don't know!" I heard her say.

As the doors swung behind me, I rushed to my car as tears fell freely. One of my waterfront spots was nearby. At this time of day, no one would be there.

I needed time to think and get my shit together from being triggered by the whole situation, and I needed to sort through it *alone*.

BECS

$(x-$

$y^2 = Z$

$\lim$

$+a)$

$(y-1)^2$

$\sin x$

$e = \cos x + tg y$

$\sin a =$

YOU ARE
BEAUTIFUL

THIRTEEN

BECS

I kicked my bare feet lazily in the water, sitting at the dock's edge. My heels sat beside me as I leaned on my arms, looking at the cloudy sky while remembering how dirty my ex did me when I was still in grad school.

We worked at the same job—different departments—and he had taken a liking to me, or so I thought.

We fucked and dated a few times until we were *official*. I thought he was into me, until I found him with another coworker, kissing in the breakroom. It was at the end of the day when most people had left, so they probably figured no one would be there, yet I was working late that day to finish my filing for the week.

I was grabbing coffee so I could go home and finish my paper for class, and I found them hot and heavy in the breakroom.

"Are you kidding me?" I said from the doorway.

They broke their kiss and the girl smirked, and he seemed irritated.

"What do you want, Rebecca?"

Why was he pissed? I caught him; the fuck!

"Are you really asking me that right now?" I raised my voice, trying to pull back on my rising temper that reminded me of my sister.

"What do you want me to say?"

I gave him an incredulous look.

"Did you really think you were the only one? Get over yourself dear. I could never love someone like you, *truly*."

Ouch, a knife straight to the gut.

"Someone *like me?*" The room began to spin, and I immediately decided against coffee.

"Do I have to spell it out for you? Don't embarrass yourself. She's clearly better than you," he said, grabbing the girl and pulling her into a kiss.

I blinked partly with shock and disbelief over the shit that was happening. *What the fuck is my life.*

"Now, if you don't mind, we'd like to continue where we left off. You can leave now. It's over," he said, kissing the girl.

"Well, your dick ain't shit anyways, so fuck you and this cunt you left me for."

I had to say something, anything to dial down the break-down headed my way.

I *knew* Belke wasn't Joseph, but when people were bitches, *could you blame me?*

The world treated plus-sized women like objects, or that we weren't the same as everyone else. It was so fucking stupid, and I couldn't stand the bullshit. I was so tired of being angry and bitter over how people treated me. Can't forget the failed relationships filled with superficial things or being told you're pretty *for a fat girl.*

I hated it here.

I exercised when I could, ate decently enough, took my

thyroid medication, but no—not fucking good enough for these pricks.

There were only certain situations where I stuck up for myself, and work-situations weren't it, because I needed the money to get me through school. *Now, it was paying these student loans off.*

Thankfully, the 2020 pandemic hit, and I got to work from home, avoiding that asshole entirely.

Thank fuck, it was over.

Graduating and leaving that fucking place was the best day ever.

I happened to gain twenty pounds from being stuck inside but still took my thyroid medication as prescribed. Yet nothing could cure the bitterness and the loneliness. Not only was the world isolated then, but I did it to myself, too. Depression sank into me deep as did the carbs. *Shit gets old when you have a metabolic disorder.*

I didn't have conventions, or anyone to talk to unless it was through social media, and I barely bothered with that.

Needless to say, that fucker went through more women, like they were nothing. I *almost* felt bad for them, but I didn't.

After the world got back to normal post-pandemic, *mostly anyway,* I went to visit my family for the summer. I lost some weight and began to feel better about myself. The insecurity was still there, naturally, as it wouldn't dissolve overnight.

I spent time with my two sisters and my parents, who surprisingly stayed married through thick and thin with their southern hospitality ways.

I was different from my siblings, the only plus-sized one. No one else had thyroid problems, and it made me hate myself even more for it when I got diagnosed in my late teens when I gained a lot of weight over the span of a year–for no reason.

I tried to lose it, don't get me wrong, but it wasn't just the freshman fifteen or *laziness*.

Merry Christmas early, Rebecca, you have Hypothyroidism.

Just fucking great.

After graduating with my master's, I got the job I was currently working in the city and had been there ever since. Then, Belke came into my life. My sex demon in the night.

It wasn't his fault, Becs, you didn't even listen to him.

I took a deep breath, my thoughts began to calm at that realization while watching the sun set.

After dark, I grabbed dairy free ice cream to cheer myself up for showing my ass and derailing completely off the train tracks.

A huge part of me hoped Belke wouldn't show up that night to talk about things and would either wait or not show up at all to spare me the embarrassment.

Unfortunately for me, when I opened my apartment door, the demon himself was sitting in the dark on my couch.

I nearly yelped, not expecting him.

"For fuck's sake," I cursed, leaning against the front door after turning on the light.

"I didn't mean to scare you, but you left... I couldn't find you. I was worried about you, Rebecca." He seemed conflicted as he said it, and I caught how he said my name. *Who knew I could be so dick-whipped.*

I really was blind for not noticing before.

"I needed some air. When I get seriously upset or triggered, I have to sort through it in my head," I told him, walking into the kitchen and grabbing a spoon to take the ice cream into my bedroom.

I sat it on my night table, going into my closet for an oversized shirt. I stripped my clothes, getting comfortable as I found Belke leaning against the wall outside the closet.

I picked up my ice cream and walked past him without a word back into the living room. Plopping on the couch with a blanket, I grabbed the remote and sought out an Adam Sandler emotional support movie, *50 First Dates*.

"Will you talk to me?" he asked, and he seemed broody. It was *cute* to see, but I didn't let myself give in to it as I normally would.

"Do I have a choice?" I grumbled, taking off the lid of my pint of ice cream.

"Always, Becca."

With a sigh, I waved a hand toward him. "You're here now. *Talk.*"

It was his turn to sigh, and I heard him come around the couch and sit at a distance.

I watched the movie, scooping my first spoonful of Oreo ice cream.

So tasty. Thank you, chocolatey goodness.

"I didn't want to overwhelm you or come on too strongly. So, I kept our visits on the weekend, and then I saw you in my human form, I couldn't help myself. You weren't mine, so I couldn't do anything other than treat you as you deserved."

I pretended like I wasn't listening with my eyes focused on the movie, but I heard and *felt* every word. My heart sank over the fact that I'm the asshole for blowing up, but then again, I found it hard to trust people in general. My eyeballs started to leak over those facts.

"Us demons feel things on a different wavelength. I was,

and always have been, addicted to you since I first sensed you... I wanted to take things slow because I could feel your pain like a magnet. Your heart was fragile and so was your soul," Belke finished.

I debated on whether to keep my mouth shut, but I heard the word *fragile* and couldn't keep my mouth shut.

Wiping my eyes, I told him matter-of-factly, "I'm *not* fragile; I'm tired of everyone's bullshit—there's a difference. The fakeness of people, the audacity and gall to treat a human being like they're absolutely *nothing!* That's all I've ever been to people. I was triggered earlier because of a similar situation with an ex. I began to think you were like everyone else..."

I rambled it all out, and my heart ached over it, but I couldn't deny what I felt to be true at the time. I went from anger to tears today at the drop of a hat.

Is my period coming? Hmm, I can blame it on that, right?

"I'm sorry, I didn't realize..."

Annoyed over my stupid leaky eyeballs, "Well, how could you? I never told you, it's not *your* fault that I never got over being treated like shit, or why I'm constantly angry at the world and bitter because of it. The world ends if you're not up to society's standards as a woman, evidently." I said the last sentence dramatically, sighing into my ice cream.

A large hand was upon my arm then, drawing my attention away from the screen as tears flowed down my cheeks.

"Can I have a bite of your dessert? I need cheering up, too." He surprised me with his sad puppy eyes, but I exhaled, feeling myself melt over him when I was so angry hours before. My earlier triggers and downward spiral were slowly easing up.

Deciding to share, I scooped ice cream on the spoon. His blue eyes were on me while I brought it to his open and waiting mouth.

"I didn't mean to trigger you, and if I see your ex... I'll be happy to switch forms and end him."

Surprisingly overjoyed at the thoughtfulness, I shook my head, giving him another spoonful and wiped my face free of tears and snot—*ew*.

"He's not worth your time. Nor mine. Just another asshole in the sea of stupid humanity. I should have trusted you not to make a fool of me, and you *should have warned me*."

"I agree. That's my fault... For a second there, you sounded like *me*." I caught his gaze with a sigh of defeat before I smirked.

"Wonder why," I suggested, taking a spoonful of cold goodness for myself.

A smile teased at Belke's lips at seeing me slowly cheer up with ice cream and him.

Eventually, I unclenched my jaw and relaxed my shoulders. I felt better after admitting where I was coming from earlier and getting his side of things.

"I'm sorry for unintentionally triggering you and not telling or showing you my human form."

"I forgive you this time. Don't make a habit of it," I told him, noticing how he was closer next to me.

"Just so you know, I've spent the past few weeks getting a position created *for you*. That's why I had you come into my office earlier. You have a master's in mathematics, someone that I need on my team. You are an asset, and a worthy candidate with the skills for *what I need*. You're smarter than you let other people believe."

Surprised by the response, I whipped my head toward him with my eyes threatening to water again. "Really?"

The warm fuzzies flutter in my belly instead. *Bels really was on my side, and I was an ass-wipe for thinking otherwise.*

"I keep my promises and I meant what I said in the beginning. *You are mine, and I'm yours.* I will take care of you in every way that I can. From now on, you'll get full honesty from me. *I'm so sorry, Becs.*"

My demon-mush boyfriend has returned. And in turn, me with him.

"I should apologize, too. It wasn't fair of me and I'm sorry. You've been mostly honest from day one, and your intentions were good. It's not your fault I was traumatized and triggered; *that's on me.* I'm sorry for projecting and taking it out on you."

"No apologies necessary, although I am grateful you didn't throw me out."

A smile came upon my face as I handed him the rest of the ice cream.

We exchanged a shared sweet look. "Like I could get rid of you; didn't you say it would be hard to do?"

"I did, didn't I?"

I sighed as he spoon-fed me a bite and I began to tell him about the situation with my ex so that he knew the whole thing. Of course, I cried and sniffled throughout.

By the end of it, the ice cream was gone, and he seemed unsettled with a frown. "I never could understand why humans treat others so cruelly and heartlessly. You didn't deserve it and if I see him and know it's him, I'll strangle him. How dare he put thoughts of unworthiness in your head."

Big scary demon, strangling Joseph—*I'd pay to see that actually.*

"Me either, but I'm glad you're different. Also, since I didn't tell you before, you're a decent human being, too —err, *being rather*. I hate one less person, compared to the rest of the world."

He smiled, leaning his forehead against mine while wiping a stray tear.

"I'm glad you think so. You are the last person on this planet I'd ever want to hate me; it's why I looked for you and waited. I couldn't let you finish the day or night thinking you deserve anything less than the best, or that I didn't feel for you as I do."

I shifted myself, turning towards him fully. The "feel for you as I do" sank deep, and I had to know.

"How do you feel, Bels?"

He caressed my cheek, giving me a fond, heartfelt look. *I'm going to evaporate with his mush-sweetness.*

"I love you, Becs, and I will do everything I need to get you to see that I do, and my intentions are only *for you*. I am yours for as long as you'll have me, which I hope extends past today."

I shrugged with a sniffle, "I suppose. It might be weird going to the convention as you *without you*."

His eyes sparkled at the reminder, and I pulled him closer to plant a kiss that spoke how I felt about *him*.

Hearing a cute needy noise escape him, I moved to straddle him, throwing the blanket off me and breaking our kiss a moment later.

"Come here and let me hold you a while," I told him.

I wrapped my arms around him, tugging him to me.

As he held me in turn, I realized that I was not only a

fool for thinking Belke to be anyone other than who he always was around me, but that I loved him, too.

BECS
YOU ARE
BEAUTIFUL

FOURTEEN

BECS

A few days after straightening things over with Belke, I put on one of my kimono dresses with a high collar, it was black and red with intricate designs that made me feel hot when I put it on.

I walked into work, still at the front desk, naturally, as Belke mentioned I'd be transferred into the position and department after Dragon Con the following weekend.

They had to hire a replacement, and I would need to train them. Interviews were being done that week and a decision would be made the day I came in feeling like a million bucks in my dress.

David wasn't too happy to lose someone he got to walk all over. When he called me into his office the day before, I explained to him that I didn't apply to any position, but that it was in my file to give me a position once it was available due to my qualifications and skills. *Can't forget the degree, too—fucking prick.*

He didn't like that answer, but I didn't give a single fuck.

David had lied. There *were* various positions all along,

but I was given something else. I was fuming after I left and it didn't help matters any when I heard Katherine talking shit again in the breakroom.

I didn't intervene, but I walked away, madder than hell. Speaking of, Belke wasn't too happy to find out either. Ever since our coming-to-Jesus moment with his human form, he's been over during the week, too.

Katherine had been acting like herself more so than normal when she found out about my transferring of departments, constantly giving me the stink eye.

I was getting a sign-on bonus and getting paid more than her. She couldn't stand it.

I basked in it, feeling appreciative of the favors that the universe was finally returning good juju to me for the bullshit I had to deal with.

After lunch the day I wore the kimono dress, Katherine covered the front desk, eyeballing me. Not that I gave her any fuel.

I had another meeting with David and then *Zavier Bel* after.

Once in his office, David had me take some surveys and fill out the transfer paperwork.

"You look nice today, Rebecca. Our team will surely miss you."

Will it, David? Really? Or will you miss having a rug to step on and you can't stand it?

I gave him an awkward smile. "I'm grateful for the opportunities offered to me in this position, thank you."

A lie, surely, but I was grateful to have a job.

He sighed, signing his name on one of the papers in messy scribble. "I almost feel sorry for you," he went on.

I pursed my lip, tilting my head to the side that he caught onto.

"Zavier Bel will be your new boss, and *he's insufferable.* I know I was a better boss than he ever will be. You'll need all the luck you can get."

Yeah, don't know about that, bud. Believe what you want, though. You're the insufferable one.

I wanted to speak my mind and defend him, but I didn't. My intuition told me to let it go. I didn't have too much longer to deal with David and Katherine's shit.

David was simply jealous of Zavier's position and how he didn't take shit from how people talked down to him, because he was considered an outsider coming in and running the show. It made people upset, David being one of them.

It gave me pleasure though.

Karma doesn't always show her cards, but when she does, it's fucking glorious.

I couldn't lie anymore, so I didn't answer or respond back. I finished the last sheet he slid across the desk, and I looked up at him.

"Will there be anything else? I don't want to keep Mr. Bel waiting, and Katherine despises working at the front desk."

He scoffed, rolling his eyes. "She could use the skills; *she'll live.* Yes, we don't want to keep him waiting."

I stood up, hiding my smirk at his sarcastic tone when he spoke about Mr. Bel.

Absolutely riveting. I couldn't wait to tell him.

I left David's office, smiling with some extra pep in my step on the way to the elevator.

I pushed the fiftieth-floor button and a few people got off and on, congratulating me on my promotion that was rightfully deserved.

Absolute strangers were talking to me. *Did I miss something?*

Maybe not strangers, but new and old coworkers alike, *acknowledged me.*

What planet was I on again? *Surely not earth.*

Shit was weird and I didn't know what to do with myself. Recognition and not harassment was new to me.

Ignoring my wandering thoughts, I arrived at Belke's office, knocking three times.

He opened the door that time with a small smile.

Adoring that one-windowed large view of Atlanta, I appreciated the fact that his office had privacy and how no one could see.

Closing the door behind me, he locked it.

I drew my lips into a flat line, holding back a smirk. *This guy.*

"You look amazing," he whispered, kissing my cheek.

"Thank you, as do you," I said honestly, appreciating his button up black shirt and black pants he wore, looking as mysterious as he always did. I couldn't help but miss his wagging demon tail.

"You are so sweet," he caressed my cheek briefly before grabbing my hand, leading me towards where he normally sat on his side of the desk.

"David despises you. But I'm sure you already knew that."

I caught his knowing look, followed by a smile as he nudged me against his large desk.

"Certainly. I only match energy. His has *all* the bad vibes. I can tell when someone is full of shit."

I grinned. "I knew there was *something* I liked about you."

Tossing a coy look to him, I sat on the desk, pulling up

my dress. He caught onto what I was doing as his look turned impish.

Since my dress was appropriate work length, I purposely didn't wear underwear to work, knowing I had the meeting in his office.

He bit his bottom lip, taking me in as I splayed my hands beside me in invitation as I watched his reactions and heat rising to those brown and blue eyes.

"Mmm, don't mind if I do," he murmured, stealing a kiss full of need before licking his lips.

He kept his eyes on me as he knelt between my thighs, the intent to devour me didn't slip past my notice.

I'd never been with him in his human form. It wasn't as interesting as his other form, but I'd take what I could get.

"You smell good," he said, breathing in my pussy which caused me to hold my breath, tugging on my bottom lip.

His human tongue slid out and onto the curve of my vulva.

Yes, steal my soul from me, Bels.

My mind sailed to cloud nine as I released my held breath and closed my eyes leaning back on my hands. He had me coming in no time with how horny I was as I kept as quiet as I could when I shook against his torturing tongue. Releasing my grip on his hair, my eyes popped open as he hummed in approval at me splayed on his desk. Zavier kissed my inner thigh before standing up, unbuttoning his pants.

"Delicious," he murmured, licking his lips with my cum.

I huffed a breath at the insatiable sight as he leaned closer, taking my lips with his and tasting myself.

When Belke pulled away to line his thick cock to my entrance, I took note that while his cock was human, it was still made for my pleasure the moment he slid home.

My mouth fell open as I looked up at him.

"You feel amazing as always, Becs," he whispered as I adjusted myself to sit up more to cup and squeeze his muscled ass.

I moved my hands up to his side, tossing my head back in quiet moaning bliss. Who knew how thin the walls were or just who was near Zavier's office.

Pulling me closer, his hands cupped and held the sides of my face, holding me against his hot, wet lips. I could still taste myself on them, but it didn't bother me whatsoever. It was somehow the sexiest and dirtiest thing all wrapped into one little bow.

His cock moved within with easy pumps, savoring our first time on his desk. My nails dug into his side as he nibbled on my ear before kissing along my jaw.

My eyes were closed in blissful *hell*, and I knew that Zavier was right there with me when he moaned in my ear.

I began to wonder how soundproof the room was as I held back my own moans with how hot this work excursion was. As if he knew, too, he captured my lips, muting and muffling them all the same.

Devils, did I love this demon man.

I quickly fell into Hell with him as my pussy clenched and spasmed in release as he filled me full of him. He squeezed one of my breasts, easing to a stop while leaning against me with his arms wrapped around me.

"You make my days and nights so much better," he whispered against my lips.

"Likewise, *you wicked man.*" I shot him a sexy look as he reached in his drawer for wipes and to clean us off.

We stared at each other; our cheeks flushed as he wiped me. The sight and care made me want more of him.

He kissed me afterward as I moved myself off his desk,

adjusting my dress and making my way to the one of the forest green comfy chairs across from him.

Watching him straighten himself up to business-as-usual-work-mode made me smirk. So much so that I couldn't help what slipped from my mouth.

"Pleasure doing business with you, Mr. Bels."

Something sinful passed through his eyes, a smile forming as he agreed with a sexy wink that was toe curling.

Zavier sat in his chair, exhaling, seeming content as he always did after any round we had, whether it was long or short.

Leaning my arm on the chair, I bit my finger lightly, holding back a grin.

He noticed it before clearing his throat. "I wanted to talk to you about the office I'm having created for you, and how the interviews went."

I placed my hands in my lap, listening attentively even though he was a huge distraction.

"Are there any must-haves that you require, or do you want to be surprised?"

"A surprise," I said automatically before asking, "How'd the interviews go?"

He folded his arms into his lap. "Well, David selected options for candidates, but I made the final decision. I think you'll appreciate who I chose."

I raised a curious eyebrow, and he smirked. "She'll be in tomorrow for training."

Eagerly, I stood and made my way towards him slowly, running my hands along his clean and clear desk that we recently made dirty, figuratively speaking. "I look forward to it... Will I be getting one of these *large* desks? I may make it a requirement, at the very least, for my new office."

I caught his eyes following me and the way my hand ran

across his desk. He seemed smitten when I climbed into his lap, grateful he had a top-notch chair that held us both.

"It's only fair I give you a desk worthy enough to *fuck you on.*"

Happy with his answer, I ran my hands through his dark locks, kissing him. He moved my dress up and cupped my ass.

"Sounds perfect," I whispered, pausing between kisses.

"One more round before you go?" he asked in my ear, tugging on my earlobe.

I shivered, turning my head to the side, nodding.

He shifted us, unzipping before entering me again.

The ride was slow and tantalizing with heated touches that had me burning and aching for him. *I hated that I had to go back to work for a couple of hours after this.*

"I expect you tonight, to finish this," I whispered after I came, clutching to him desperately while muffling our noises with passionate kisses.

"I'll be there," he said breathlessly, cupping my cheek with starry looking eyes from post-sex haze.

We cleaned up again, straightening up after another sweet kiss.

My lips stretched upward, leaving him at his desk with his own satisfied look. I admired the looks he gave me, how smitten he was, and how lusty in love I was.

We were both heathens, and I was more than okay with it.

BECS

YOU ARE BEAUTIFUL

FIFTEEN

BECS

The new girl was *just* like Katherine, and I bit back a laugh when she walked in.

Thank you, Bels, you're the best.

The only difference between Katherine and the new girl, Ashlee, was that Ashlee was *actually nice* to me.

Although, as her trainer, I would certainly hope so.

Katherine loved her immediately, of course, overly complimenting her and her nice clothes and the Coach bag Katherine didn't have.

David was also kind to her, ignoring me completely. I rolled my eyes as they walked away, and I found Ashlee rolling hers, too.

We caught each other's look, laughing in unison.

"This should be fun," she breathed out and I grinned in approval.

"I like you already, Ashlee. I dealt with them for longer than I'd like, and you can only imagine how they treated me for being plus-sized *and* having a brain."

"Are you kidding me?" Her scowl gave me internal life for injustice.

I shook my head.

"That's the stupidest shit I ever heard. There's nothing wrong with you, Rebecca, and if I hear anything from her mouth, I won't let that shit slide. This is 2022, *not* high school. For fuck's sake."

I blinked at her response before nodding in agreement. "You're my kind of people, Ashlee. Consider me your friend and fellow coworker. I'm hopeful my new boss is way better than David," I told her quietly even though I already knew the answer to that, but I had to pretend otherwise.

"He's certainly more handsome, *goodness*. Also, *since we're official*, call me Ash. Only people I like call me that, and you're good people in my book, too."

"Then, call me Bec, or Becs, *because same*."

We beamed, doing a cheesy handshake.

I'm sucking your dick tonight, Bels. Hells yeah—a work bestie, finally!

"I'm glad you're here, you'll be fantastic; the only hard part is juggling the influx of appointments and calls on the busy days," I went on to explain while showing her the routine.

I took her to lunch with me that day and the next, showing her my favorite spots, and it turned out she was like me with lattes.

Things are turning around after all, Bels. I could get used to this.

The weekend before the cosplay convention was spent making sure to get the final touches together on the cosplays I made, and Belke agreed to help me the following

Saturday with the body paint. He seemed overly eager for it, too, but I wouldn't complain having his hands all over me.

On the weekend of, we loaded up the car before driving to the hotel near the convention in the city. I wanted to be fancy and experience a true getaway even if I lived not far from where the Dragon Con was being held.

When we arrived, he checked us in, and someone began loading and bringing our things to our room on a higher floor.

Inside the room there was a large living room, and then the door over led to an even bigger bedroom with a California king bed, nice neutral décor, and a large tub in the bathroom. There was a fancy standup shower, too, and a toilet in a separate area with another set of sinks.

"You didn't have to get so fancy, Bels," I said, grabbing the wine on the table near the coffee pot by the door.

"Yes, I did. I wanted us *both* to enjoy this weekend away, and my very first convention *with you.*"

There's that big demon mush.

I showed him my sweetest smile, popping the bottle open with a giggle.

"It's most appreciated, and I always have a fun time at these things. I'm excited for you to meet my friend, Figgy. They are bringing their girlfriend, who I haven't met. Don't forget to use they/them pronouns for Fig and she/her for Figgy's girlfriend." I reminded him politely just in case he forgot.

"Of course, I'm flattered you want to introduce me to your friend."

"I'm always happy to show *you* off. I just hope no one from work shows up, or it might be awkward."

He walked closer. "Fuck them. They can kiss my

demon ass. I can't wait to spend this time and show you off either."

My toes curled at his words, taking a sip of wine before handing it to him.

"Cheers to my hot demon boyfriend," I said sweetly. He seemed thoughtful, taking the bottle and chugging some down with a happy sigh.

"Cheers to my hot girlfriend, although *a she-demon* tomorrow. *Hells, I can't fucking wait to see you in full form.*" Zavier licked his lips as if picturing me standing before him then.

I grinned unashamedly because he was in for a treat.

"Let's get ready for this evening and the after-party. Are you still going to match with me?"

"You know it. Always."

We killed the rest of the bottle before getting ready.

I did my gender-bend of Howl, putting on my wig, matching earrings and makeup, and Howl's famous cape at the beginning of the movie that I proudly made myself. I ended up adding a plush Calcifer to sit on my hip because how could I not include Calcifer?

Belke did a gender-bend as the character, Sofi, wearing the hat, a shirt, and plain pants. His hair was already dark, so it worked out.

We put in our respective character contacts, mine being the color of Belke's eyes, and his being brown.

"We look hot," I told him as I put on my boots.

"Agreed, although, you put more effort than I did."

"You're still precious," I said, booping his nose.

He said nothing even though he was certainly amused by my gesture.

As we made our way towards the convention, I recalled how I made him watch Howl's Moving Castle, both sub and dubbed versions. He enjoyed the movie, saying he'd go as Sofi as she was from the beginning of the movie when she ran into the wizard Howl. I agreed, feeling admiration and appreciation pass over me. I leaned my head on Zavier's shoulder since he was in human form.

"Blonde looks good on you, I wouldn't mind you weaving your magic over me," he purred, and I caught his cute stare.

"Thank you, and maybe I will," I winked in turn, enjoying his playful mood.

He kissed my cheek as we made our way into the convention center. People were already filling in and dressed as various characters from shows, anime, and movies. The best part about it? *People looked like me.* It was *my* safe space to exist creatively.

As Bels and I stood in line, he held my arm as Sofi did in the movie which was *adorable.* I loved how he meshed well into my life and my passions. The support he gave was insurmountable. A math equation I couldn't name.

The compliments from people who enjoyed Howl's Moving Castle brought me back to life. Here, I was a real person, not some plus-sized nobody who got bullied at work. Having a handsome being at my side worked wonders as well.

Once we were inside and badges given, I found an anime art table with prints and posters and Figgy, who was dressed as a Kawaii anime character, same with Figgy's girlfriend.

We squealed upon seeing each other.

"BECS! LOOK AT YOU!"

"Look at *you!* Figgy!"

Figgy did a spin for me before grabbing their lady.

"This is Marissa, *my lady*." I told her *hi*, before I indicated my head towards Bels.

"Here's my man, Zavier."

He gave me a sweet look before telling them hello.

"Now that the introductions are out of the way, let's go grab our cute fandom stuff before it's gone by tomorrow!" I giggled at Figgy's suggestion, following behind them and their girlfriend with Bels beside me.

Everyone knew that part of the conventions and cosplays was wandering around and buying all the merch of fandoms and favorites, plus seeing the cosplays and cool things people came up with. All shapes and sizes–*it's the absolute best*.

"The Zavi-name is okay, right?" I asked so only he could hear.

He nodded while looking at various stalls that were set up all over the place. The stalls of artists and handmade items, plus actors and actresses from TV shows, movies, and the voice actors for anime.

It was overwhelming in the best of ways, but the four of us spent the next few hours buying plushies, posters, and fan art from various shows. *There was also a demon plushie that reminded me of Belke.*

Zavier was amused with me the whole time as I caught his gaze while on our way to drop all the shit off at the hotel room before meeting up for dinner.

"What's that look for?" He inclined his brow, and I turned my face away, whispering, "*I blame Figgy*."

His grin made me feel light as a feather. "Uh-huh. I'm hardly judging, I got some fan art that reminded me of *you*. And the fun cartoonist drawing of us together."

I tossed him the demon plushie from one of the large

bags as we rode the elevator to the room. "It's a demon-mini that made me think of you."

The blush he gave me was out of this world as I grinned at how flattered he was to receive a plushie from me. "I'm also not judging myself either. I always save money for these events, and only get stuff I can't live without..."

He chuckled after looking at my hands full of bags when we dropped off our stuff at the room before heading back out to a steakhouse close by.

Figgy and Marissa were already there waiting, and we went in as a group. We received some weird looks, but the workers knew about the convention, saying nothing. *They better not anyway or else I'll put my southern sassy foot up their asses.*

After being seated, we ordered alcoholic drinks, our food, and made idle talk as everything began to arrive.

"Is the rave tonight or tomorrow, Figs?" I asked later after receiving our food.

"There's a normal dance-night tonight, and tomorrow is the rave. Or it could be both... I wasn't paying attention to anything other than tomorrow's... What are you two going to be tomorrow?" Fig asked, looking between me and Zavier.

"A fun surprise that you'll have to wait for," I told them nonchalantly.

Figgy scoffed, "Then you can be surprised, too! We chose a gothic Lolita from our favs."

"Ooo! I like it!" I nodded towards Fig and Marissa in approval.

"Sunday is school outfit day, as per usual," Figgy added, and I agreed.

"We're predictable, aren't we? Do you have rave outfits planned?" I asked, looking between Marissa and Fig.

"We do, I'll be a cute rave bunny," Figgy piped up.

Marissa rolled her eyes playfully with a sigh, "I will also be a rave bunny."

"That's cute," I told them, and they grinned, exchanging a cute look between themselves before sneaking a kiss. *D'awh!*

"What about you two?" Marissa asked.

"We'll be leather bunnies," I said quietly, hiding a grin.

"Nice," Marissa mentioned as Figgy gave me a knowing look and a wink.

I couldn't even look at Zavier, who patted my thigh, squeezing lightly.

"Well, cheers to my first convention, and what will most certainly be an interesting weekend," Zavier said, holding up his drink as we all cheered.

"It's your first time, really?" Marissa asked, and Figgy seemed curious, too.

Zavier nodded. "I'm a cosplay virgin."

I nearly spat out my drink, and they laughed at the comment. I turned my face towards him, giving him a playful look, and he looked like a playful kitten, stealing a kiss from me.

"With her help though, I think our cosplays are well-paired."

"Agreed!" Figgy concurred as with Marissa.

"Now, let's go get drunk and dance our asses off," I mentioned to everyone after we paid and got our checks upon finishing up our meal and drinks.

Everyone agreed as we left back to the convention and to where the dancing was.

There were a lot more people than I imagined when we walked into the huge room of flashing lights.

I had never danced with my boyfriend before. Hopefully, he didn't mind dancing.

There was a side room to put our coats and stuff, so I handed over my cape, plush Calcifer, and Zavier's hat. After, the man himself went to grab us some alcohol at the bar.

Figgy and Marissa had already made their way to the dance floor. I smiled, thinking how great they looked together. Marissa gave off huge introvert vibes, but she seemed nice enough to me.

Bels appeared next to me with a double shot.

"I didn't ask what you liked, sorry," he went on.

Sniffing it, I asked, "Tequila?" He nodded as I downed it.

"Works for me!"

He blinked, a smirk forming before doing the same.

I unbutton my top slightly, feeling hot, but also feeling mischievous with my favorite demon boy.

Certainly not a boy, but *damn, was I lit.*

A fun song came on, and I began to move my hips slowly, raising my hands while walking through the crowd. I turned to find Belke making his way over with a look of desire at my drunkenness. My look matched his as I indicated my finger towards him.

He reached for me, pulling me closer with a sexy look. I sighed, looking up at him before he stole my lips, holding me tightly.

My arms held his sides as he slipped his tongue in my mouth. Drunk brain was buzzing with thoughts of him. I felt like a main character in a movie after he released my lips from our kissing rendezvous.

The song changed, and I placed my arms on his shoulders, swaying my hips in sync with his.

As the next song came on, I turned around, placing his hands on my hips. Moving my head to the side, leaning into him, I felt his lips on my neck before tugging on my ear. I sighed out as he leaned his head against mine. The music, our bodies pressed tightly, and his heat.

I began to get overheated and horny after a while, and I grabbed his hand, leading him to get our stuff before leaving.

"It's so hot, Bels," I pouted once we were in the elevator of our hotel.

It was after midnight, at least.

I started unbuttoning my shirt all the way since it was only us in the elevator. I still held the cape, and Calcifer, leaning against the wall. My eyes were closed, but it wasn't long before I felt him run his hands over my midsection, trailing up towards my bra.

His hand kneaded my large breasts as his fingers trailed upward before licking up my neck, stealing a kiss as the elevator stopped and pinged.

Opening my eyes slowly, I could see his blazing look.

"Let's shed these clothes," he whispered before moving away and me behind him. He held his hat in his hand, and my hand in the other.

I admired his backside, appreciating that he was well built for a human so that I didn't overshadow him with these hips that didn't lie.

I smirked once we were at the door to our room, and I grabbed his round, muscular ass.

He pulled me inside, closing the door and nudging me against it.

I took my shirt off and Belke began undoing the rest, sliding the pants down as I kicked the shoes off.

His lips were on my skin immediately, pulling my

underwear down, and the rest of it off, kissing the top part of where I ached. I almost felt embarrassed about all the sweating I'd done, but Bels didn't deter or move away.

Why are you thinking about how your vag smells right now, Becs? Don't kill the sexy vibes!

Pushing the thoughts far from my mind, I ran my hands through his hair, and I heard a moan slip from him.

"Let me see my demon boyfriend," I breathed out and he looked up at me before kissing my inner hip.

"As you wish."

I took my wig off and the earrings as he undressed.

"Do you have a preferred form?" I asked, standing in front of the full-length mirror, completely nude.

"It depends on who I'm around."

I turned around to see him in full form with his *wings*.

"I love how you look at me in my true form, so it's probably my favorite... I also can't double-penetrate you in any other way. I'll happily be in any form that you want me to be. I don't mind either when it comes to *you*, Becs."

I'm so in love with him, it's stupid.

"You are my truest treasure, Bels. I've never met or seen anyone more beautiful than *you*. You've been something else this entire time, not that I'm complaining. You continuously show me what it means to be loved."

I moved closer to where he stood, and I knew instantly why he chose our particular room, to stretch out in. His gaze followed me as I circled him, admiring him in all his magnificent, hellish glory.

Belke's tail was semi-tucked near his feet, horns were out, naked with his cock hard and waiting, and wings outstretched.

Fuck me. I was speechless.

I ran my hand lightly over his dark, soft feathers, placing the lightest kiss there.

Moving to the front of him again, I wanted to gaze at his face as I told him what I needed to say next.

"I realized I haven't told you yet..."

He tilted his head, waiting with bated breath. His eyes lowered to my lips.

"I love you."

His tail moved, reaching me, and I stepped into his embrace.

In that embrace, I felt his wings around us both, and his tail. It was like being hugged three times, all wrapped in one. He felt safe, his arms, and his warmth.

I found a place of belonging with him, his sincerity, and *love* with his horns and heat.

BECS

YOU ARE
BEAUTIFUL

SIXTEEN

BECS

We made love to each other that night with love-filled gazes. Saying those words was freeing for me. I wanted to weep at how he looked with his dark wings opened wide as I stared up at him, pumping inside me. Slow and sensual. Those blue eyes full of love. A vision, another mathematical equation I couldn't conjure.

"Let me touch you," I whispered as he leaned closer, moving his wings within reach so I could.

As soon as I ran my fingers on the top of one, he came immediately.

He nuzzled his face into my neck, heavily breathing.

"I didn't realize they were so sensitive," I said to him stroking his hair, then his wing that laid on either side of us.

I felt him twitch inside and moan, finding it fascinating.

His hand made its way to my clit, realizing I didn't finish.

"You have nerve endings here and you can seek paradise from it, yes?"

"Y-Yes-s," I managed to get out, feeling his lips and

breath on my neck. *I'm so turned on right now, I can't even think.*

"It is the same for when you touch me. With my horns being touched, I want to fill every hole of yours. When... you touch *my wings*, it undoes me completely. There isn't a sensation quite like it. Perhaps, someday, you'll get to experience it for yourself, but there's nothing else like tasting hellful bliss."

I arched into him, feeling my build and at the right moment, I ran my hand on the other wing in the same spot. Another orgasm shook him as mine found me instantaneously.

I held his head to my chest, gathering myself.

"I love you, Bels," I said gently, running my hand through his soft demon hair. A view I never wanted to leave for the rest of my days.

I felt his lips on my neck. "I love you, Becs."

We laid there for a few more moments. "It's going to be a long day today, and a long time getting ready... Snuggles and sleep?" He kissed my cheek before pulling out and groaning. I missed his cock filling me already.

"Tomorrow night, we're continuing this," he said, and it almost sounded *pouty*.

I smirked, sitting up on my elbows. "Whatever you say, horny-demon-man."

He grunted and I couldn't help but watch him walk away into the bathroom and turn on the shower. *Hate to see you go but love to watch you leave, you sexy ass.*

His wings disappeared as did his tail. I lay there, dozing off until he came back out, tapping me with his tail.

"You'll feel better and more relaxed after showering, then we'll sleep."

I groaned in protest, realizing he was right.

Slowly, I made my way to wash my makeup off, then I made sure to scrub myself good, washing my hair and everything in-between.

He was right though, I felt more relaxed, and sleep tugged at my eyelids once more.

Belke held the covers open as I climbed in, snuggling close as his unknown scent enveloped me into comfort. Someday, I'd figure out what his scent was. It was probably something otherworldly. Something that suited his kind and him more than what my human brain could name.

"Goodnight. I'm glad you're here," I murmured to him.

"Me too. I love you, Bec."

"Love...you." And it all went dark as I passed right the fuck out.

Night one—spectacular. Ten out of ten.

Belke

SEVENTEEN

BELKE

"Bels!"

I grinned wickedly, teasing her as I painted her body. I couldn't help myself. Her curves were perfect and each trace of them wasn't enough for me. Despite the insecurities she held, I loved every inch of her.

"Focus," she huffed out after the release from my tongue-side excursion before painting her thighs and legs. It was in my nature to pleasure, so naturally, I had to taste her before leaving the hotel room.

It took a lot longer to paint her body, because I kept getting distracted with the way she looked at me hungrily. A demon without horns herself, she was *always* on my sexual wavelength. A dream on two luscious legs that I wanted to lick and taste for the rest of my life.

I found her to be the most fascinating and beautiful human I'd ever met. I was selfish with her; I couldn't take her soul and give it away to anyone else. *She was mine to have.* I didn't care what I had to do for it.

It's uncommon for demons to fall in love with *anyone*. But not impossible. With sex demons, our goals involved contracts and energy exchanges, but that wasn't all, we had duties to uphold for our realm and tasks to be completed.

Rebecca was an ocean, a current that had swept me under and into her depths. Her mind was her own. Her soul was honest, sweet, yet broken in a way. Broken by a world that lived and thrived on being their own energy-sucking demons. Her body was a playground worthy of exploration to touch and taste. She was an obsession with a label that came with, *"For Belke Only."*

We had both lived a lonely life doing what needed to be done or what was asked of us, so when she whispered those words last night, *"I love you," I was captured.*

Forever.

My soul was officially taken. She didn't realize it in the beginning, but I knew I wouldn't take her soul; I had to keep my big, scary demon persona, after all.

Her energy and scent of *home* attracted and reeled me in from the beginning. Seeing her reactions and intrigue to me were remarkable and surprising, too. I didn't view her for the insecurities she battled with herself, I saw the ethereal being within; a spirit like mine. A goddess I worshiped for as long as I had her.

As I continued painting her, my thoughts continued to drift, thinking of how angry she was in my office that first day.

I don't *ever* want to see that look again or have her angry with me. That moment was scarier than some of the scariest demons I've seen, and I don't mean in looks either, *but killing-specific ranked demons.*

I wasn't violent unless I had to be. It's why I chose to be a sex-demon and not another class. I could justify pleasure from both parties before I took their soul and exchanged energies, but not just outright *taking*. Our *soul-taking* wasn't terrible either way, it just promised a place in our realm for the afterlife. We didn't take years off or anything crazy like the heretics said.

I was born and raised in Hell.

There were stories of earth and humanity, the wars and love. I never had the pleasure of experiencing it until the past decade.

Some of us were allowed up here, if we brought back souls and worked on getting back the hordes that escaped as an act of rebellion and hate.

So, I traveled around doing as much, until demons in Atlanta started showcasing themselves to the public eye, then it brought me there specifically.

I could see some of my brethren's viewpoints, humans were vile and filthy, sometimes worse than what I've seen in other worlds. *That* I could understand but eradicating *all* of them? Not even all demons were alike and the same, so it made sense that humanity was similar. There were pros and cons to all of it. But I made a choice to be here, and I had no regrets.

Rebecca was my destiny because her soul and energy healed me. *She's mine, no matter what.*

"You did good, Bels," she mentioned, looking into the mirror's reflection as my thoughts shifted to the present with my woman standing beautifully in front of me.

Around her, I was easily distracted, yet grateful to fate that brought us together.

"I can't wait to see you in *full* form." My tail brushed up against her leg in loving approval.

"Let's get to it then," she said with a smile that reached her eyes.

I nodded in turn, going to grab the black dress I found.

It had a deep plunge that would accentuate her lovely

breasts. The back had a fun jeweled pattern, and a leg slit with an added slit for her tail.

I was giddy, handing it to her while handing the other items she would need to use to hold up her breasts without wearing a bra. I didn't know about all things women, but I had help in finding what was needed while shopping for her.

"You did good, Bels, I'm most impressed." She encouraged me with the flash of her teeth.

I beamed proudly as she got dressed and began working on her hair and getting the horns to stay in properly so that movement could be more manageable.

"I'm liking this look more and more," I purred in her ear, placing fun earrings in her ears and then ones that matched in mine.

"I could never be a sexy demon of *your stature,* but I'll take it." She winked and put on platform shoes to give her some height.

I found it alluring as she did her makeup; I changed into my normal demon wear of black with the full form without wings.

That I saved for her, and her only.

"Will you help me with the tail, please?" She asked quietly, and my own tail swished back and forth happily.

I grabbed her well-made tail, bringing it over to where she stood. This talented woman even got the soft texture right, my beautiful, creative genius.

I began to assist, stealing a kiss from her neck. Huskily, I whispered in her ear, "You have no idea what this look does to me. All my desires and affection are *for you*, and what you have in store to look forward to tonight *before and after* the rave."

I heard her sigh out soft and steady as I stepped away,

letting my touch linger on her smooth skin before we finished getting ready.

"You are my match in every way," I whispered in the elevator later as I admired the she-demon beside me. She had slipped a black garter on her open-slit leg, and I noticed it peeking out with how she leaned in the corner. *My demon.*

"I'm going to enjoy teasing you all day, Bels."

"A torture I'm willing to suffer with," I countered back with a needy look, my cock begging to bend her over and fuck her right there in that elevator.

"Hmm," was all she said, and I shivered, anticipating the night ahead. I could even picture her as one of us back in the home realm, living comfortably and happily alongside for the rest of our existence both here and after death. *A beautiful nightmare.*

"Let's go get chaotic, Bels, and show em' that demons are sexy and not as evil as they think. Emphasis on the *sex* part."

Yep, I'm in love with this demon woman alright.

"Right behind you, Becs," I told her as the elevator pinged, and we stepped out towards the hotel lobby to make our way to the convention and begin what would most certainly be an interesting day.

$$(x-$$

$$y^2 = z$$

BECS

$$e = \cos x + tg y$$

$$\sin x$$

$$(y-1)$$

$$\sin a =$$

YOU ARE
BEAUTIFUL

EIGHTEEN

BECS

"Well, damn, Becs! *Zavier*." Figgy wiggled their eyebrows as I grinned shamelessly.

"I tried really hard to look like a sexy demon that shows up in strangers' rooms at night to lure them to the dark side," I said teasingly to Figgy and Marissa, who grinned while also looking fabulous in their gothic Lolita character outfits.

I snuck a side-glance at the demon himself, winking. Belke cleared his throat not bothering to hide his amusement.

"Well, you both pair well together either way," Marissa commented honestly. Offering my thanks to them both, my heart soared at the thought, and the rest of the day I was on cloud nine. Not five minutes went by before various people asked for pictures with us.

Some good photos were tagged and sent to me of Bels and I. We were swoon worthy, and he looked as beautiful as I've always seen him. I didn't look too bad either. Belke was ethereal and otherworldly. I was lucky to be beside him.

I held his hand most of the day, and I think he enjoyed being able to waltz around as himself. It was adorable to see his tail *wagging almost* every time I caught a glimpse, and it reminded me of a happy puppy.

I think I have a confused boyfriend, part-demon, sometimes cat-like, and now has cute puppy energy. What sort of cinnamon roll was he? My mind immediately conjured up a demon with horns but with cat and dog features with big sad puppy eyes and a cute nose.

I giggled as we walked through a crowd, and he gave me a questioning glance.

"I can see your tail wagging," I told him quietly, and he narrowed his eyes playfully. His tail stayed to his side then, but not before gently rubbing my leg.

"I'm happy, what can I say?" He shrugged, and I brought his hand to my lips for a quick peck.

"I love you. Happiness is a good look for you." I gave him a heartfelt look as we stood waiting in line for snacks.

He relaxed at my words, looking thoughtful. "I love you. Contentedness works well for us both, doesn't it? It's certainly a treat to have a sexy she-demon at my side."

I made a kissing noise, half-giggling before he leaned down to steal my mouth in a sensual kiss. *Mmm.*

The afternoon was spent getting stopped by *plenty of more people,* which was completely fine by me. I worked my ass off to look like my demon man. Strangers could take pics all they wanted. *And send them to me.*

I couldn't deny how grateful I was to finally leave back to the hotel room though.

Figgy and Marissa had said they'd meet us at the rave and that they needed some time with no socialization.

Which I totally got. I wanted some time alone with Bels, too.

He said he had plans for me, after all.

I leaned in the corner of the elevator, revealing my sexy

thigh from the slit so that it was fully out and exposed. I wanted to tease him more inappropriately, since we were alone.

My intentions quickly hit their mark as his eyes traveled down me slowly, taking in the eyeful I was giving. I could clearly see desire prevalent in his eyes once they met mine with how they simmered and lit up.

"I was told... you had plans for me?" My tone was low as he snuck closer, kneeling.

Frozen with my thundering heart, his lips trailed up my thigh before taking the flimsy garter off with his teeth.

I converted to fire instantaneously.

Raising my leg slightly, he pulled it off with his hand and put it in his pocket, standing back up.

"Why yes, *I do*. To answer your question." The low gravel of his husky tone was delectable as the elevator pinged. I stepped out first, doing a sexy walk in front of him while running my hands through my hair.

"I wonder though, would *I* grow a second cock, if *you* rubbed *my* horns?" I gave him a smug look, leaning against the door as he opened it with a knowing glance.

"A thing of dreams I'm sure... however, why don't you touch mine and let me demonstrate how good it feels to be fucked by *this* sexy demon."

I shivered. I always loved it when he talked dirty to me.

"Show me what you've got horny boy," I cooed, walking into the living room area.

He grabbed my hand, quickly turning me around, moving me quickly to the oversized couch. Those lips claimed mine rightfully, and I was hooked into his demon trap. *Not that I wanted to leave.*

"I've waited all day to have you *in this form*," he said against my lips.

"I want your wings out," I demanded quietly, meaning every word.

He growled and grunted, undressing quickly. I moved my dress as he kneeled on the couch, cornering me against the back of it as I straddled him, placing him inside. Already wet and needy from that torturous elevator ride, I couldn't wait for his blessed cock. I arched backward slightly as he gripped the edges of the couch, keeping me in place while increasing his thrusts.

Out of my periphery before I closed my eyes, his wings appeared gloriously. A dark angel of his own accord, but I supposed my own conceptions of angels and demons were wrong, however I'd take Belke no matter what he looked like. Who said demons couldn't have feathered wings that were soft and sensitive to touch?

I was moaning louder than I expected as he filled me fully. His hands moved towards my hips, holding me steady.

Belke had one hand behind me and the other at the center of me while leaning forward to kiss and lick my chest. I used the back of the couch to hold myself, leaning over it backwards.

It didn't hurt, but damn did it feel *amazing. I guess I'm more flexible than I originally thought.*

My first orgasm found me rather quickly with his expert touch, and soon after, he grunted for me to turn around.

Not before I stroked one of his horns though.

As I turned around, a low growl slipped from his vibrating chest. I faced the back of the couch, pleased with my sneaky deed. Knowing what was coming, I parted myself as he slid home once more.

Still sensitive, I moaned, taking every glorious inch of his demon cock. I blinked open my eyes, noticing another cock near my face. Smirking in sheer ecstasy, I licked the angled soft tip and began sucking cock-number-two off. It was shaped like it was last time which made him feel that much more pleasurable once he put it in my ass. I got to the point where it was hard to focus on sucking him as he really gave it to me in fast, intentional strokes.

Nearly screaming from it, I tossed my head back, feeling his hand cup my breast. At the same time, his other hand found its way into my hair, tugging me back toward him. I arched my back more, delighting in the noises he was making while he hit deep within me with how I was arched.

That self-lubricating cock did wonders, that's for sure. Who needs lube when you have a dick to do it for you? *Sign me up–forever.*

Hearing him exhale behind me with those hands tight around my hips, I inhaled that unnamable scent of his that was too great and special to name. I thoroughly enjoyed it when he was unbridled and passionate.

"I love you, Becs, you have my soul with you *forever*," he whispered before biting my shoulder. I cried out as I tumbled down the length of a strong-as-hell orgasm that left me blind as my mouth fell open wide, unholy sounds leaving my lips.

"Touch my wing, so I can join you," he added in a sultry tone.

I reached my hand out blindly to the side and felt feathers immediately. Stroking firmly, but not to hurt him, I felt him shatter, too, moaning louder than I'd ever heard him before. A demon roar that caused my soul to leave my body if only for a while.

It was music to my ears, a sound that felt like a blessing to my soul, too.

"You also have my soul, willingly and fully, Bels. I love you," I told him moments after.

Belke removed both cocks, hugging me close to him. He buried his face in the crook of my neck, breathing me in. I wondered what I smelled like to him with how often he breathed me in, whether it was my cunt or at my nape. Who knows what it must be like for him.

But instantly, I knew I'd never love anyone else the way I loved him.

In such a short amount of time, I was captured sexually, but also by his mind, kindness, and most of all, his *love*.

I lost track of how long he held me, but eventually he let go. The Belke cloud I was sailing on; I never wanted to be without it.

"Let me scrub the paint off you before this rave?" He offered his hand as I turned around with a heavy sigh, reluctant to move from the couch.

I was tired already from the weekend that wasn't over, but I was enjoying his company most of all.

"Right behind you, Bels," I told him half-heartedly, losing steam from the long day.

I moved to stand, feeling overly fucked. I wasn't gonna complain though. I got my second wind of sex in the shower until being scrubbed down.

I flopped on the bed later, post-shower. "You wear me out, Bels. Geez."

He huffed a quick laugh, kissing my cheek.

"Do you need caffeine to get through the rest of the night?"

I nodded in agreement. "But first, sexy leather bunnies."

He shook his head in amusement, moving away to get dressed and change forms.

For the rave look, we ordered bunny BDSM masks, and I made a harness that made me feel sexy under Belke's gaze.

The only thing I added was a red lip stain and another black dress that went with the harness.

"How am I supposed to last tonight and not leave this room when *you look like that?*"

"Oh? And how do I look then?" I played coy.

"A sex kitten, *or bunny,* rather."

I unleashed a smirk of flattery.

"You do realize you're making me drool, too, right? How am *I* supposed to keep my hands off?"

He wore a chest harness with a netted shirt and tight leather pants that accentuated every feature.

Totally dying over here.

Even in his human form, he was jaw-dropping. His eye colors were a thing to dream about. Same with his demon form.

"Two beautiful people, waiting for a continuation of earlier," he teased, and I rolled my eyes playfully.

"Let's go, you horny bunny, before I say to hell with this rave, and fuck you all night," I warned.

He announced his approval low in his throat as I took his hand. We stepped out into the night for more shenanigans.

BECS

YOU ARE
BEAUTIFUL

NINETEEN

BECS

"Alright, you two look incredible." Figgy nodded with approval as I posed playfully.

Marissa and Fig were dressed as bright colorful rave bunnies, *as I like to call them*. They had those fluffy leg warmers and PLUR gear since Figgy's a regular.

For the first time in like—*ever*, I was doing a couple outfit; not that I minded. It was the best in a cutesy cheesy way, and I could tell Bels was enjoying his first convention. Belke had been giving me cute glances, hand squeezes, and cheek kisses throughout the day that made me feel more loved than anyone before him. Feeling special and cherished was something I could definitely get used to.

After a few drinks with our group of varied rave bunnies, we collectively danced and drunk giggled before Marissa and Figgy danced with just the two of them, and I made the moves on a very eager Zavier.

His eyes were glued to me the entire night, and I couldn't wait to tease him. With all the grinding against him hot and heavy on the dance floor until the late-night hours, it was a relief when he whispered, "I'm ready to leave *now*."

With how needy he sounded, all I heard was, *"Let's continue our sexcapade from earlier."*

Which was totally fine by me.

I nodded against him before he took my hand, pulling me through the dancing crowd and outside. The crisp night air was amazing as I pulled off the mask.

Buzzed from booze and my horny boyfriend, I outstretched my arms and leaned my head back to inhale deep. The city and him was all I needed. "It feels amazing outside, Bels," I exclaimed.

"It does," he went on, and when I was all smiles, catching his gaze, he pulled me closer, kissing me under a streetlight. In these late morning hours, it was only him and I that existed. Returning his affection, he deepened the kiss, slipping his tongue inside where mine was waiting.

Until he interrupted the moment to speak. "I'm ready to have my wings open as I'm buried deep inside *you*," he whispered, tugging on my earlobe.

My toes curled in response as I gave him a sexy eyebrow wiggle, making him grin and shake his head. He led us back to the room, pinning me to the door once we closed it behind us. It was seconds before my dress was pulled over my head and tossed randomly.

"Such a sexy look on you, Becca," he purred in satisfaction.

"Likewise. Feel free to dominate *me*, my big demon boy."

He grunted, licking my neck in one swift motion while running those large, *now demon hands,* firmly down my body in rough sensual caresses.

An exhale of satisfaction leaves me while I grabbed one of his hands.

"I have something for you, Bels," I drew out in a needy tone, dragging his hand to my wet and aching pussy.

With an eager kiss, demon boy got the hint and teased me with a finger, then two, before slipping inside me, using his thumb on my clit.

"Bels," I said in calling, moments later, feeling a quicker than normal build heading my way.

According to my body, I wasn't as tired as I originally was earlier. The two of us were teasing each other all night, so it was only fair, *I supposed.*

I was near throbbing in release when he stopped abruptly, and I pouted in protest. Belke was in partial-demon form with just his hair and body.

"Together, Becs," he breathed out.

Before I could get mad and more frustrated, I pushed him backwards towards the living room couch.

I forced him to sit, springing him free as I kneeled between his legs.

"Not before I torture you," I told him wickedly before placing that demon dick in my mouth. The grooves and ridges worked with me as they pulsed and throbbed against my tongue.

"Fuck me, Becs," he managed to huff out, leaning his head back. Those luscious lips opened with soft sighs which would drive anyone wild. Belke was made for sex, that was for damn sure.

I managed to peek upward and Jesus, the expression on his face was to die for with his mouth open and moaning; his eyes were closed blissfully.

My inner feline was grinning evilly as I focused in, basking in his low moaning, sighs, and the way his hips moved as he fucked my mouth.

"Bec," he urged on in a cute pleading way that made me stop at once, making direct eye contact.

His eyes were furnaces of blue as I saw his form changing completely. I was mesmerized as his horns and tail appeared until he was in full demon form. Belke scooted to the edge of the couch, pulling me into his lap immediately as his wings appeared.

Nearly coming from the sight of him alone, I eagerly placed him inside, sinking down as his arms went around me in turn. We united in a shared gasp while he gave me fiery, deep kisses from my neck to my breasts. My hands went to his shoulders, then his hair before soft feathers brushed against me.

As I kissed him with everything I had and brushed my fingers across the top of one of his wings. Poor Bels crumbled with a startled cry out.

That's a neat little party trick.

As I rode him, I heard him call out my name as I touched his other wing and we climaxed in sync, something that I enjoyed a lot when it was with him. There was something special about bodies being in sync together.

"Fuck," Bels leaned his forehead against mine breathing heavily. *"You have no idea how much better release is when you touch my wings."*

"You like when I ruffle your feathers, do you?" I grinned against him while his low laugh reverberated against my skin.

"Always. Ruffle me anytime."

He stood, holding me as if I weighed *nothing, which still mentally messed with me,* but before the thoughts lingered, I felt the bed under me suddenly as I dropped onto it. A yelp left me as I took in his wings, lost in his beauty; a cock-tail was heading towards me at the same time.

Belke's Cock-Tail or a BCT for short.

I smirked over the thought of this eager-to-please demon as his eyes became even more enticing.

"I want to take you to new heights, Becs."

I raised my eyebrow, offering a funny to go with it. "I *do* enjoy our *religious* experiences together."

"Will you do the sixty-nine-position with me? It's more comfortable for you if you're on top."

I quivered over the thought, sitting up to begin to take off the harness I wore.

Belke moved to lay on the large bed, and I crawled towards him.

"Are you sure about this? What if I smother you?"

I know, I sounded like an idiot. Stupid insecure brain.

"Then, I'll die doing what I love, *and that's you.* Please smother me with *you.*" Seconds later I felt a BCT pet my leg briefly.

"Ohh," *my,* "Okay."

Before I combusted over his words, I maneuvered myself over him. I scooted myself to where his mouth was ready and waiting. *Okay, here goes.*

He gripped my thighs in a way that made me groan at his first eager lick.

Angling myself better, I used my hand to aid as I began my tantalizing licks to his cock. Tasting our own concoction of a sex *cocktail,* I closed my eyes not minding the taste in the least.

The taste of him and I drove me further to focus on the task at hand. *Sucking that demon dick.*

I may have started this encounter, but *damn-n-n.*

Out of my periphery I noticed his tail got *longer.*

Did my eyes deceive me?

Before I thought to ask, a BCT entered my ass while he licked my pussy.

I paused momentarily to moan loudly before reminding myself what I was supposed to be doing. I leaned my head on him, taking his demon cock out of my mouth, using my hand instead. I struggled to talk.

"How...am I supposed to *focus* when... you're doing things like *that?*"

He gave me a fierce lick in response that made my thighs quiver.

I continued to stroke him, my build growing from deep inside me. The sensations of his tongue and cock teasing my ass were almost too much. Immediately, I knew this orgasm would obliterate me. It was then I realized that his hands held me so that I was hovering in a way so that both his dick and tongue could stimulate me at the same time.

Then, he stuck a finger in my butt, putting pressure on a sensitive spot as I shook and screamed. My vision went dark, putting my head into his groin while steadying myself with my arms.

"Guh-goddamn-mn, Bels," my words slurred and muffled together. I gritted my teeth as my eyes rolled back.

There was no functioning for me after that.

He slipped out of me, releasing his hold on my thighs as I pulled myself up and away to roll onto my back. I didn't open my eyes again until I caught my breath and my soul returned into my body.

My head was at the edge of the bed, and he was sitting there playing with my hair with an expression that made him appear as if he won a gold medal. His wings had disappeared, and I basked in the post-sex daze.

Here's your gold medal, Bels, you win.

"Alright, now that I can focus," I said after however long

it was as time didn't exist, not when I got fucked into a different dimension. "Let me finish for you, my mouth is ready."

He smirked, standing up as I moved slightly to angle myself better, opening my mouth. We matched gazes, and he nudged his dick snug into my mouth.

Caressing my hair, I was purring in delight and post-orgasm bliss. Feathers enclosed around us, and I took the hint, grateful for his consideration of my tiredness. *My sweet demon, Belke.*

I reached up blindly until I touched feathers and felt him fill my mouth instantaneously. An idea came over me then.

Testing out a theory, I waited a few moments for him to find his breath as his hand gripped my hair in a way that made me touch his feathers again.

He spilled into my mouth once again with a louder moan that made me blush. *So fucking hot.*

Looking up once, I caught his gaze, and I swallowed him down.

"How am *I* supposed to focus when you do things like *that?*"

I gave him a smug stare, twirling my hair, and sitting up so my legs were at the edge, dangling.

I sent him some of that sass, "Guess you'll figure it out, won't you?"

He let out a short growl and before I could think, I was quickly pulled by my legs and was once again on my back. With more demon dick in my immediate future, I whimpered as he guided himself inside eagerly.

I gazed at him with his wings outstretched. He was dominating me and unfurling. It was everything to witness him in a full sex demon state—*my favorite view of him.*

A demon, not of this world, beautiful with that bronze skin glistening with sweat, and those black and gray horns spiraled away from his perfect human-like face. The way he gazed at me as if I'm someone to be cherished and worshipped.

"I *love* when you look at me as if I'm a masterpiece of art that belongs in a gallery to feast your eyes upon."

"You are," I whispered sweetly, meaning every word.

He thrusted harder, leaning down to claim my lips. He cupped my breasts at the same time before moving his mouth to tease them, too.

When my climax found me again, I took him down into orgasmic oblivion, touching his feathers. Seeing him undone as wildly as I was, did unspeakable things to me as I smelled cum and delicious debauchery.

Done with reality and happily spent after out-of-this-world sex, I quickly passed out with Bels snuggled up behind me.

Night two—Belke's trying to kill me—with pleasure. 10/10 will fuck again.

BECS
YOU ARE
BEAUTIFUL

TWENTY

BECS

Belke attended the last Dragon Con day as himself while I did my student outfit that involved a red plaid skirt with thigh-high socks and garter, plus the white button-up shirt, tie, and a bra that could be seen to appeal to the anime-waifu aesthetic.

I wore fake glasses and made sure to put on a show for Bels while popping gum and twirling on my braids. Seeing him squirm and narrow his pretty eyes, gave me motivation and life.

Catching his coy, seductive looks, it was noticeable in those blue eyes of all the wonderful things he wanted to do to me.

I teased him so much that after we went to the car garage, he sat in the driver's seat and patted his lap. No one was around to witness a large demon in the car leaning back in the seat and angling himself for me, but I arched myself more comfortably so that he had access.

Belke parted my underwear and slipped inside my wet heat. I faced away from him, holding onto the car as he held my ass in a way that he went hard and fast. *Fuck me, I could get used to this.*

"You live to tease me, don't you, little one?"

"Mmhmm," I sounded out in my throat, because little did he know how much I enjoyed his reactions and that wagging demon tail of his.

My mind went blank as he stuffed me full of him, and I wasn't quite ready to come yet.

Once he caught his breath, he moved himself to the back seat. I scooted the driver seat forward, shutting the door and climbing in the back with him. In a swift motion, I straddled him, rubbing his horns sensually while stealing a quick peck before having him guide himself inside once more.

There was nothing better than when he was filling me up or how he held me close and tight.

Belke blew out a deep breath and the windows fogged immediately.

"So full of surprises, aren't you?" My lips twitched upward, while those large calloused hands paid special attention to my breasts.

I held myself in place, using the car roof, grateful that my car backseat was big enough for the both of us to fit in to finish the job.

"Fuck, Becs," he said through gritted teeth, trying to control himself.

I leaned forward, trailing appreciative kisses down his strong jawline before moving to his neck, suckling in a spot that made him groan.

Falling quickly into a steamy sensation, he squeezed my ass and rubbed my clit. The rise and fall of orgasm hit me fast as we flew off the edge, coming with a sharp cry.

Moaning in his ear, I soon nestled my head into the

crook of his neck, breathing in that scent of his I still couldn't name. One day, I swore I'd figure out what to describe what he smelled like, because fire and brimstone weren't the right words. Nor was any masculine or feminine scent.

"We can't be taken anywhere, can we?" I asked him, and a small laugh escaped his pretty mouth.

"No, I suppose not," he said with a satisfied smile.

I caught his blue eyes with the turn of my head. "Never a dull moment with you around, Bels. Not that I'm complaining one bit."

"Good. Cause I wouldn't change us for the world," he said lovingly, kissing me once more.

"Do you feel like driving? It's not a long drive, but I'm tired."

He placed his lips gently on my head in agreement, "You've got it, Becs."

Getting off him and making my way to the passenger seat up front, he changed back into his human form dressed casually as he slid into the driver's seat.

"I have the best weekends with you, Becca. Thank you for bringing me and using me for inspiration. I'll attend with you *anytime, anywhere.*"

Happiness soared through my entire being. "Anything for you," I crooned, sharing an equally mischievous look that he wore, remembering our sexcapades, including the most recent one we finished.

Once he got us on the road, I turned up the tunes before deciding to tease him again. Having never done it before, *there's a first time for everything.*

I took off my seatbelt, and he gave me a quick look wondering just what I was up to.

With my face blank, I ran my hand firmly over his thigh

and slyly moved up and over towards his zipper, rubbing and cupping him. I heard him suck in air through his teeth.

"Do I need to pull over?" He asked, and I leaned in closer to his face to whisper, "No, *you* just focus on the road and not killing us on the way home."

He made a small noise, and I began with the first button before springing his human cock free. I placed a sweet kiss on his cheek, then his jaw before using my hand to stroke him and it didn't take him long to spring back to life. *My eager sex demon.*

"Becs—" I put my finger to his lips, shushing him quietly.

I moved my head down to replace where my hand was to continue my torture.

Please, don't kill us, Bels!

"Fuck," he grunted out moments later.

I rejoiced in his noises and sighs, especially when he combed his fingers through my hair, a combination of confused gestures of slight grabs and pets. I tried not to be smug over it, but it was my greatest joy to feel him squirm and come undone because of *me. My Bels was distracted with my road head.*

His hand was on my upper back when he finally came with a hushed sigh.

"What am I to do with you? You are practically a sex demoness in human form."

After swallowing him down, I casually moved myself back into my seat, putting my seatbelt back on just for him to arrive in the parking lot at my apartment complex.

"Only for you, Bels, *only for you.*"

He adjusted himself as he killed the engine. A Cheshire cat smile overcame me as I spoke, "Thanks for not killing us, Bels."

He shook his head before narrowing his eyes playfully.

"Love you," I said sweetly, leaning my head on his shoulder.

With a sigh of defeat, he returned the affection. "I love you...evil woman."

"I'll take the compliment," I said with innocence, batting my eyelashes.

"As you should."

I closed my eyes as he kissed the top of my head. Teasing him was one of my favorite activities, and he gave me the reactions I craved. He didn't seem to mind the little games we'd play, because at least we both were getting off in good fun.

For our getaway weekend, it was all worth it. The best Dragon Con by far, with my favorite demon.

BECS

YOU ARE
BEAUTIFUL

TWENTY-ONE

BECS

The buzzing from my phone woke me up. I reached over to tap it, but it kept going. A grumbled complaint escaped me as I sat up with my eyes closed and answered the phone. *It's a Saturday morning, who is calling me at this ungodly hour?*

"Hello?" I greeted to whoever was on the line.

"*Rebecca, are you home? I'm in town for the weekend. I have breakfast!*" The sing-song voice shouted into my ear.

Rubbing my eyes, I sighed at the realization of my eldest sibling, Penny. "What time is it that you're calling so early?"

"*Rebecca, it's nine a.m. in the morning; who even sleeps in anymore?*"

"What kind of breakfast?" I ignored her statement, thinking that I could be convinced to be social if breakfast were involved.

"*Good things. Are you home?*"

Her version of '*good*' made me roll my eyes. "Pen, yes, I'm home but—"

"*Okay! I'll be there in five!*"

She hung up the phone before I could protest. Falling back on the bed, I'm more awake and aware enough to the warm demon heat beside me all curled up. It humored me that Bels tall demon self could even fit in my bed.

I rubbed his side briefly before reluctantly getting out of bed. Belke watched me get up and head into the bathroom. After using it and washing my hands and face, did I hear his sleepy voice from the doorway. "Should I leave?"

Hugging my muscled demon lover a good morning, I responded, "Normally, I would say no, but...I haven't told my family about you. I've been blowing them off lately, claiming to be busy with work stuff. Sorry about that, Bels. *I'll work on that today.* I bet that's why my sister, Pen, is popping over—to make sure I'm still alive. No doubt forced by my mother, but still."

A gentle stroke of his tail ran down my leg gently as he patted my head. While I was grumpy, he remained a big demon mush.

"I'm not mad. I can only imagine the conversation of a *demon boyfriend,* or even a boyfriend for that matter. Something women gossip about."

A smile formed as I glanced up in his arms. His blue eyes were just as sleepy as how I felt. *"Exactly."*

"I'll go do demon-things then. It's okay, Becs. Enjoy the day with your sister."

He kissed the top of my head as I walked past him towards my closet to throw clothes on.

While putting on deodorant and a spritz of one of my body sprays, curiosity brimmed, "What things are those anyway?"

I heard the sink running before it shut off as he poked his head out. "Check-ins, supervisions, report updates, that kind of thing."

"But you're a sex demon... Don't you have to *do your job?* You aren't going to get into trouble for my distractions or wasting time with me, are you?" A sinking feeling over the thought grew while I anticipated the answer.

Belke leaned on the door frame with an arm raised above his head, gazing at me.

"No time with you is a waste. Demons don't always do things solo, there's always others involved for whatever the cause is."

"Bels..." I gave him a look of disapproval, noticing how his tail began to wrap around him as if he were tucking his tail as if I reprimanded him.

I tried not to smirk over the cute gesture, fixing my facial expression.

"You're dodging... I don't want to get you into trouble, Bels. If you have to—"

A knock came at my front door.

I pinched my nose in frustration at my sister's poor timing.

"We're not done with this conversation," I told him earnestly.

He stared at me, giving me demon-puppy vibes.

I can't with you, Bels—stop.

"Don't let her see you, Bels," I whispered while walking towards the front door to let Pen in.

"About time. Mom sent me down this weekend to make sure you're alive since you've been *busy* all these months."

All I did was sigh heavily with defeat, holding open the door for her to enter.

"Sorry to disappoint you with my mundane and unexciting life," I muttered as she walked past with her long blonde hair bouncing in a high ponytail and her athletically toned body moving toward my kitchen. She was a couple inches shorter than me as I was the tallest of my sisters. I was also the youngest sibling. BJ was the middle child. Each of us was born one year apart.

I stared toward my bedroom, wondering if Bels was still in there as my brain drifted on if he had sex contracts to fulfill. I had been so distracted with feeling loved, that I didn't even think to ask the important questions about my demon boyfriend. *Am I that lonely?*

Pen fumbled through my cabinets, finding the paper plates before putting what she brought for breakfast on them.

"So, cut the bullshit, why are you ignoring everyone? Something's going on, even if you do live the solo, single life. You never ignore us this long." I caught her blue-eyed gaze as she sat down at my dining table. Penny also reminded me of a second mom—*the mom-sister.*

"It's not like that. Things are complicated at work right now with the big merger. I got promoted recently, and it's been a lot of work. I'm not doing it on purpose. Dragon Con wasn't that long ago and I made my outfits. Give me a break. Also, why do you always assume that I'm single?" I puffed my cheeks dramatically.

She half-laughed, nudging my plate and coffee to the other side of the table.

"You've been single since Joseph, Becs. You can fool Mom and Dad, and hell, even BJ, but *not me.* Work, I can see, and we've heard the news about it. *There's also news on demons being rampant.* How were we supposed to know you weren't taken away by one? Mom's worried sick, you need to call her tomorrow after I leave. What's really going on? You do seem *different.* It looks like you've lost weight, not that weight is everything. Are you still taking your Levothyroxine?"

"*Yes, mom,*" I sassed, avoiding the other questions. It

could be all the hot demon sex I'm having, but I wasn't telling her that.

She sighed heavily when I didn't answer her other questions, eyeing me as I continued to avoid her gaze. I grabbed the plate of breakfast foods and plopped down for a sip of cold brew coffee. At least she loves me enough to remember the importance of needed go-go bean-energy.

"Rebecca, I'm serious. Are you okay? *I'm* even worried about you. You haven't texted in weeks."

I swallowed down the bite of food I took which was turkey bacon and egg on a wheat type of bun. It wasn't too bad. Penny was a health guru-nutcase, after all.

"Pen, I'm fine, seriously. You sound like mom right now. *Please stop.* I just woke up, and you know how I get without my coffee."

"The coffee is from your favorite place," she said to me, sipping on whatever she ordered. It smelled like some type of tea.

It was a peace offering. I should be grateful she remembered.

We ate in uncomfortable silence, well mostly from me because she had questions, and it was too early for that shit.

Even though Penny was like our mother, BJ was like me in a way that we *minded our business.* Most of the time anyway, unless it came to family. We're all nosy, deep down. A southern thing, I supposed. We had that sweet, southern belle charm with sassiness if needed—*well, me mostly.*

Penny was one of those women that went to the gym consistently and took care of her body and what she put into it. She ran her own business and went to school for fitness and nutrition, so it all made sense when I truly thought about it. I could do without the lectures though.

Unsure if Bels was still in the next room, it didn't feel

right to talk about him without him there. *It was rude. Let my sister fret about it a little longer.* The minute I uttered the words *dating* or *boyfriend,* the whole family would be calling about it.

My sanity returned after a few sips of coffee, and I finally had some energy to respond. "I appreciate the concern, and I'm sorry for being distracted and busy lately, but I assure you, I'm fine. I'm just a busy working adult with the new promotion. And I like to spend my weekends in the quiet silence of my apartment—sue me."

She eyed me curiously, *almost* believing me.

"Please tell me they increased your pay at least?"

I nodded, finishing my plate and focusing on my caffeine intake.

"That's good. After all your hard work with school, you deserve it. Plus, it will pay down those student loans faster. Have you thought about leaving Atlanta?"

I shrugged, swallowing my last bite of food and chugging down the remaining coffee. Pen was still observing me like a science project when I finally looked up at her. "Have you been working out though? You look good, sis."

Having not heard my sister compliment me in a while, I couldn't help but perk up at it. "Thanks, Pen. Yeah, I have."

With sex that is.

"Awesome! You know that makes me happy to hear. I've been pushing Mom to take better care of her health and to stop eating out with Dad since they're getting older."

"Your health and nutrition degree keeps us all in line, Pen," I said with a smirk.

She grinned knowingly. "Fitness and Nutrition, *thank you very much.* Well, I'm glad you're doing good, sis. Congrats again on the promo. Did you have any plans today? Aside from your normalcy of hiding away in your apartment?"

"No. Why, what are you scheming?" I narrowed my eyes as she finished her tea.

"Come out with me and have a girl's day. Break your normal cycle. If you say no, I'll drag you to the gym and make you suffer *with my exercise knowledge.*"

I held my hands up in defeat. "Okay, okay. Let me grab my shoes and a hair tie. I'm all yours, no need for boring me *to death.*"

Happy with my answer, she leaned back in her chair satisfied as I stood up.

Walking into my bedroom, I slipped on my sneakers and grabbed a hair tie before she got any bright ideas on coming in further.

I caught Belke leaning against the wall in his human form. I put my finger to my lips, and he seemed like he had something to say, *but it would have to wait unfortunately.*

"Don't say a word," I mouthed to him.

I quickly walked back out while twirling up my hair in a messy bun.

Grabbing my bag, Pen began throwing our trash away.

"What do you have in mind?" I asked, grabbing my keys.

"Mani-pedi. Shopping. Girl stuff—*duh.* I haven't done shit with you all year!"

"Alright, lead the way," I told her, ushering her out and locking my door behind me.

Sorry, Bels.

BECS

YOU ARE
BEAUTIFUL

TWENTY-TWO

BECS

"I lied earlier, I left out something," I admitted quietly as we sat in the massage chairs with our feet soaking in the spa.

Since I was mostly awake and relaxed, I supposed it was only fair to be somewhat more honest with how I'd been spending my time.

"I *knew* it! Spill, now!"

I shook my head, suppressing a shy giggle. "I'm seeing someone I work with... He was over when you showed up, and I told him to hide in the bathroom."

She swatted my leg. "REBECCA!"

I shushed her, looking around the spa awkwardly. "Don't be *so loud*."

"You're *terrible*! But... Do you think that's a good idea considering what happened with Joseph?"

Meh, probably not, but I also didn't care. She didn't need to know Zavier, *Belke*, was actually one of those *rampant* demons.

"He's not Joseph, Pen," I told her with a thousand percent of confidence in that statement.

She gave me the stink eye. "Uh-huh. I'd be careful with that though."

Ignoring her comment as if I didn't know that already, I also knew that Belke wasn't just anyone. He wasn't even human.

"Well, *tell me about your new person!* I'm assuming it's a male, right?" She asked as I nodded.

"Yes, his name is Zavi. I think things are serious..."

She gave me a raised brow look, indicating that she wasn't done. "Text him, invite him for dinner, and tell him I'm sorry for dropping in and making him hide in the bathroom; *only if he accepts dinner, though.* If he says no, I'm *not* sorry."

I laughed, shaking my head. "Alright, one sec."

I tapped my phone, texting Bels himself, who gratefully accepted. I told him how I gave his nickname of Zavi instead, to spare myself the *longer* lecture if she found out *who* he was. Penny would really freak out if she knew it was my *boss. Oops.*

"What'd he say?" she asked while looking at her own phone for dinner potentials.

"He said he forgives you, and he'll be happy to join us for dinner."

She turned toward me, flashing a bright smile. "Korean BBQ sound okay, around 6 p.m.? I want to go to my favorite spot."

I agreed, letting Bels know.

"Alright, done," I told her as the salon workers began working on our feet.

Pen chose a pink color for her nails and toes, while I chose a blue that matched Belke's eyes.

I'd become a sap—*I'm so delightfully gross.* I blamed Bels for rubbing off the mushiness.

Who are you, Rebecca?

"So, you're not off the hook. Tell me about this, Zavi, what's he look like?" she asked, casually looking from me to the lady working on her toes.

"He's alright looking..." I honestly didn't want her to know just how handsome he was.

"Go on." She gave me a narrowed-eyed look that said she wasn't having my simple-answer bullshit.

"Dark hair, pretty eyes, taller than me... I don't know, you'll see him later. Ask him about *him* yourself."

After an unamused look from my sister, I winked, typing a message to Bels, *"Now, she won't stop asking me questions about you... Send help."*

He sent a laughing emoji, and I sighed, catching my sister's eyes peeled to the side of my face.

"What?"

"I'm going to get answers, whether I have to pry them from one of you... Now that I know *who* has been occupying your time, I'll let it slide for now. At least answer me this... Does he treat you good? If I find out he's another Joseph, *I will fucking lose it.*"

You aren't the only one, Pen. Yet, I had a good feeling he was nothing like that asshole.

"Put your unmanicured nails away... Yes, he's wonderful. A bit unconventional, but I'm *not* complaining." I smirked recalling Bels in his demon form and his cute house-pet mannerisms.

"Okay, I lied, *one more question*," Pen went on catching my drift, wiggling her eyebrows, "How is he in the bedroom?"

"Penny! *You really want to have this conversation here?*" I lowered my tone, and she nodded, not caring.

The ladies working on our toes, also weren't objecting, pretending not to listen. *Great—this is fine.*

Rolling my eyes, I gave in. *"Fine."*

Pen beamed, leaning on the arm of the chair, staring at me in waiting while she indicated her hand for me to spill the tea.

"It's phenomenal. He's rather *talented* and I have no complaints. He gets a five star rating. Joseph was like two stars at best."

She snorted at the last comment, and I caught the ladies smirking at our feet as their usual chatter was absent. *I swear people are so nosey in the south.*

"I can't wait for dinner tonight to see your new man. What time is it now?" she mumbled to herself at the last part, sounding overjoyed.

"We have five hours," I told her at the same time she figured it out.

She giggled. "Now, I'm excited to find an outfit for our dinner tonight and pick out yours, too."

"I suppose I'll allow it," I said playfully, and it was her turn to roll her eyes.

Thankfully, Penny dropped the conversation on Zavi, and we finished things up at the salon after another hour.

"I feel better after our mani-pedi, sis," she told me, and I nodded in agreement. When my sister wasn't acting like our mother, she wasn't too bad to hang out with.

"Where do you want to go first for shopping?" I asked as she drove us away from the nail salon.

"To the mall—duh. I know you're picky on clothes."

She wasn't wrong, but she'd be surprised to know the things I've worn for Bels, or lack thereof.

"I'm sorry you have an inconveniencing, plus-sized

sister," I told her, looking out the window as the buildings blurred by.

"All this time, and you *still* talk like that? *For fuck's sake, Rebecca.* You have a medical condition! You take your meds and do what you can, give yourself a break. You know that shit pisses me off."

Shit, yeah, it does. I totally forgot.

I've been saying the same shit for so long, it's an old habit. However, with Bels around, it hasn't slipped out as much, and I'm beginning to like who's looking back in the mirror. I said nothing after mumbling a *sorry*; I didn't want to argue with her today.

Penny sung out popular lyrics to the radio station until we arrived at the mall nearby.

"Alright, let's find you something first, do you still go to that one store?"

"Yep," I tell her as we parked and headed inside the mall.

Ten minutes passed before I heard her squeal in excitement about seeing something cute in one of the store windows, quickly dragging me inside.

I half-laughed at my sister as she grabbed ten things and tried them on, showing me each one as I sat on the bench outside for her to model for me. It reminded me of an 80s/90s movie montage while that genre of music played in the background.

"How's this?" she asked at the last outfit, it was a cute romper that could be dressed up or down.

"It looks good," I told her in approval, feeling slightly envious that she didn't have to try as hard; clothes just looked good on her and her size was available in all the quantities anywhere and everywhere.

Nope, stop it, Rebecca, we're not going to have this battle today.

Thankfully, I didn't have to as Pen grabbed her haul and gave me a grateful smile. "Thanks for being here. I've missed hanging out and shopping with you."

Offering her a small smile in return, I followed her to the checkout counter until we left with her monstrous bag of cute clothes that she got at a discount.

"Sorry, I know I said we'd find yours first, but you know I have a squirrel brain sometimes when I'm out shopping. *Plus, there was a sale!*"

I shook my head, laughing. "It's okay, Pen, I'm not upset. You got some good deals, and we're spending sisterly time together."

She gave me a look, trying to see if I was lying—which I wasn't. I knew how my sister was when it came to shopping. She hugged me to her side anyway. "That's right!"

Continuing with said sisterly time, we made it to my favorite plus-sized store that was my go-to. As we browsed, I noticed the same purple-haired lady from before, only this time she was in a cute little black dress.

"Welcome back," she said with a grin as I appreciated her style once more.

I waved to her as she came over to me with a smirk of appreciation, "How'd the outfits from last time work out?"

Pen caught on as my face flushed. "Great. Thank you for the recommendations."

She winked as Penny stared at me, noticing my awkwardness. "Well, let me know if you need any more recommendations, I'll be around!" The lady took a hint from the interaction, and I thanked her as she walked away. I pretended to browse, avoiding Penny's stare.

"*What* recommendation did you get?"

"A cute fit, obviously."

"Uh-huh, it wouldn't surprise me if it was *lingerie.*"

I shot her a look and she grinned knowingly; I continued my browsing more seriously rather than getting more flustered.

Since before the cosplay convention, I hadn't been by for any retail therapy, so the store had a ton of new stuff out, *plus sales.* Something I seemed to inhabit from Penny's eye. It made me miss BJ since she was the most fashionable one out of all of us. She lived in that world with her creative self. Miss professional photographer. Just briefly, I realized I kinda missed my sister and parents. I did enjoy my space more though.

"What vibe are we feeling for tonight?" Pen asked, holding up several options for me.

"I like the blue one," I told her about the cute babydoll-shaped dress she held up.

"It *does* match your nails," she said in agreement.

We picked up a few more items, and I may have lingered in the *sexy* section. Penny came over immediately grabbing things.

"Oh, *these* most definitely," she said, wiggling her eyebrows again.

I shook my head, feeling amused and embarrassed, but I grabbed them anyway. An underwear sale, *don't mind if I do.*

"Alright, sis, let's see if there's any shoe sales, grab more coffee, and then head back to your place to get ready."

"Sounds good, Pen," I said in agreement as I left the store with my own big bag of stuff, although not as monstrous as hers.

On our shoe excursion we found some cute sandals and Pen grabbed two pairs of sneakers on sale. There were two hours remaining by the time we left and pulled into my apartment parking lot.

"Alright, let's do this. I'm so fucking stoked right now," I heard her say, clapping her hands before rubbing them together as if she were formulating some new exercise regime for the world to know about. *Always scheming, that one.*

It was so ridiculous how my family got about my dating life.

"Calm down, Pen, you act like this is my first date..."

"It might as well be! Shit it's been *years*, let me be happy for you!"

I held up my hands in defeat as we got out of her rental car, grabbing our bags and making our way inside.

"Go wash your ass," she said as soon as I put my bags down.

"Okay! Damn." I lifted my arm to smell my pits just to be sure, and I recognized that she was right.

Boy, did I *love* having a mother-like sister. Sheesh.

Belke

TWENTY-THREE

BELKE

I wore a dark blue, business casual outfit for the dinner gathering at a tasty Korean BBQ spot. I was to be meeting Rebecca's sister.

I overheard their conversation that morning and how her sister caught her off guard. After our interrupted conversation, I could tell her concern for me *avoiding responsibilities*, yet I didn't want her to worry about me. I had friends amongst the ranks, so it wasn't a problem—*mostly*. Not that I had ever been in this sort of position before.

I hadn't touched anyone else after our first encounter. Once she agreed to be *mine—that was it for me*. I knew I didn't want her soul the way everyone else gave me bits of themselves.

Since I thrived on sexual energy, I was still able to get by. It's not exactly forbidden to do so with one person just as long as that sexual energy is exchanged, that's what my purpose was when I wasn't on a mission of some sort from our home realm, Donte, or what was instructed of me.

Putting away my thoughts for later, I opened the door to

the restaurant and quickly found the two women tucked in a quiet corner.

Rebecca waved me over, standing up to reveal a short pale blue dress. It stopped mid-thigh, and I couldn't help my lingering gaze.

Keep it together, Belke; don't get hard in front of her sister—reel it in.

When she originally texted earlier, I happily accepted that she wanted to bring me more into her life. I couldn't tell by her exchange that morning if she was ready for that, but my guess was that Rebecca wasn't awake enough to process much. I was hoping to lay in bed and fuck her that day, but there was always later. I'm a simple being in my tastes.

I admitted our relationship was...mostly sexual, but I wanted to dive deeper into the life of the woman I loved. I wanted to tell her more about me, but I also didn't want her to worry either, so I still debated on how much to reveal. She knew about demons which was half the battle. Becs had already seen me at my most vulnerable, but sometimes it was hard to explain more truths about myself.

Once I got to their table, I saw how beautiful Becs was with her makeup and her hair, plus new shoes. I appreciated her efforts, although unnecessary as I loved her any way she came. *Naked and undone, especially.*

She introduced me to her sister, Penny, Pen for short, and she shook my hand as if it were a professional interaction.

I sat in the circle booth next to Becs, and her sister was on the other side of her.

Feeling their eyes on me, we then made casual conversation while we put our order in.

"So, tell me *Zavi,* what are your intentions with my

sister?" She asked after we ordered, and drinks were brought out to us.

I heard Becca sigh, and I lightly rubbed her exposed thigh, indicating it was no bother.

"Well, purely *carnal,* of course, and making sure she feels loved and appreciated every day."

I felt her energy shift next to me, eliciting a small smirk, and her sister nearly spat out her drink.

"I like you already, Zavi," she said with a grin, tossing Becca a mischievous look.

"Your girlfriend here has been ignoring *us* for months, so our mother sent me here to check on her... You seriously downplayed his looks, Becs," she said, shifting her eyes between me and Rebecca.

"Oh really?" I quipped, catching Becs shooting her sister a look of *did you really have to say that?*

"She said you were '*alright,*'" Penny went on with a smirk.

I coyly drew circles on her thigh, "Am I really, *just alright,* Bec?" I playfully grabbed her thigh, purring into her ear.

She tensed up slightly, and I knew her sister meant well with not only her teasing banter but in showing that she cared for her sister.

It reminded me of how I cared for my brothers, too.

A groan of disapproval reverberated Rebecca's throat. "Yes, I couldn't exactly yell out that you're a sex kitten, now, could I?"

A low laugh erupted from me as I squeezed her leg, and her sister's eyes glittered at the knowledge.

"She did give you a five-star rating, Zavi, so I think you're doing just fine. I'll be sure to tell Mom you're taken care of." she winked at her sister, and Becs groaned loudly.

I kissed her cheek, patting her thigh gently before moving my hand away.

"I'm happy to hear it, *along with my five star rating*," I said to them with an air of nonchalance, but deep down I was extremely flattered.

Penny giggled, finishing her beer while Rebecca began drinking hers.

"Are you from here, Zavi?" Her sister asked casually.

"Yes," I said, taking a drink from my glass.

I could tell Rebecca was listening closely, probably realizing that she didn't know much about my history just as much as the blonde-haired sister across from me.

"I don't mind Atlanta, personally, but I prefer the west coast," Pen went on.

"Let me guess, California?" I asked, making light conversation.

"That obvious, huh?" she replied, smirking.

"You do look like a California girl," Rebecca piped up in a singsong voice.

I stifled a laugh.

"Zip it, I'm interrogating your boyfriend here. I bet you haven't even told him anything about *your family*, have you?" I could tell her sister was starting to bring the sass, and I knew it wasn't just Rebecca who was like that.

I hid my amusement watching the sister's bicker.

"Keep it up, and I'll ignore you for another month."

"I fucking knew it, Becs! You're the fucking worst."

"*You're the worst for interrupting my morning!* Leave Zavi alone."

Before Penny could continue, I put my arm around Becca, "Ladies, it's quite all right. I don't mind the questions. I have nothing to hide. Also, at least I had clothes on when you arrived this morning." I grinned as her sister's look soon matched mine.

"Thank you, Zavi. I'm only curious anyways, but I appreciate your permission. What's your last name? You work with Rebecca, right?"

I nodded. "Bel."

She pulled out her phone, and I knew what was about to happen.

"Don't take offense to what I'm about to say, Zavi," Penny went on before shooting her sister a serious look while leaning closer in a hushed tone, *"Really, Becs, your boss? Are you crazy?!"*

Rebecca stared daggers at her sister. "It's 2022, not the ninety's, what's the big deal? We're discreet, and *you're the one asking all the fucking questions!"*

I stepped in briefly for some damage control. "She's right, we are discreet, and I've been working on reshaping the working environments that existed *before* the merge. Rebecca earned her position through nothing other than her own merit and talents. She shouldn't have been at that front desk when there was a finance position suitable for her the whole time. Her old boss is on my shit list because of it, but don't you worry—*I'm working on it.*"

I felt Rebecca freeze, and saw her sister do the same. She didn't look taken aback, but more satisfied with my answer than anything.

"You failed to mention *that*, Becs," Penny rubbed between her eyes in frustration. "Were they bullying you this whole time?" She directed the question towards Rebecca.

"I'm used to how people are, Pen," she said dismissively as the waiter brought refills and our food to cook on the grill in front of us.

They lit it up, and it began to warm immediately. We had ordered a sample of lean protein and vegetables.

I removed my arm from behind Rebecca and placed it in front of me.

"Mind if I start?" I asked them, taking the tongs to start preparing the food.

They said nothing as they stared at each other, and I decided not to interfere and continued with my quest of cooking. It sounded like the two women had some things to sort out without me.

"That's bullshit, Rebecca, utter *bullshit*. Why are you always like this, just letting people walk all over you? *It's not okay.*"

"And you wonder why I don't come home..." She grumbled, "I don't need another lecture."

Penny glared at her. "I wish you believed in yourself more, you deserve more—that's all I'm saying. What I always say."

I wish she did too, Pen. I certainly believed in her. More than she already knew.

"I pick my battles, that wasn't one of them; give me some credit. At least Zavi gave me the opportunity to do what I'm good at, *and that's numbers*. Believe me, karma's a bitch, and she serves that shit on a hot plate. Don't worry about me, things have been improving. Even without him around." Rebecca points her thumb toward me. "I would've found another job. There are assholes everywhere I go. *Seriously.*"

"Whatever you say, Becs. You know I just worry. I'm sorry. In case I haven't said it, or enough of it rather, I *am* proud of you. I don't know how you deal with it, because I wouldn't," Penny said, seeming calm but sighing into her beer in defeat.

"I'm proud of her, too," I chipped in, flipping over the varied meats once they were cooked enough on one side.

"Thank you," I heard Becca whisper as she watched me cook. She continued to stare off into space, lost in thought and no doubt wanted some of the heat taken from her.

"So, since you're asking questions, what do you do?" I asked Penny casually.

"I do many things. I'm a nutritionist, personal trainer, exercise coach, and life coach. An entrepreneur of health if you will."

I gave her a small smile. "Aside from your parents, any other siblings?"

"Our other sister is BJ. She's a professional photographer. She works for various magazines and runs her own business specializing in portraits and landscapes. She's overseas right now for one of the fashion week shows."

"Nice. Where did you grow up?" I asked, placing some of the cooked meats on their plates, and began adding more to the grill.

"Wilmington, North Carolina. Where our parents live still," she mentioned casually, beginning to eat what I placed down. Rebecca was silent and said nothing as she slowly grabbed a fork and took a bite.

As the meat cooked, I lightly rubbed her leg again, kissing the side of her head to offer her some comfort and hopefully some cheering up.

Catching her brief gaze, she gave me a small smile, which was all I needed to confirm she was okay.

After flipping the meat, I took some bites of what was already cooked, approving of the flavors and spices.

"Do you have any family?" Penny asked between bites of food.

"I didn't know my parents, but I have an uncle, and a brother, a few cousins—normal stuff."

Her ears perked up. "Is your brother single?" I heard her ask immediately.

I chuckled. "I haven't checked with him lately, but I shall let Rebecca know if he is."

"You're terrible, Pen," Rebecca piped in, shaking her head.

"It was just a *question,* excuuuuse me," she drawled out, but I gathered that Penny was serious.

My lips curled up, taking the rest of the meat off the grill with the added vegetables and dispersed it onto our plates.

"Thank you, Zavi," Pen said and Becs joined in on the thanks.

"Of course, ladies," I said politely, feeling useful.

We ate in silence, and finished dinner without any more fuss. The sisters seemed to get it out of their system. *That's a relief.* It made me uncomfortable when Rebecca got unsettled, and I wanted to spare her of that, no matter who or *what* was the cause.

"I'm glad you came out tonight, Zavi, I feel better knowing that someone is looking out for my sister. I apologize for our bickering; we get like that sometimes. It means a lot to me though, and I hope you stick around for a while." Her smile was bright as my heart warmed at Penny's approval.

"Thanks, I'm glad to have met you. Next time you're in town, we'll have to grab dinner again."

"I won't pop over unannounced either next time," she answered with a grin, moving to hug her sister before she side-hugged me.

"I'll be heading to visit our parents tomorrow, so expect

a call from Mom within the next week," she said, glancing at Rebecca, who nodded.

"I'll make sure she gets home safe," I said as she smiled and waved, heading to her car as I took Becca's hand, giving it a light squeeze.

"Ready?" I asked, leading her to mine after she nodded.

"I'm not surprised you drive a Cadillac," she said with a small smile as I opened the door for her.

"I'll take the compliment," I responded sweetly once she got in but not before sneaking a quick kiss.

As I shut the door and climbed in the driver's seat, I asked her quietly, "Want to go somewhere to talk?" After this morning's interruption, I could sense that we had a lot to talk about. I had promised her more honesty, and I needed to keep that promise.

"Yes, I'd like that."

I sent a quick text to a contact I knew and began driving to the aquarium. It closed soon, so I made sure they'd leave it open after hours for us.

"Do you like aquariums?" I asked as I opened my hand for hers.

She took it, squeezing briefly. "I do. I haven't been in years though."

"Good, let's continue this date then?" I caught a quick glance from her as the city lights shone all around us making her appear more ethereal and unreal. *So fucking beautiful, my woman.*

That moment was one I wanted to freeze in time, because it's how I'll always see her, beautiful and perfect under the Atlanta city lights as we drove downtown. I love her so much, it'll hurt when I finally reveal more truths.

"Sounds good, Bels."

BECS
$(x-$
$y^2 = Z$
$\frac{\Delta x}{\Delta y} = \lim_{\delta} \frac{\Delta x+2}{\Delta y-1}$
$+a)$
$sinx$
$e = cosx + tgy$
$(y-1)$
$sina =$
YOU ARE
BEAUTIFUL

TWENTY-FOUR

BECS

What a day.

I couldn't deny the relief as we walked inside the aquarium right before it closed officially. Belke pulled some strings so that it was just us in there after hours.

We began to walk through the place when he spoke. "The workers will be here for another hour, but that's okay, we can stay longer without any issues."

I nodded as I wandered slowly through the various exhibits, trying to gather my thoughts on what *and* where to start with my questions.

Bels must have noticed a disturbance in the force as well, because I could feel his eyes lingering from me on what I was looking at.

It bothered me that Belke and I didn't know each other in the sense that most normal relationships did. It began sexually and slowly changed these past weeks since Dragon Con. Not that I didn't know anything about Belke, but I didn't know about the world he came from or his history, family, or things like that—*I wanted to know more.*

Until Penny's visit, it didn't cross my mind. Maybe it was the shock of someone expressing wants and needs that involved me, someone that cared for me, but did that make me terrible for focusing on the sexy positives?

I had been living in a fantasy world, one I adored, and one that held Belke and I together. We didn't have to be anyone or anything other than ourselves. None of it was normal by any means, but I craved *knowing* more ever since this morning. Penny asked questions and suddenly I felt as if I knew nothing about the demon in my bed *or my heart*.

His actions and words had already proved his worth, and whatever else was up his sleeve, but I didn't really understand the full scope of him. *Boy did I want to.*

Standing in front of the jellyfish tank, I sighed deeply. Lost in thought, I wondered what it'd be like to be one of the jellyfish, simply existing in my own underwater world. Do jellyfish dream? Do they even know of their own kind or other worlds outside of that fish tank tube? Would they even care?

"What's on your mind, Becs?" I heard his voice echo quietly.

I saw him through the glass, a lovely reflection upon that jellyfish tank. A distorted but beautiful vision of the man in front of me. There was so much that I didn't know but wanted to.

"A lot, actually. I don't know where to start. Until my sister's visit, I thought I was content with where things were, but now..." I watched the jellyfish existing in the tank as words failed me.

"I don't have anything to hide from you. Yes, there's things I don't or haven't mentioned, but it's not for *you* to worry about. I don't want you getting involved in things, because you're human, and I don't want you to get hurt. I hope knowing that doesn't upset you."

Catching his gaze in the glass again, I lingered a while longer before turning around to find him there in front of me. Belke stepped closer and I ran my hands up his chest, staring up at him in those human brown and blue eyes.

"I worry about you, Bels. I understand, *sorta,* but I don't want you in deep shit because of me either. I wouldn't be able to live with myself if you got in trouble."

He cupped my cheeks, rubbing them lightly while offering sweetness like that of a cinnamon roll. "I appreciate your intentions more than you could possibly know. The demon world is in chaos and even *here* on Earth. Part of it, I already told you. There's a rebellion, and many hands are on deck. I'm up here for multiple reasons, so even if I'm not claiming the *energy of souls,* or contracts for the afterlife, I have a multitude of excuses in my bucket pool. You are not keeping me from anything."

I took a deep breath as he leaned and kissed my forehead before pulling me into his chest with a light squeeze.

"I love you. I want to protect you. Being with me *protects you.* I don't want anyone else to have you. You are *mine. I* am *yours.* I protect your soul from others as any lover would—a good one, that is. Besides, I still have to fix things as promised. The demon stuff, there's not much for you to do about it."

Releasing each other, I couldn't ignore my own helplessness and what it meant to be human. He still wanted to be around a useless human like me when he was there because of the demon rebellion. My brain couldn't fathom. My mathematical brain could only conjure up so many scenarios and the possibilities of other realms and existences. *Scientists and physicists would lose their fucking minds, and probably were, to be honest.*

I tilted my head up in invitation before his lips found mine, seeking solace there.

"Saying you had siblings and an uncle, was that true? I hope you don't think I'm an ass for never asking about your history and life story. Just like I hope you aren't upset I haven't told you mine. I wasn't expecting her to show up this morning. I would have said something eventually, I swear. I just...wanted you all to myself. I'm selfish, in that sense," I told him honestly as he petted my hair once with a small smile.

"*Sort of.* I figured if it came up, we'd go at *your pace.* I'm not offended, I enjoy being with you no matter what we're doing. Although, I'm built for *fucking,* amongst other things, I'm not a bad companion either."

A fond smile drew upon my face at the thought. "No, you aren't just those things. You're a sexy demon-house-cat-puppy. You're my favorite person—*being.* Demon, too, not that I know any others. I love you, Bels. You make me feel special, and at *home.* I don't have to pretend to be anyone or anything. *I can just exist with you.* Not that we were ever *normal,* but like, who cares, right? *We're* happy, aren't we?"

"I most certainly am." He stole a kiss, seeming at ease before giving me a humored look, narrowing his eyes. "Is that what I am now? First, I act like a cat, but now it's *a puppy?*"

"Not my fault you act like both," I said playfully, making a kissing sound with my lips.

"You are special to me, Becs. I've explored *every* last inch of you, and there's nothing that I don't love. I *love* when you get sassy, the way you look at me when I'm in my most true form, and even in this form. You still *see* me. I can also just be myself with you; that is something I've never known. I certainly don't care about relationship standards; I like that we go with *our* flow. We have our own bubble, and it is my favorite place to be—I hope you know that."

"I do now," I said with heartfelt emotion at his sweet words, pulling his head towards mine.

I couldn't help but kiss him after he said all that mushiness. He pulled me closer, deepening the kiss as I clutched him to me.

A soft groan escaped us both before I broke the kiss to mention, "We should wait until the workers leave and make sure there's no cameras on us."

"*Yes, ma'am,*" he whispered, taking my hand, and leading me down another hallway.

"I do want to know about your history though, if that's okay?" I asked quietly, my emotions were more settled now but never my curiosity.

"Are you sure? It's not exactly *pretty*. Plus, with who I was before *you...*"

I sighed, realizing what he was getting at, and it didn't deter me. I pictured him in demon form with his tail close to his body—like a scaredy cat.

It made me smile. "As long as you feel comfortable, I want to know all about you. Tell me while we sit in front of the big tank of fish?"

He nodded in response, leading me to the enclosed tunnel for the big tank in the aquarium. There was no one else around, and no workers lingered by either.

I released his hand and looked around at the various fish and sharks in the tank all around us. It was always magical to view aquatic life as such. I could be close, without being close—it was great. I wouldn't want to touch a shark, but behind a reflection was fine by me.

"I do have brothers, but it means something different than it does to humans. Brothers, to me, means we were *made* into what we are at the same time. Like being born, but without a mother's womb. Whatever I was before being a demon, I don't remember. Time exists differently in Hell. I *feel* old, but we don't time things as humans do on earth. That's the simple way to explain it."

I turned my head, considering him as he spoke. He was looking at the fish lost in thought.

"I'm a mathematician. I know all about complex things, cut me some slack. Time and space function differently here versus where you come from. *That* makes logical sense," I rambled on, letting him know in a subtle way that I understood complicated things. "I'm not as dumb as David looks." He grinned at me, mentioning that he never thought such about me. Internally, I knew, but I didn't want him to hold back his knowledge in the event he thought I wouldn't understand. "So, parents and stuff, isn't a thing, in your...Hell?"

He shook his head, not looking at me. "We have our leaders, aka, *my uncle*. Although, I told Penny that for simplicity purposes. The gentleman you met a week before meeting me in human form, Donte, is my superior, but also my brother. There are people above him, too. It's a weird hierarchy, so I'm not even sure how to explain in a way that makes sense, but he's a sex demon like me. There's rank, yes, but we still operate on some equal lines, like not everyone pulls power or rank cards just because they can."

Donte, Donte... Oh! I recalled those piercing blue eyes of the man in black that greeted me during that day of the important first meeting—*now it makes sense.* Are all sex-demons handsome, or what? *Again, logically it made sense how sexual energy rises within people because of their phys-ical attractions. Okay, Becca, cool it.*

People loved to talk about not judging books by covers, but we were all idiots and did it anyway.

"That's interesting. Is there a hierarchy? Like royalty, or anything like that? Also is Hell a place or do people have to die and sin to go there? Are you underground with burning flames and torture like people think?" I dared to ask the big dumb questions and hoped he wouldn't judge me too much by what we're taught here on earth.

A low chuckle erupted from him. Hearing it was sexy to me, so it was no surprise when I heated up internally.

"*No.* It's another dimensional plane. You're a math-ematician. I'm sure you've seen and read about multiple realities and planes—time travel. Some can die to go there, but not by sin and damnation. Demon, as humans refer to us on earth, is short for *dimensional* for us. So, technically where I'm from, we spell it d-i-m-e-n." He spelled it out for me as I processed the information he gave.

"It's not in this solar system or anywhere close that a satellite could go, unless you add a thousand plus years and more advanced technology... Random portals occur throughout time and space, that's how some dimens escaped. It wasn't some plotted thing and there's no specific spot they show up. Of course, with advanced mathematics, I'm sure those calculations could be calculated." He grinned at me, running his long, graceful human fingers through my hair. "I suppose it's similar to those 'glitches in the matrix' conspiracy theories. Think of Hell as its own planet that exists outside of your known plane. Not the religious Hell of sin and damnation." I heard his teasing undertones of how religious heretics sounded, and he had a point on how ridiculous people can be, but whatever, to each their own, I guess.

Finding his information absolutely riveting, I wondered about those math equations and if I could figure it out. I've certainly looked and calculated many complex equations. It wouldn't be impossible. Hmmm...

I turned towards him more intrigued than ever before. "*How* do you get there?"

"Well, we're told when we are needed by our brothers and sisters, and then we go..." *Okay? What are you hiding, Belke?* "Most of us were created in that world. So, to answer your question, not fiery flames. In fact, there's a lot of climate and beautiful scenery. Due to the gravitational and magnetic field, we have multiple moons. Not as close as the Earth's Moon, but we have them."

I stared at him as if he held all the stars and galaxies in his hands. I was lost in his wonder, his dimensional creation. I supposed demons could be aliens, for *aliens* described something unknown or belonging to another place, wherever that might be. *A fucking alien-demon-cat-puppy being.* 'Dimensional being' was right on the money. *How fucking cool!*

Belke considered me as I held the great debates in my mind of all the things that humanity had yet to discover. He spoke, distracting my musings, "I was sent here with my brothers and sisters to aid in the investigation of the proclaimed *demon* rebellion. It's unclear to me *when,* but eventually, I'll have to return to Hell. Each world we are sent to, we must learn and blend in, hence *this* form."

This form was certainly beautiful, that was for sure.

My heart sank over that thought. "I hope it's not any time soon... Would I be able to come with you?"

He placed a hand on my shoulder, giving me a reassuring look. "We'll worry about that when the time comes. I'm happy with any time spent with you, Becs."

The thought was deeply unsettling with how my heart clenched together with invisible strings. "If you had to go back, would you ever return?" My throat had grown tight.

Not looking forward to what he says next.

"I'd find a way back to you, if I knew you wanted me to." He rubbed both of my shoulders, seeming sad as I swallowed the lump in my throat. Anyone with working emotions could sense my tension at that moment.

"I tell you this before and after my ignorance. Without hesitation, Bels. I'd like you to return. I love you, *dimensional* or not. My *soul* is yours."

It looked like his eyes were misting which made my own do the same.

"Then, I'd fight for you—to be *with* you. To love that soul with all of mine. *All of the Hells be damned.*"

A small smile formed upon my lips as I wrapped my arms around his waist, gazing into those eyes I adored.

"If a measly human like me could battle the world—I'd fight for *you*, Bels," I told him honestly as his arms went around me, holding me as if I was the greatest treasure to him.

"Then, that's more than enough for me, Becs. It means a lot to hear that. *I love you.*"

"I love you, Bels, I mean it."

"I know you do," he said so quietly that I shivered as those vocal tones traveled their own wavelength down my body.

"I'll spare you the past talk. I can grasp context clues that you had a violent and sexual history, but somehow, you changed over the course of your lifetime."

"Smart woman, but yes, you're not wrong—it wasn't in

my world though, but other worlds. Remember rankings and duties? Just like here, there's jobs and duties, some of us can have a multitude. Donte and some of my brothers can be sent on various missions to other worlds depending on what needed to be done. Think of it as being a sort of peace-keeper and stopping conflicts and wars."

I laid my head on his chest, rubbing his back. "We all have our histories. Mine isn't anything special either. My parents are together, my sisters are smart and beautiful, *skinnier,* and without the health problems that I have. I'm a math-cosplay nerd, and I enjoy my solitude. I was bullied throughout my life, because *bitches be bitches*, and eventually I developed an attitude as I grew older—sass, if you will. Then, the whole thing with my ex, Joseph... I didn't want to bother with relationships anymore. *I stopped caring.* Until a sex *dimen* appeared in my room, wagging his tail."

He squeezed me, grabbing my hands and leading me to sit on the platform behind us. We soon faced one another.

"It really makes me sad when you talk about yourself as if you are anything less than perfection. People on this planet are such assholes, and their idea of beauty is so fucking skewed. It isn't fair that you've had to deal with that shit. But if I hear it in my presence, *I'll lose it.* Your brain is brilliant, you're creative and smart. *You* are beautiful; your soul is *beautiful.* Those bullies can answer to me, Belke, and I won't hear anything else about it. You deserve happiness, Bec, and a relationship that makes you forget the why or how the past went wrong—what matters is right *now. You have me for as long as I'm able.*"

My eyes misted with pent up emotions from the entirety of today and all the new information. That moment was so special, beyond any human words I could ever form. "I am yours, Bels. *All of me.*"

He reached and wiped my falling tears, scooting closer as I adjusted myself so that my legs were draped over his. Bels and I were fishes in the sea of the universe, and this moment was our aquarium exhibit. All the energy in the time and space continuum could watch for all I cared.

Cupping my face in his hands, we peered into the depths of windows to our souls, frozen in our fish tank. "Everyone has left; *it's just you and me.* Cameras are off at my request. See there's no red light?" He indicated toward the camera further down the tunnel, and once I saw it, I scooted even closer to him when he pulled me into his lap.

Our arms went around each other, and our lips forged together in silent promise. My tongue sought out his as I moaned, an intense need crawling up my spine with desire.

His hands went into my hair holding me to him passionately, deepening the kiss and I fell into his hellish adventure.

"Did I tell you how beautiful you look tonight in that dress?" Bels placed featherlight kisses down my jaw and my neck.

"I don't remember, perhaps we were both distracted from all those thigh rubs under the table at dinner," I got out breathily.

"I've been thinking about being between your thighs all evening."

I hummed in approval at the back of my throat as I tilted my head, nudging my hips towards him to show exactly what I wanted.

"Then, by all means, slip between them." My tone dipped low and luscious.

Belke pulled up the dress over my hips, squeezing my thighs.

"Don't mind if I do," he purred, almost like a kitten.

I held him as he undid his pants, parting my underwear not long after. Teasing his cock at my entrance, I exhaled impatiently.

"Keep going," I beckoned him; I was wet, ready, and waiting.

As he did, my hands thrusted in his hair as we moved in sync once he laid me flat on my back.

Fuck me, Bels.

As the most romantic date *ever*, I basked in the glow of the large tank and fish and those perfect eyes on me. We met each other at the joining of our hips. One hand was on my ass and the other began to tease my breast, eliciting a groan from me before his lips nibbled on my nipple. I tipped my head back slightly, closing my eyes in silent delight. Belke was unlike anything else, and *fuck* if I let it leave my grasp.

He cupped the back of my head as he marked my other breast. *A mark that said, "Mine."*

"You're hell on earth," he whispered, bringing his lips back to mine in heated passion.

"As are *you*," I panted as he pumped his cock harder. "Fuck. Bels, you feel so good. *Don't stop.*"

Absolute hellish bliss it was. My orgasm was already brimming from deep within, my organs ready to overtake my soul just like Belke had from the first moment he appeared at the edge of my bed.

I tried to stifle my moans, which only made him thrust up harder until I couldn't hold back when release came tumbling from my lips and my pussy.

"Some of my favorite sounds from you," he said before moaning in a way that made me blush as he joined me.

I held him to me, mewling in his ear. He squeezed my

ass one more time before kissing me again as we slowed our movement.

"This is a cute place to have sex in," I said quietly, a smirk forming.

"It is. I know of a couple of more discreet spots if you're open to it?"

With my most wicked grin, "Lead the way, Bels."

His eyes lit up, and we made sure our stay over the next few hours were well worth the while.

$(x-$

$y^2 = Z$

$+a)$

$(y-1)$

$\frac{\Delta x}{\Delta y} = \lim_{\delta} \frac{\Delta x + 2}{\Delta y - 1}$

$b^2 + 2ax + a^2$

$\sin x$

$e = \cos x + tg y$

$\sin a =$

BECS

YOU ARE
BEAUTIFUL

TWENTY-FIVE

BECS

"Hey, Ash!" I waved, making my way to reception. It had been a few weeks into our new positions, and it was still a bit weird to see her where I always was.

She smiled, saying "Good morning," as I handed her a cold brew.

"You're the *best*, I love you," she groaned out, wiggling her fingers on her fresh cold brew.

"I was already there so I figured I'd bring one for you. Want to do lunch today?" I asked in invitation, knowing Mr. Bel had an important board meeting.

"You bet I do!"

I grinned, clinking our cups together. "How's the *new* team?" I asked her quietly, and she rolled her eyes, giving me a knowing glance.

"They don't bother me too much, but Katherine's *fake nice* to others really irritates me. She's okay with me, I guess, but I don't exactly stop to have a chat with her even though she offers to do lunch and things. I always tell her I'm busy."

I huffed a laugh. "Well, at least you're being treated better than I ever was."

She offered a consoling look. "I'm sorry, Becs. How are you liking your new boss and department anyway?"

"Real answer is that my boss is certainly *nicer,* less condescending, and listens to my ideas. The others on the team are also nice to work with, and each of us brings something to the table. The to-everyone-else-but-you answer is that Mr. Bel is the *worst and that I'm miserable.*" Ash and I basked in a shared grin. "There's a big budget meeting this week which should be fun. Wonder if we need to cut people?"

She nodded, taking a sip of coffee, and sighing in pleasure. "He's not bad to look at either, I'm sure."

"You aren't wrong," I said with a sly smile, and she wiggled her eyebrows suggestively.

"*None* of the people here would turn *that* down. You know, if they weren't afraid of him." Ash went on playfully and I giggled, agreeing, but also not giving anything else away.

"Well, let me escape before the two gremlins come in and harass us both; I'll see you in a few hours, Ash."

"I'll grab us some salads and meet you in the break room at lunch," she said with a smile and a wave. I returned it, heading towards the elevator. I pushed the fiftieth floor button and waited for it to ascend, lost in thought.

Positive changes were happening, and I knew it wouldn't have happened if Belke hadn't arrived with Donte.

When the ping finally came, I headed towards my desk which was two doors down from Bels at the end of the hallway. I had a fantastic view of the city, *and privacy* for spontaneous horny-demon visits.

I smirked as I settled in, remembering last week where he had me bent over the very spot I sat.

Focus.

Opening my computer, I dove into working on the spreadsheets that I had been working on for the budgets, along with how much people were spending in each department. It didn't take me long before I began to get lost in the numbers.

Not knowing how much time had passed, a knock sounded at my door, and there the handsome man was, dressed in a pale gray.

"I'm about to head into the board meeting, it's been busy, but I wanted to say good morning, at least."

I smiled happily as I gave him a thumbs-up and wished him good luck. He saluted me in a way that was super cute, walking away. Another coworker in our department paused near the doorway as soon as Bels left. He was a blonde-haired gentleman named Tony.

"Good morning, Rebecca. Did you get the chart I sent over in preparation for our big meeting in a few days?"

I nodded, confirming I did. "Yes, I merged it with what I had and created this," I turned my second monitor around to show him as he walked inside to peek at it.

He looked it over once he was closer and grinned. "Perfect, I should've known you'd weave your little math wizardry magic."

A well-deserved praise, I'd say. "I think we're going to kill it. We all bring great ideas and plans to the table; it makes sense to continue down the path we're on as a company—*a merged company*. The numbers don't lie, Tony."

"Agreed. If our meeting goes well, I think the new investors will throw a benefit party and get other local companies on board to work on future projects with Toom."

"Well, here's to hoping!" I crossed my fingers visibly, and he cracked a smile.

"We have a good team; we've got this. I'm going to work on some more numbers to double check what you send over this morning and see where some budgets can be squeezed or worked around. Can't forget the cuts either, along with the discrepancies you found."

"Sounds good. Thank you, Tony," I said as he walked out with a wave over his shoulder.

I checked the time and realized lunch was soon. I finished what I was working on before locking my computer and closing my office up behind me. Making my way down to the first floor break room, I met Ash at a table in the center of the room.

Not too many people were there, and I didn't recognize anyone but Ash. The woman herself slid a salad toward me as I sat down.

"I got you the Greek one, hope that's okay?"

I thanked her. "Of course! Lunch will be *on me* next time."

Ash and I chatted over assorted topics ranging from my degree to her childhood in Florida before moving to Georgia. I was mid-laugh over a story involving childhood embarrassment with a bottle of water in my hand, when Katherine walked in with two random women that looked just like her. They might as well have been the work version of *Mean Girls*.

As if the world needed more bitches and bullies.

"Well, look who it is. *Miss Accountant.* Enjoying being someone else's problem, Rebecca?"

I saw Ash stare down at the remainder of her food, biting her tongue visibly.

"Why don't you tell me, *Katherine?*"

She scoffed, ignoring my comment as she and her crew walked towards the large fridge, grabbing their lunch bag.

Ash side-eyed me like she was two seconds away from talking shit, and I gave her a look that said *"I got this, girl."*

"I don't know why you ditch us and hang out with her, Ashlee, she's so boring and dull," Katherine remarked, and I sighed heavily as Ash threw what she didn't finish in a bag, standing up.

"Oh, so we can talk about where to get our nails done, and what the newest season of Coach is in? *No thanks, Kat.* Rebecca has more brains and interesting things to say than *any of you.* So, keep your comments to yourself, otherwise I will report you to HR for workplace harassment and for not growing the hell up."

I stood up at the same time with a small smirk on my face, deciding I was done with the rest of my food, too. Katherine stiffened at the sound of her *Kat* nickname she hated and glared at the two of us.

Her friends scoffed, tossing us dirty looks, and I could see Katherine's wheels turning for some sort of remark, but I followed behind Ashlee out of the breakroom.

Once we were out of earshot, I told her, "You didn't have to do that, Ash, I could've taken care of it."

"I know, but that shit makes me so mad. *Like grow the fuck up,*" she mumbled under her breath.

We shrugged in unison, making our way to our favorite café.

"I'll buy," I said as we stood in line. Ash said nothing as I could tell she was trying to calm herself down with the tapping of her foot.

My heart warmed fondly; it was nice knowing someone else was on my side.

While waiting for our drinks, I sarcastically asked Ash, "So, what do you do on your weekends when you aren't getting your nails done and talking about the newest in-season Coach?"

She smirked, relaxing her shoulders finally.

"I hang out at the mall and look at the girls and boys, *duh,*" she mocked, and I giggled over it. "On a serious note, though, I do roller derby on the weekends. It's my shit."

"Really?" *That's fucking awesome, work bestie.*

"I know, despite professional appearances, *I promise I'm fun.*"

I released a hearty laugh as our order was announced and we walked over, leaving the café shortly later.

"I wasn't saying that, but I wasn't expecting you to say roller derby of all things either. It's a compliment," I told her honestly.

"Well, *thank you.* Believe it or not, it helps work out my anger issues. There's only so much help my therapist can offer."

I laughed at her remark as she followed up with, "What about you? How do you spend your free time?"

"I'm boring. I like to binge-watch shows, and work on cosplays when it's convention time. Nothing crazy," I shrugged it off and she paused.

"That's awesome, Becs! You're not boring at all—despite what that bitch says."

I huffed a laugh as we walked into our building, nearing the end of our lunch break. "Thank you. It's a hobby of mine."

"Well, I have no doubts of your talent, Becs," she finished, walking to her receptionist area.

"Thank you for the lunch company. Try and have a good rest of your day?" I told her and she gave me a goofy, sarcastic look of a thumbs-up. "You too. See you later, Becca."

I waved, and made my way to the elevator, sipping on my coffee.

The elevator pinged and people came out, minus one person.

I stepped in, seeing Bels eyes light up as I hit our floor.

"I'd rather spend my lunch with you," he whispered once it was us alone and the elevator moved up.

I smirked, taking a sip of coffee before offering it to him. "Long meeting?"

He took the coffee and sipped it for a minute before handing it back. Bels dropped his shoulders in defeat, "*Yes.*"

"Good or bad?" I took the drink and chugged the rest.

"Both, but it'll work out. Are you prepared for Friday?"

I nodded. "I worked my numbers magic and I'm polishing up the slides today and tomorrow."

He seemed relieved as the elevator pinged and a few people got on.

David stepped in and noticed me and Zavier. He nodded towards him in a semi-dismissive manner and locked his gaze onto me.

"Hello, Rebecca, how's the...*new* department treating you?"

"It's going great, thank you," I said with my warmest smile, and his look changed to a two-faced-vibe then.

"Glad to hear it. The other elevator was full, so it looks like we have to ride up together..."

"How's everything on your end?" I asked, making casual conversation since there were some floors left.

Belke kept his face neutral, crossing his arms, pretending not to pay attention to our conversation as cringy as it felt.

"Ashlee is great, and well, things are as good as they can

be. I have no complaints. You are certainly missed, but I'm glad you're happy..."

That's awkward, bud.

"I am. It's nice to be doing a job I'm more suited for with my skill set *and degree.*" I gave him a fake smile as he offered his own unsettled one.

"Of course," was all the rest of what he said as the elevator let him off at his floor before we continued upward.

Thankfully, I didn't have to engage in any more awkward conversations, because we arrived at our floor not too long afterward.

I didn't look back as Bels kept a safe distance to not let anyone think anything *sexy* was going on. Even if there was, it was no one's business.

Throwing my cup away, I made it to my office to drop my bag off, and Bels pretended to head to his office. I checked my emails to see if I had anything urgent, and I grabbed an empty folder to pretend I needed a reason to go to Belke's office.

I shut his door behind me after noticing no one was around, locking it, too.

"Was that awkward for you as it was for me?" he asked while leaning against the front of his desk.

"It was more awkward for me, believe me. *It's bullshit,* I tell you."

Bels beckoned me closer. "Come here."

I tossed the random folder into a chair and went up to him.

"I'd probably lose my mind if I didn't see you at least once a day," he admitted quietly, and I gave him an appreciative look before he pulled me towards him into a cherished embrace, kissing me tenderly.

"You certainly make the days and nights better." I nuzzled my nose against his.

"Likewise," he said between kisses as I drew my arms around his neck.

"Mmm," was all he got out before I paused. I released my hold on him, and a flash of concern appeared on his face.

"Let me cheer you up?" I offered, sinking to my knees in front of him, undoing his belt and zipper.

Before he could object, I glanced up between my eyelashes, seeing him bite his lip.

I rubbed him, but as always, it didn't take him long to *grow* underneath my touch. Kissing his inner hip briefly, I took him into my mouth as he sucked in a breath.

"Fuck," I heard him mumble out as his hand gripped my hair, leaning his head back. I caught that delectable closed-eye expression of bliss.

"I love when you surprise me with that hot mouth of yours," he whispered as I stroked and curled my tongue down his cock to his tip. "Too bad I can't make this last... I'm going to come soon. Swallow me down, pretty lady." I heard his hushed sighs before he began twitching slightly in release, spilling his hot cum in my mouth.

I supposed my man was ready and waiting for it, after all.

Swallowing slowly so he could visibly see, I tucked him carefully back in his pants before I stood up. I straightened myself out, walking away towards the chair I tossed the folder in.

"Pleasure doing business with you, *Mr. Bels.*"

He grunted, starting towards me, but I straightened my hair quickly, unlocking the door before disappearing towards my office with a grin plastered on my face.

I received a text message that read, *"You're evil. Maybe I wanted to return the favor."*

"I'll be waiting at home," was all I sent back, so I could get back to work.

He may have walked past my office once or twice with pouting glances, and all I could do was smile innocently. *I'm not the demon here.*

$y^2 = z$

Bees

$\lim$

$\frac{\Delta x + 2}{\Delta y - 1}$

$e = \cos x + tg y$

$(y-1)$

$\sin a =$

YOU ARE
BEAUTIFUL

TWENTY-SIX

BECS

I wore my fancy black pantsuit to the important budget meeting on Friday and gave my speech on the numbers I ran. I added in where costs and spendings could be cut and distributed along with potential partnerships. My slides showed the numbers, and the numbers and facts didn't lie.

The first cut being David's department. The fucker had the audacity to falsify his spendings. *Can't deny the possible retribution I felt over my findings.*

Tony and our other teammate, Dani, showed the charts and trends added to the PowerPoint, plus windows of opportunity based on the numbers I produced.

Donte and Zavier both looked impressed as did the other board members. Admiration flashed through Belke's eyes at one point, along with Donte's approval in his blue-eyed gaze.

"We have a lot of good things to work with here. Splendid work. Thank you," Donte went on with his deep masculine tone, and a few others in the room agreed.

"We have the foundations, now we just need to build

up from there. Excellent work everyone," Zavier said as the room rose, bidding farewells and exiting.

I shot my team members smiles that they returned, and we grabbed our things. Zavier walked with Donte, discussing things out of earshot, and they followed other members out of the large meeting room down the hallway.

"Celebratory lunch?" Tony offered.

"Rain check this time; I have some things I need to finish up before the weekend."

"Of course, what about you, Dani?" he said, turning towards her.

Dani agreed as we followed her out towards the elevator. I appreciated her professional outfit which involved a pencil skirt and blouse. The way her dark red hair looked in a tight bun—total librarian vibes. My power pantsuit and her fit, we passed the badass women check. *If I did say so myself.*

After the crowded elevator ride to our floor, I left them there as I made my way towards my office.

Due to my nerves, I couldn't eat anything, but I was relieved once I made it through and sank into my desk chair with a sigh.

I happened to look up to see Donte in my doorway moments later.

"Impeccable work today, Rebecca. I'm going to look into those partnerships mentioned, and I will arrange for a soiree of some sort in the oncoming weeks which will be great for networking and forging those contracts."

"Sounds great, thank you."

He nodded, a handsome smile appearing before disappearing from my doorway.

I jumped back into work, turning on a random music playlist. Humming off and on to it, the sky grew darker out, and I worked later than expected. *At least I got everything done.*

I shut everything down, feeling satisfied when Bels poked his head in. "I was wondering when you'd be done..."

I frowned, a feeling of guilt creeping in for keeping him late on a Friday night. "Were you waiting on me?"

He nodded, inclining his head. I grabbed my stuff, turning the light off and locking the door behind me on my way out.

"I'm sorry. If it helps, I got a lot accomplished," I tried to explain while he seemed conflicted.

"Don't overwork yourself, Rebecca."

I puffed out air. He used my government name, which he only used at work. *Still irritated me.* "I'm not. You forget, I love doing what I went to school for. *I'm a math geek.*"

Humor passed over his handsome face while we stepped in unison into the elevator and made our way downward. "If you say so. At least the week turned around —all thanks to you. I'm proud of you, Becs."

Heat rushed to my cheeks. "Thanks."

"Any weekend plans?" I asked quietly as we made our way towards our cars in the parking garage nearby.

"*You.*"

"Can't wait," I teased back as his eyes flicked to his demon puppy ones reflecting the parking garage's lighting.

"See you shortly," he said innocently, and I knew he'd be there before I made it.

Naturally, I was right.

Walking through my door later, I found Bels in his naked demon form. His horns were out, along with his tail wagging behind him, all while coming towards me.

I giggled as he took me into his arms squeezing me tight. "*I love you.*"

I squealed as he still held me tight before releasing me. Looking up, I caressed his face. "I love you, Bels."

His tail rubbed against my pant leg. "Are you *sure* you're a demon and not a domesticated house pet?"

He pouted and I giggled, finding him adorable and not scary before reaching up to rub his horn. He hugged me closer, making a cute noise as I smirked devilishly.

"*See?*" I added as he pulled us into my bedroom and suddenly my back was against the bed.

"You started this, by rubbing this house cat behind the ears," he said, standing over me with his growing cock. I couldn't help but be proud of myself.

"*You* started it!"

"This I have to hear," he said, tugging off my pants as I took off my blazer, revealing my matching set of black lacey undergarments.

"For showing up here all those months ago in this very same spot, *wagging your tail!*"

He mumbled under his breath as he tugged my underwear off, too. "I don't know whether to take it as a compliment or..."

"You are precious. *Please,* don't stop. Continue wagging your tail when I come home from a long busy week at work, where I have a very demanding boss."

"Oh, really now?"

"Yes. Zavier Bel is the worst boss, *so I've heard,*" I exhaled in quiet relief over his tender touches as he kissed up my body, unclasping the bra I wore.

"You love me," he whispered against my skin.

"I do. I love our surprise sessions at work and teasing you endlessly. You make it so easy."

He grunted, reaching underneath me to pull me closer

to his waiting cock. "You're the demon here, and you don't even have horns."

I gave him an innocent look. "Not my fault you corrupted me."

He raised an eyebrow, looking up from where he leaned down to kiss my breasts.

"Please elaborate," he said with wicked playfulness, narrowing his eyes.

"Lean closer, pop those wings out, and I'll be happy to show you." My tone was a summoning.

A low growl left his throat, and it took two seconds for those black feathered wings to appear. Belke licked up my chest toward my waiting lips.

I lightly rubbed both horns at the same time as he bit down on my shoulder right when I brushed my fingertips against his wing.

"Seeing you come undone is my favorite experience," I whispered seductively as his eyes opened in a flash with a hot-as-hell moan. I became one with his horns and heat.

"Likewise," he said needily before I rubbed his cum over my entrance.

I gave him a look that told him he was the object of *all* my desires when he finally entered me.

"I'll be happy to show *you*," he crooned, leaning back down and increasing his pace as I ran my fingers up his horns again. The out-of-this-world low growl that left his chest made my toes curl.

Fuck, I couldn't ever picture Belke not being with me.

"Open your mouth," he commanded in a low tone, taking one of my breasts into his mouth, nipping lightly.

I did so as he served a BCT for me. My tongue lolled out in response. His soft sighs grew louder as he squeezed my sides and lifted my leg up to plow deeper.

Moaning around his BCT, I toyed with the grooves and angled tip. I took my *evilness* too far when I ran my hand up his horn before sneaking a single stroke down one of his wings.

"Fuck," he drawled out, pumping my pussy and my mouth full of warm demon cum.

Humming around his BCT, his eyes narrowed in on me.

"Okay, that's it. Bend that ass over, you're about to get it."

I gave him a pouty, innocent look. *Oh, who, me?* Bels motioned his fingers for me to turn, taking my BCT away from me. My pussy was throbbing from all the teasing, but I assumed the position, exposing my ass high in the air for him. After my rear got licked and prepped, I was double-demon stuffed with cocks.

It was moments like these while moaning in sexual bliss that I took note how we were two in the same, human and demon—*or dimen, rather*. We may have had our differences and origins, plus histories, but we were *made* for each other.

$(x-$

$x^2+2ax+a^2$

BECS

$y^2=z$

$\lim\limits_{\infty}$

$\dfrac{\partial x+2}{\partial y-1}$

β

$+a)$

$\sin x$

$e=\cos x + tg y$

$(y-1)$

$\sin a = b^3$

YOU ARE
BEAUTIFUL

TWENTY-SEVEN

BECS

"What color?" I asked, holding up three options to the demon in front of me.

The color choices were red, purple, or midnight blue.

I stood in my underwear, waiting as he considered *me* in what I wore, along with the dress options. It took a purring sound and a longing glance over me for Belke to lick his lips like I was a tasty treat.

"You look great in all of them. I'd love to see you work the room in red though. Wish we could skip..."

A smirk appeared while I glanced down and caught how his tail moved with what he said. *A wag of approval.*

"Red it is, then," I said aimlessly, tossing the others on the bed.

To coordinate, my makeup was done nicely with red lipstick that matched the dress and red heels. I pulled on the entire fit, giving Belke a final turnaround. No longer the demon, Zavier's blue-brown eyes reflected in the mirror dressed in black and white.

"A demoness in human form. Weaving your magic over

me and everyone else there tonight. *Perfection* is what *you* are, Becs."

Giving him a cheesy grin, I leaned into his side. "You clean up well yourself, *Mr. Bels,*" I purred in his ear as he snapped a picture of us both on my phone, sending it to himself.

"I love you. Let's go kill it." He kissed my cheek in return.

"Let's turn heads, Zavi-Bels," I added, swiping up my gold clutch.

I followed him down to the limo he had waiting, and he mentioned he'd be picking up Tony and Dani, too. Once we did, Tony donned a dark blue suit, and Dani wore a nice dark purple dress. I saw Zavier smirk as if he noticed me making notes of their wardrobes, and I shook my head. Red was definitely a good call.

"Tonight's goal involves smiling; the rest of us will do the talking. If people mingle, of course, smile and be friendly, typical stuff. Enjoy yourselves, but don't treat it as a non-work function completely. *We're paid to be here on the weekend.* If all goes well, I'll give you Friday off," Zavier mentioned casually, pouring champagne in small glasses, and we clinked our flutes in agreement.

"Network and smile—easy, right?" Tony mentioned, as Dani and I nodded with our glasses in hand in salutation.

"We have a talented and capable team; we wouldn't be here if it weren't the case," Zavier told them.

"Cheers to us," I added, clinking with Dani and Tony, downing the bubbly.

After the short ride to one of the high rises, Zavier told us that he'd check in later.

"We've got this," Dani mentioned to us quietly as we walked in sync after Mr. Zavier Bel.

The work squad was rolling up in style.

I knew various departments from our company—minus David's—would be in attendance as well as potential companies and clients for future partnerships.

We made it inside the fancily decked-out hall before making our way towards the area up a few floors for the event. The event room had a spot for dancing, a glass bar on the opposite side, dark romantic lighting aside from the dark blue lighting above the dance floor; it was modern and fancy with *tons* of people.

Great, this is fine.

The three of us mumbled how we needed another pick-me-up. The one bubbly in the limo wasn't cutting it.

Exchanging similar looks between us, we laughed, heading towards the bar.

"I need liquid courage to get out of my introversion," Dani mentioned on cue between songs.

"They sure go all out, don't they?" Tony asked as we waited at the bar to order.

"Seems so," I mentioned as the bartender took our drink order.

"First round is on me," I added, paying quickly before they could object.

I went lighter with my drink that had a vodka base; it was fruity, but not too strong. I could easily drink four and still stand up straight. *I'd surely need it to deal with this crowd.* I knew I had to space my drinks if I were to last longer than two hours.

"Cheers, team, let's meet up in a bit," Tony went on as we agreed in unison before parting.

I sighed heavily, finding a spot near a fun sculpture that was near the entrance to the room.

Sipping on the drink, I looked up, observing it while

making note of the artistry, trying to decide its origins. It reminded me of a Michelangelo sculpture in a way.

"The artists in Atlanta always fascinated me," I heard a voice I wasn't expecting from beside me.

Noticing it was Donte, he raised his glass. Naturally, he'd be here tonight—*duh, Becs*.

A thought occurred to me then as I offered a polite *hello*. "Donte, can I ask you something personal?"

His brow quirked curiously. "Shoot."

I stared at the sculpture again, taking in the shapes of muscles, and how it looked older than time itself. "Do you know when Belke has to return *home?*" I tried to hint toward him that I knew everything without coming out and saying it in public.

Donte swallowed down his drink and sighed. "Unfortunately, I do not at this time."

I frowned with defeat while he leaned closer to speak into my ear so no one else could hear, "Thank you for not outing our kind. You also look great tonight. Come, let me introduce you to a few potentials, they're anxious to meet the brains behind the math."

I huffed a laugh, following close with him. Donte wore a white suit which was a lovely contrast with the black attire he normally wore. Not that it was hard for him to look good in anything I've seen him in so far. *Damn sex demons.*

As he introduced me, I shook hands with people at various companies who were impressed and happy to work with Toom. As we chatted, I noticed Donte kept a protective stance at my side, occasionally placing his hand upon my back when we laughed or took sips of our drinks.

I didn't know how I felt about that.

Uh, Bels, come check your boss! I couldn't tell if he was pulling the moves or what.

After another conversation, once another twenty were to be had, Donte led me to another group, and I froze.

"Rebecca," Donte went on, "Meet Joseph, a potential client."

I blinked, and Donte tilted his head with a smile, catching on to my *outside face.*

Fix your face, Becs!

With my best fake smile, I extended my hand as he did the same with his own knowing cocky smile.

"It's a pleasure to meet you, Rebecca, I've heard so much about *you.* Lovely to meet you." *Don't punch him in front of the big boss. Act cool, Becs.*

I inclined my head politely as I let Donte do most of the talking. My ears were pounding along with my heart. *Slug bastard.*

Super proud of myself, I played it fucking cool—*as a professional woman should.*

"I'd love to talk to you more about partnering with some added ideas. Take a walk with me, Rebecca? I'd love to hear your ideas."

I looked towards Donte as if in permission, but also a *please, say no* silent plea.

He didn't get the memo though, nodding and leaving us there as I begrudgingly followed Joseph.

Goddammit. I sure wish I had a demon named Belke to save my ass right about now.

He led us to a small high-top table without chairs and placed his emptied glass on it. It was near a fancy structural beam by the dance floor.

"You look great, Rebecca... I don't remember you looking this way, *ever.*"

Ew.

He looked me over, impressed, and I wanted to smash

the glass against his face and see him bleed for all the shit he'd done.

Of course, I'm fucking living my best life, and this motherfucker steps in.

What. The Fuck.

But no, the glass stayed in my hand as I smiled awkwardly, taking a sip and finding something to look at in the distance.

"So, you work for Toom now. Using your degree finally, huh?"

"Yes," I said simply, and he sighed, not taking any fucking hint. Egotistical asshole.

"It's been a while. How are you doing?" He took a step closer, and I shot him a more serious, warning look that time.

"What do you want, Joseph? I don't want to talk about the weather with you. Are you serious about working with the company or not? Don't waste either of our time, because I certainly don't have enough to drink to have any other conversations but that—*with you.*"

I finished my drink quickly, walking away towards the bar.

Thank fuck, it's over.

I ordered a double-shot of tequila once the bartender came over. *What I had wasn't strong enough.*

I downed it quickly, ordering my first drink again because it's all about balance.

Good, that should hurry the booze along.

Someone appeared next to me, paying for mine and theirs, and I heaved a sigh, seeing Joseph again.

Thank-uh-oh-fuck, it's not goddamn over.

"*This* doesn't fix you being a fucking prick to me, or mean that I forgive you," I told him, taking my drink, and walking off to hopefully disappear and pretend I could be anywhere else.

"Rebecca," he said as he caught up to me where I stood next to a pillar near the other table I was at previously.

I shot him an unamused look, trying to be professional as I could without causing a scene.

"I'm sorry for hurting you."

Yeah, and hell froze over, you fucking twat.

I simply gave him a look of disbelief. Like what did he think I was going to do? Suck his dick in front of everyone? *Ew—no.*

Now, if a certain demon showed up and asked nicely...

"I was an asshole, and you have every right to hate me. I hurt you and was a piss poor excuse of a boyfriend before, never appreciating what I had."

I took a sip, making a face of agreement into the glass yet saying nothing. I took in his appearance and wondered what I ever saw in that receding hairline. Joseph put on some weight in a muscley way. *Sucks to suck doesn't it, Joey?*

Feeling his eyes on me, I said nothing, finishing my glass when I felt an arm go to my lower back. I stiffened, thinking it was Donte or someone else, but it wasn't.

Belke

TWENTY-EIGHT

BELKE

I was speaking with clients, making my rounds, when I spotted Dani chatting with two women, laughing casually. Then I looked for Rebecca—nothing. As I thought about looking for her, I saw Tony coming towards me seemingly worried with a serious expression.

Once he was upon me, he spoke, "There's something going on with Rebecca. I think she might need some sort of assistance. I saw her walk away from a gentleman, and he kept following her. She seems upset, and I wanted to bring it to your attention just in case it's an important client or not."

I nodded, gritting my teeth and keeping my face neutral. "Thank you; I will take care of it and smooth things over."

He inclined his head, pointing towards a pillar where I saw the red-dressed beauty herself. Sighing in relief, I straightened myself, exuding all the *hot human boss* energy.

Depending on what the guy said and did to upset her, it varied on how I would handle it.

If he so much as touched her inappropriately...

I snuck up beside her, placing my hand upon her lower back, feeling her stiffness. Confused by her reaction, I realized how tense and distressed she was from the encounter.

"*There* you are," I spoke warmly to her before moving my eyes towards the gentlemen across from her, who was standing far too close to *my* woman.

"Yes, I'm *here*," she got out politely before adding, "Mr. Zavier Bel, meet Joseph Blake, a potential candidate for future partnership."

"Ah, yes, *Joseph*," I extended my hand, being polite and the dumbass didn't get a clue, shaking my hand *as a professional does*. Her fucking ex was *here*? The universe had its jokes.

"Pleasure to make your acquaintance, Mr. Bel. You have an exemplary employee here, who I was just speaking with about—"

Joseph winced at my tight, firm handshake. *Weak human.* I withdrew my hand and interrupted.

"Yes, if you'd like to continue, Donte, would be happy to discuss it. He's at the bar if you'd like to speak with him further. Rebecca here is certainly a star-employee and is needed elsewhere, if you'll excuse us. Please enjoy," I said in a tone that was polite, *professional,* and that I wouldn't hear of any answer other than his dismissal immediately out of my sight.

We smiled politely at Joseph, and I led her away toward the opposite side away from that prick.

She seemed relieved once we paused out of his eyesight. "Thank you," she said with the utmost gratitude.

I sighed heavily. "*That* was him? *I should wring his neck.*"

Her lips perked up, pleased with my answer. "I'd pay to see that, Mr. Bels."

I couldn't help but smile then, enjoying that little nickname of hers that made me want to crawl in her lap and *purr*. "The night is still young."

We shared a knowing look. Becca exhaled, releasing her scrunched up shoulders. "If it wasn't *you*, it would have been *me*."

That's my girl.

I gave her a mischievous look as I finished my drink. "Good thing we're behaving tonight then, hmm?"

She winked as I looked for Dani and found her chatting with someone else.

"I think we'll ease up on your mingling tonight, I'll have Dani keep you company if you feel like dancing. I don't want you to be alone with that creep again or risk him bothering you," I grumbled, going into protective mode. *If only my tail was out.*

"Good, because I might strangle him and risk losing this job."

We smirked in unison as I mentioned that I had a few more guests to greet before we could leave. I didn't want to leave her, but she made her way to the dance floor. I found Dani quickly, mentioning that there was a creep following Rebecca around, and if she could keep her company.

Thankfully, it didn't take much convincing. She appeared ticked off that there was a creep on the lurk as she walked towards where Rebecca was.

I momentarily watched her dance from where I stood on the incline seeing how she looked without a care, moving her hips in sync to the tunes. I loved her and instantly wanted to be down there pressed tight against her, and before too long I would be once the important people left.

With enough alcohol, others wouldn't care as long as I didn't *fuck her* in front of everyone...as enticing as it would be. I decided to behave as I turned away from the marvelous sight of her, enabling myself to get more conversations over with.

It was another hour, and I was done. Donte mentioned how Joseph gave him his contact information and left —*thank fuck.*

He soon left as I gave him a nod, and he disappeared while I made my way to where Rebecca was still dancing. No one else important was in attendance that I had to hide anything from.

I gave Tony and Dani the go ahead to leave if they wanted, and I told them I was on my way to tell Rebecca, too. Thankfully, they left together in the limo we arrived in —which I encouraged.

Now, I could be myself with her.

I slipped in behind Becs, hands on her swaying hips, and kissing her neck.

She giggled, realizing it was me, and it was then I knew she had more to drink by the smell of vodka. Leave it to my Becs to turn her damper of a night around.

"Did I tell you how sexy you are tonight?" I whispered in her ear between beats so she could hear me.

"No, but why don't you continue to tell me?" she asked in invitation, turning around towards me.

Slipping her arms around my neck, I pulled her closer.

She was completely feline—the devil woman herself and the woman who held my heart and soul in the palm of her hand. My universe dangled from her fingertips as she smiled at me, lights reflecting the same love I felt for her.

I leaned closer. "Beautiful demon in red. I can't wait to take you out of that dress, and..."

Moving my head, she laughed, lighting up, so beautiful

and happy. "And-d? What then?" She rested her head on my chest, gazing up at me.

"Dance with me, and I'll show you," I coaxed as the song changed and a salacious gaze emanated from me causing her to sigh with contentment.

We spent some time pressed up tightly to one another, dancing and kissing until the limo arrived back to pick us up. I told the driver to drive around until I said otherwise. The window between the driver and the back portion of where we were went up. Alone with one another, Becs climbed into my lap immediately without warning.

"You said you had something to show me, *horny boy?*" Her voice was velvety and smooth.

I stared up at her with intrigue, cupping her ass while her hands settled upon my shoulders. I could smell the alcohol, but it didn't deter me. I appreciated how eager she was, her sexual energy rolling off her in waves. That same energy that originally lured me to her in the first place. The energy that gave life within my veins and soul.

"I do. I want to show you what you do to me." I tugged on my lip as her glazed-over eyes took me in. I squeezed her ass before moving one of those hands to hers.

"Yeah? What do *I* do then?" Her voice lowered as we stared at each other, and I moved her hand down towards my hard cock.

She released a soft sigh, grinding against me with her pubic bone. "If I was a hot demon, I'd feel the same way, too." She was soft spoken, leaning closer before rubbing me as my hand traveled up her thigh.

Hovering those luscious lips near mine, I held my breath.

"I may do things *to you,* but do you know what you've

done to me?" she spoke quietly, leaning back slightly to catch my gaze.

My eyes lingered from her lips to her eyes back to her perfect breasts, uncertain of what to devour first.

"Tell me," I whispered as she paused her rubbing to undo my pants, taking me out.

"*You*, coming to my rescue. Getting *bossy* and telling that prick to fuck off. Getting *protective* over little ole' me." She wrapped her hand around my cock, beginning to work her magic.

Closing my eyes briefly, I let out a slow breath. Suddenly, I was hyper aware of where every inch of her was and where she touched.

"*You like that, do you?*" My tone was low, gravelly.

"It was some sexy shit... Slide your hand up further and you'll see."

Eyes locked eyes with hers, I maneuvered my hands as she continued to stroke me, and I snuck two fingers between her thighs. I went under her slip of lace underwear, ran them up and down twice, enjoying far too much of the moisture between them along with those delightful sloppy, wet sounds.

I heard her breathe out before biting her lip. Pulling my wet fingers from her, I brought it to my lips slowly before enclosing my mouth around them as she watched.

"Mmm. Sexy shit, indeed," I purred, seeing her eyes change from hot and bothered to *unhinged*.

I gave it less than ten seconds before I was inside her.

Sure enough, after I removed my fingers and tasted *her*, she moved her underwear to the side, climbed into my lap, and quickly placed me inside.

We blew out a breath in unison, cut short with quiet moans as my hands went around her and hers around me.

"Goddamn, Bels; you and your sexy shit," she breathed out before I stole her lips and dove my hand into her curls. Tightening my grip, I devoured that sexy little mouth, breathing in that sweet pheromone scent of hers that drove me fucking crazy.

What she didn't realize, although I told her, I felt the exact same about her. All I thought about was *her*. Being near her, *in her, inside and filling her up,* in her company, doing *normal* things, and fucking her in all the places we frequented—I couldn't get enough of her.

I always wanted more.

Tangling my tongue with hers, I basked in the glory and stretch of how she rode and claimed me as hers. After she began to moan, I broke our kissing rendezvous. "I'm crazy about you, Becs. You also do the sexiest shit."

I moved my kisses down to her neck, then shoulder before nuzzling my face into her bosom. *One of my favorite places to be.*

Her hand went immediately into my hair, tugging my head back. Becs gave me a look that told me all I needed to know. I moved one of my hands to her clit, stimulating her more. There was nothing better than climaxing together.

Becca stole my lips as she tightened around my cock, clutching to me in a beautiful finishing moan. Holding her to me, I came right along with her.

"Fuck," I grunted out as she cradled her head into my neck, catching those breaths that belonged to me.

"Fuck, indeed," she mumbled, nuzzling her face into my neck.

I made an *mmm* noise, leaning my head against hers.

"It's you and me, Becs. You. And. Me."

"Sounds good to me, Bels."

Bees
YOU ARE
BEAUTIFUL

TWENTY-NINE

BECS

"Hi, Mom," I spoke into the phone as I cooked dinner one Thursday evening after work. Mom didn't call after one week like Penny had predicted, it was even longer.

"About fucking time. Thanks for letting someone know you're alive. Had Pen not stopped by, I would've been left wondering! The pandemic didn't go anywhere! What if you got COVID, and died, and I never knew!"

I heaved a sigh, adding coconut oil to the pan. *So dramatic.*

"Sorry, Mom, I'll work on it. It's been busy around here..."

I paced around the kitchen, not letting the lecture bother me.

"Yeah, so I was told... He seems all right, but I haven't met him yet. Penny approves though, so I'm sure I'd approve, too. Why don't you bring him to visit sometime? Come visit your family, or are we chopped liver now because you're high and mighty like your sister, BJ?"

I rolled my eyes. Why leave Penny out? *She had her own business.*

"Sure, I'll ask him, and squeeze you into our *busy* schedules. There's nothing high and mighty about Atlanta, Mom, calm down. It's not New York or L.A."

"For the south, it is."

Grumbling to myself, I mixed the frozen bag of stir fry together in the skillet. Something I knew would make Penny have an aneurysm over getting frozen foods.

"If you say so. Enough about me. How are things on your end?" I steered the conversation away from me.

"Aside from being an empty-nester, your father and I are trying to take better care of our health and working on not eating out so much. We go on walks, visit the beach when it's not cold, and we planned our first cruise that leaves next month. Somewhere in the Caribbean for seven days."

The scent of stir fry filled the air as I inhaled a deep whiff. My stomach answered in a grumble. "Sounds like it'll be fun. Take lots of pictures. I'm sure Pen is being more than helpful on diet and food recommendations, hmm?"

"Your father sucks ass with pictures, no one wants to see his feet. Or random photos of walls. You know I'll take pictures of the scenery and of us, like always."

I heard a male voice in the background on her side, asking who it was on the phone. I heard mom mention it was me.

"The old man wants to say hi to his daughter who left us for the state of Georgia."

"Ain't no old man over here!"

I shook my head, hearing my dad take the phone from mom.

Please, stop.

The whole family is dramatic and cringy.

"What's up, girl scout! Long time no chat and see. Your

mother says you have a new man? He has a job, right? Does he cook and clean or answer to 'yes, boss?'"

I heard my mother curse in the background as I snorted. "Dad, please *stop*. Yes, he has a job, and I think so... He's a domesticated house-cat."

I heard his laugh echo as I turned around to peer over my shoulder to see Bels himself with his tail out beside him, no doubt debating on whether to wag it or not at the mention of my comment. He stood there giving me a sassy look, crossing his arms, and tugging on his lips.

Returning a smug look of my own, I turned back around toward the stove, seeing that the food was almost done.

"Never heard that terminology used to describe a man before, hope he didn't hear that."

I giggled, *he sure did.*

"I'm creative sometimes."

"Horseshit. You were always creative when you played dress up. Stealing your mother's makeup and jewelry... Anyway, are you thinking of visiting before our cruise next month or after? Bring your house-cat with ya."

I sucked in my lips, holding in my laughter when Bels appeared beside me. He leaned on the counter near the stove, giving me his most amused look.

"Maybe after your cruise; that way you can spend two days explaining what walls and ceilings we're looking at when you show us pictures."

I heard my mother in the background laughing as dad mumbled something incoherent.

Then, they bickered in wholesome fun before I heard him tell her, *"You better cut that shit out!"*

I shook my head again. "Alright, bicker later. This is why I don't call."

"I'll hand the phone back to your mom. It was good to hear from you, Becca. Ever since the pandemic hit..."

"I know, Dad, *I know.* I'm fine and safe. I'm vaxxed and waxed."

It was Belke's turn to laugh then, but my dad didn't catch it because *he* was laughing.

"Well, we're your parents, we're allowed to worry about you. I love you. Here's your mom back."

I told him I loved him too when she got back on the line.

"Damn old geezer," I heard her say then I heard a smacking sound.

"Did Dad just smack your ass? Also, you're not even fifty-five yet!"

"That he did... Yeah, that's old enough."

I turned off the stove, realizing the food was done.

"I'm glad you all are doing okay though. Maybe I'll visit after your cruise next month."

"Sounds good, honey. We love you and make sure your house-cat behaves otherwise you'll have to put him out of the house."

I huffed a laugh, seeing Belke pout and lowering his tail to the ground as if in defeat.

"Of course. Dinner is done, and I'm hungry, so I'll chat with you soon. Love you."

"Love you, too."

I hung up the phone. My family means well, but lord have mercy, they can be too much.

"That's my parents for you, Bels. Now, if you ever visit, you will always be referred to as a cat. *You're welcome."*

"What's the difference when you call me one versus them?"

"I'm cuter."

His laugh was low as he grabbed two bowls and kissed my cheek. "You are."

I smiled sweetly, letting him grab what he wanted as I set the phone down on the counter.

"Do you really want me to meet your parents in the near future though?" he asked, grabbing a bowl full and walking to the kitchen table.

"Only if *you* want to. I doubt it's every day that a demon gets introduced to his lover's parents...or even has a solo lover. Whatever the case, if you want to stick around long-term, it's an option. Although, I'd never willingly sign you up for *that* torture."

I grabbed my bowl, turning to find him smiling from his seat as I joined him at the table.

"I'd love to meet them, assuming I'm still here..." He mumbled.

I froze. *Uh, what?*

Belke swallowed and hesitated briefly, looking down into his bowl. "I got word earlier that I may be needed back home soon. I'll find out more in the upcoming weeks..." Belke grew quieter.

His home—Hell—*it was happening.*

"*How?*" I asked all choked up, staring down in disappointment at my bowl of untouched food. Nausea seeped its way in, replacing my earlier hunger.

"It hasn't been decided yet, so I can't answer that, Becca."

My eyes watered while I played with my food.

Belke reached his hand across the table for mine. I stared at his outstretched hand for a moment before taking it. "*I will* find my way back to *you*. It's easier for me to come back than for you to come to me. When I know specifics on when, you'll be the first to know." He squeezed my hand, rubbing his thumb over mine. "*I don't want to leave you.* I hope you know that."

My eyes filled up then. "Worst break up ever."

Words were hard, and I wasn't sure *what* to think. I pulled my hand away and grabbed a napkin to wipe my stupid eyes.

He frowned, standing up and appearing at my side, holding out his hand. "Come here," he said gently, taking my hands into his and leading me towards the couch.

Once he sat down, he pulled me into his lap, holding me to him. My head was cradled in his neck, and I couldn't help the rising emotions of what I had learned when silent sobs consumed me. He was still here, yet it felt like I was losing him before he was even gone.

"I love you, Bec. The total time up here was nothing in comparison to the time I've had with *you*. It's been a year, and it's been the best. All this shit was *worth it*. Humans suck, but not you—*never you*. You've captured me completely down to the very depths of my soul. You showed me love, and humor, and accepted me as I am. I will never forget it *or you*. You once asked if I'd come back. *I would. I will. For you—always*."

I cried harder as he held me, stroking his fingers through my hair. Not knowing what lay ahead, I didn't think our time would end *this soon*.

Whatever that meant.

Drying my tears, Belke adjusted himself and we managed to curl into one another on the couch.

With a whisper while facing him, I couldn't help my honesty even though his latest news was utterly devastating. "I love you, Bels. I'm glad you caught my sex-vibes, showing up here and wagging your tail."

He smirked, leaning to kiss my forehead before I snuggled close, wrapping my arms around him with my head tucked under his chin. I inhaled him in, still wishing I had the words to describe his otherworldly scent. Describing the elements on earth as I knew it, didn't scratch the surface of what he was and smelled like to me.

Perhaps, I'd never figure it out.

I wasn't sure what specifically lay ahead, but all I knew was that if I could do something to stop it or keep him—*I would do it.*

Belke

THIRTY

BELKE

"Donte," I spoke as calmly as I could, feeling a sense of desperation that it was all ending too soon. My undying heart couldn't take it. I couldn't bear to see Rebecca's face and sadness. Last time was rough enough, but I promised not to keep things from her, no matter what... I debated holding to that promise.

I sat across from my brother in his office ladened with black furniture, including the chair and desk that separated us. His office was dark and moody. As a leader, he had a lot on his plate, not just from home but here on earth, too.

Blue eyes met my own. "It will happen soon, Belke. As you know, I got word from others who have arrived. I'm not sure why you're needed back home, but the Elders requested it from their latest messenger. Whenever the time comes, I do believe you're allowed to come back here, but the messenger didn't say specifics. The Elders can be quite cryptic." Donte paused, looking off towards his view of downtown Atlanta. I followed that gaze, my heart in my throat.

Generally, the Elders stayed out of things. They helped

facilitate and guide, offering wisdom when needed, but never to rule over Hell.

"I know of your relations with Miss Stone. Not that I disapprove, but while you're home, you should seek out the Elders council... Soul mates do not only exist in our plane, but across space and time."

Soul mate. It echoed on repeat in my head as I met his eyes, shock searing through my entire being. *That explained so fucking much.* The irresistible urges and energy fluctuations. No wonder it felt impossible to be apart or knowingly leave her.

For the first time in well, *forever,* hope filled me, but not before the looming sense of dread in having that knowledge.

"Consider it, as I expect Miss Stone will not be too happy with you, Belke. If the Elders confirm and approve, then I'm sure some sort of arrangement can be done. Maybe you'll be removed from your rank and given something else that doesn't involve what we've done for all these years."

I caught his gaze again and nodded. *I didn't even think about that possibility.* Yes, I felt unimaginable things, but was she truly meant to be mine forever? Only the all-knowing Elders, who were top-tier dimensional beings would know.

"I will look into it as you suggest, brother. Rebecca won't be too happy with me when she finds out specifics, and someday I'll tell her as I don't want to get her hopes up in case we're wrong. For us, returns are temporary, but for humans, I may not see her for the rest of her mortal life."

The burning truth of that fact made me want to disrespect orders. It all depended on what the Elders told me, and if I got the once in a lifetime chance to come back to Earth *again.*

"What do we do with the aftermath once I'm gone? I'd

like to know she'd still be taken care of with the rebellion still going on."

Donte interlaced his dark fingers, settling them into his lap.

"You don't even need to ask. I find her humor...most refreshing. She's useful, and I'll be more than happy to give her your position within the company. Just make sure you send it in an email when you *transfer* departments, since the world can't know you're a proclaimed *demon,* too. We're already exposed enough." I nodded, knowing all too well how this world was. "Then you have the religious fanatics muttering things they don't truly understand about the concepts of Hell," Donte added. *"There's more than one as you know.* We are not even in the same realm as what they perceive, so we look like villains no matter what. The unending battle to humans who don't have the capacity to understand, not when they run around with judgments, slavery, and prejudices."

I gave him a look of understanding. We lived in the south; unfortunately, racism still existed. It was something our kind quickly learned when we took our human forms on earth. White privilege existed, along with the realities that Caucasian-appearing humans wouldn't understand about minority groups in general. I couldn't possibly understand what it was like to be in Donte's shoes as a black human male nor our other brothers and sisters. Unfortunately, worlds like this one had their prejudices and stereotypes, but as dimensional beings, we were so much more than labels. In our demon forms, we were equals and looked similarly with the eyes and bronze skin. Due to Donte's rank, brotherhood aside, he was slightly taller, and his horns were a different shade of gray. Regardless of what we looked like externally, we knew of bigger and better things than what made us different. All of us existed with a brain, body, and love to give. The inner heartbeat of the universe, reminding us of the same beautiful things that connected us all together from atom to atom.

"A losing battle, if you ask me." I sighed, giving him a look of bittersweet understanding of dimensional duties and obligations. My only hope was that the Elders were gracious and that I got to come back to Becca in this lifetime. I'd never met the Elders of Hell, but I heard varying things that made me wonder about the truth. *That they weaved time themselves. The keepers of portals and peace.*

"Thank you, Donte. No matter how long it is this time, it's always good to do business with you, brother."

Donte chuckled, revealing his perfectly straight set of human teeth. "Brothers, always. I'll keep your woman safe, although she'll probably try to kill my ass when she finds out... If and when you come back, she'll be unharmed. You have my word that no harm will come to her. Given what we are, I won't touch her either. I'll swear that oath to you now."

My lips drew upward. *Okay, it lingered in my mind.* He's like me, after all.

A sex demon was the easiest way to think about it when describing what I am to humans, but the truth was far more complex.

In Hell, dimensional beings—*dimens*—if you're on the energy track that involves the sexual kind, we were powered, attracted to it, and stronger with it, but we also returned the feel-good energy. It was all about give and take. We were made for pleasure, but not in the objectifiable way, unless someone was into that. There were duties to uphold, and we didn't get *in trouble* for not stealing souls as religions might think. No torture was to be had unless it was the pleasurable kind. It was more of a consensual exchange.

We could recruit other dimens with soul contracts, but not everyone got the pleasure to go to Hell. Sometimes the contract just involved the wills of the soul. It varied for everyone, some wanted to feel hope or loved, and sometimes they wanted peace knowing that there was somewhere, someplace to go after death.

No whips and chains, *kinks aside*.

I debated on asking the obvious question, but I had to request one thing, if only to spare my potential soul mate. "Thank you, Donte. That helps me get through the next steps... I don't want to traumatize Rebecca any further. Please, don't let her see what happens."

He nodded in agreement. "You have my word."

I counted to five and took a deep inhale and exhale. I made eye contact with Donte. "I feel a little better knowing that someone is watching out for her. I know the terms of us coming here were limited anyway, but it's certainly been an experience that's for damn sure. More so in the past year," I told him, shaking my head with a laugh.

He chuckled. "It sure has; the humans are chaotic. What world isn't though? That's the nature of things. I know it won't be long before I'm due back. Eventually, we'll be back home together, brother."

I nodded, rising up. The two of us exchanged a look of understanding and compassion. We've fought battles in other worlds together, while learning and growing. So many different forms we've taken and being able to be ourselves back in Hell. There was no one I'd rather go through eternity with as family.

"Back to work I go then," I joked as Donte inclined his head, hiding a smile.

Leaving his office, I shut the door behind me with a sigh, then I slowly made my way to the elevator and pushed the fiftieth button.

Donte was a superior, but we were also made at the same time. Although, ask anyone else that wasn't from our world of Hell, *the one not in flames,* they'd call us *crazy.* Delusional. Perhaps we were to any outsiders. We had a world—*a planet*–of our own.

I reflected back on my connection with Rebecca. Yes, sex could be an emotional connection, or not, but with any of my previous soul contracts—*as I called them*—most people wanted a night or a few. I think I had a weeklong contract on Earth once. But that was it. In my years of being what I was, *I've never felt as I did like when I'm with Becca.*

Yes, it began as a sexual thing, but even in the beginning, I couldn't *take* her soul in the way she hypothesized a demon would. I knew how I wanted to keep it, and her, safe. I wanted her with me. I used a play on words before when I told her about contracts. I should've known what she was to me. I couldn't explain our energetic connection, other than a beautiful stroke of fate.

A soul mate.

Of all things, I certainly wasn't expecting *that,* and I was more than willing to fight like hell to find a way back here.

It bothered me to leave her at all, but not this... I only hoped she wouldn't witness my departure.

You did that on purpose, Donte, because you knew I couldn't lie to her.

I sighed when the elevator pinged, and I walked towards my office. Rebecca's office door was cracked, and I heard her humming to tunes, which could only mean she was focused on something. I smirked, walking by and an idea came over me, since my time was drawing up short.

I strode into my office with determination, shutting the door. A quick call to the front desk, and Ashlee gave me useful information.

Thanks for not telling me about Katherine, Becs.

I rubbed between my eyes as I listened to Ashlee talk about recent experiences with David and Katherine, including the breakroom incident with Rebecca.

I should fire all of them.

There was a decision to be made about working with Joseph. *The Prick.*

Before I'm gone, I needed to prepare for unfinished business, if only for my Becs. *I hope our time isn't up.*

I wrote the necessary letters, making certain arrangements and placing them carefully in my desk. Plans were put in place so Rebecca would take over for me, and I made sure to backup files and place them on a secure thumb drive for her information only. It would help her navigate many future tasks, but it also had demon information and last known locations for the rebellion groups, minus the leader of it. *That fucker was trickier to find.* The leader of the rebellion was more of Donte's wheelhouse, so I wasn't as involved as he was. Donte had all the information, of course, but I wanted Becca to know a little bit more than she did about what I didn't want her involved in. I even put up a note for her to find about how I would fight to get back to her in her lifetime. Timing is always the hard part. I could be gone five minutes, five years, or *fifty*. There was no tangible way to gauge how long it would take for me to come back to her, but I had to give her some sort of hope.

All I knew was that I would fight *like hell*. Time and space would not stop me from *my destiny*.

BEES

YOU ARE
BEAUTIFUL

I gazed out of my office window, debating on the numbers and whether I could make my calculations better than what I had.

David's department got a huge cut—*sponsored by yours truly*. If that fucker hadn't falsified his costs and budgets, lying about the receipts when we could pull up the accounts and see for ourselves.

Katherine would soon be out the door, especially if I had anything to say about it. They were already doing lay-offs within the company anyway since the merger last spring.

Ash was still the best, and Bels... I swallowed the lump rising in my throat.

Bels will be going home soon. The only question was *when*.

I couldn't deny how everyday felt like it could be the last, a type of anxiety I didn't know was possible.

We hadn't really talked about Belke leaving back home as he didn't have specifics. Our time was ending, that much I knew. It was a deep gut feeling that I couldn't explain. I couldn't talk about it, because then it would be *real*. I wasn't ready to let him go and risk never seeing him or that wagging tail of his again.

After the discovery of him leaving, I could see a lingering sadness settled into Belke's expression. It bothered him too, even though we didn't speak about it; we still felt it deep down.

My Bels.

An otherworldly...dimensional force waltzed into my life, and I wasn't ready to let the happiness go that had spread through my life like wildfire. Because that's what it felt like. My soul was understood and nurtured by him. *Never* had that been the case for me. Until him.

I didn't have to guess with him, minus the beginning and my own insecurities which weren't his fault. Yet, we worked through them, and he didn't leave, *he stayed*.

For a while, the battle with the mirror didn't rage on. I wasn't constantly questioning myself or my outfit choices. I felt beautiful and more secure in myself. All it took was one tail-wagging demon. My spirit understood his, just as he caressed mine, loving me wholly. *Fucking me into another spiritual plane, too.*

I hoped it was in the cards to see him again, but for now, I'd take what time I had, then break again while he was gone.

Whose to stop me?

There would never be another Belke, and after him, I wasn't sure I'd want anything else. It felt like *fate* that he ended up in my bedroom all those months ago. Sexual energy woo-woo aside, I'd been worshipped ever since that fateful moment. I'd carry it with me for the rest of my life.

I laid on Belke's chest tracing random abstract shapes on his bronze skin, and his tail was rubbing my side in the soothing way I enjoyed.

Belke finally showed me his apartment in the city, which was where we were then. It was only a little bigger than mine, and it was the cutest. He had a simple living room that was modern, decked out in brown and blue colors, not too fancy, and the kitchen was plain except for a single coffee pot. *He knew how important go-go juice was.*

His bedroom and bed were big enough to hold his wings. The amazing sex we had not too long ago with them outstretched was overwhelmingly good, too.

I called him beautiful at our release, and he pulled me close while soft, black-feathered wings cocooned around us both. It was the sweetest, and my heart ached knowing it would all be over soon. Every moment with him was lovely, especially with the thoughts in the back of my mind that it wouldn't last.

"What do we do, Bels?" I asked after however long of silence as I adjusted myself to lay my head on his stomach, staring up at him—still tracing shapes with my fingertips on that chiseled bronze chest.

He reached his hand out and began playing with my hair. "I don't know, Becs. For once, I'm without answers. I'm loving every second with you while I still have it."

I closed my eyes, trying to take a calming breath. Under my lids, I could feel my sockets filling up with tears, but I opened my teary eyes anyway.

"Remember what I said, no matter what happens, I will return to you someday."

My fingers traveled further up his chiseled chest.

"That's what worries me, the *time*. I hope I'm lucky enough to see you again before I'm dead and gone, too," I whispered sadly, letting the tears slide out.

A bit morbid, but I couldn't help it. All I could see was the gloom ahead.

"Me too," he admitted quietly.

"Whatever lies ahead of us, Bels, I will wait for you, and there will be no one else. Whether it's forever or our time we had, I'm grateful. Now, I finally know what it means to truly be loved and worshipped. You changed me for the better, and I will take these experiences into the unknown future ahead. *I love you.*"

He sat up immediately and cradled my head in his arms, gazing down thoughtfully and with a heated touch.

"I love you. You say these sweet things, but you also changed *me*." He tucked a strand of hair behind my ear, rubbing my cheek with his thumb. A cute smirk drawled upon his sweet cinnamon roll demon face. "I wouldn't have known what it was like to be a domesticated cat, with puppy energy, but I'm glad *you're my owner.*"

My lips curled up at the same time he finished his statement.

"You're welcome. You're still a big demon mush."

"Only for you, Becs."

BECS

YOU ARE
BEAUTIFUL

THIRTY-TWO

BECS

It's going to happen soon, Rebecca.

The words echoed endlessly in my brain.

I tried to be positive, but it felt like my heart and soul were in disarray. Yes, I was happy I *knew*, but then part of me wondered if ignorance would be bliss instead. *It was already traumatic enough.*

I was on edge as the days passed since. More than ever before.

Belke could feel it too as we spent all spare moments together. At work, my place, *his*, and going to our favorite places such as *our* café for our coffee.

On one particular Friday night, Bels mentioned he'd be late to my place.

So, when it was eight p.m. and he still hadn't shown up, I felt myself being pulled back into my car towards the office. I drove fast, thankfully not getting pulled over, and as I got closer, the sinking feeling grew more. Of course, he'd spare me mentioning the exact moment. *Asshole.*

He must've known I wouldn't have let him do this alone or without saying goodbye.

"I'm coming, Bels," I whispered as I pulled into the parking garage, nearly running into the building when something caught the corner of my eye.

I froze, seeing *Belke* turning around a corner, briskly walking away from me.

Oh, no, you don't!

I ran as fast as my legs could carry me, shouting his name once I got closer.

He stiffened with a short pause, turning around toward me with a look of terror.

"No, *no*. You shouldn't be here, Becs." His tragic tone broke my fucking heart.

He glanced around desperately before staring at me with anxiety that matched my own.

"So, what, you were just going to *leave?* Are you fucking kidding me right now?" I hissed out, making sure he caught my anger to go along with it.

"It was better this way, Rebecca." He sounded as if he was in physical pain, *just like how I felt knowing he was just going to leave me without a word.*

"I call *bullshit.*"

He sighed as I stepped closer, taking him in, knowing that it would be the last time. Belke seemed fidgety, constantly looking around us. He was still in his human form. "You were supposed to find out tomorrow morning, *not come here. Dammit, Rebecca!*"

"You're an idiot if you think I'd let you leave willingly. *I'm not leaving you. I don't want you to be alone.*" My voice cracked as my eyes watered.

"I won't be alone... I can't willingly leave you if you're here," he pleaded quietly as if he was seconds away from breaking with me.

"I'm not leaving you; *I love you. It's me and you.*" I

needed to remind him. For him to feel the words I was saying to him.

Tears leaked out of both of our eyes then as I reached for him, and he shook his head, backing away.

"Becca, *go*," he warned, a silent plea.

"I'm not leaving you," I insisted.

Tears brimmed his lashes. *"Please,"* he begged.

A silent sob escaped from me, and the world shifted from under my feet.

"Don't go," I pleaded as he pulled farther away from me.

"You know I have to go. You don't need to see this; I'll see you again. It will be okay, Becs. I love you." I could hear the same heartbreak in his voice. A reminder that we were from different worlds.

As I still sobbed, he walked away, turning the corner towards an alleyway, disappearing from me.

I tried to gather myself, but the world was moving in slow motion as I ran after him. Like time and I were not on the same side for once. An equation I failed to calculate. The calculation of my heartache. A world without Belke in it.

Before I could process and think anymore, I heard strange noises and a gunshot sound as I rounded the corner. Donte was standing over Belke, who lay dead at his feet, and with him, lay my heart. Belke was in demon form before shifting to his human form in a slow succession.

I saw the man who killed him walking towards me as I felt the walls closing in, and the world spun before I met the pavement as the world went dark.

Bels was dead.

BECS
YOU ARE
BEAUTIFUL

THIRTY-THREE

BECS

Weeks passed, and I couldn't remember anything. I fell into a deep pit of despair, and I couldn't even look Donte in the eyes without wanting to sob. All I remembered was him saying, after I gave him a look of disdain, "We have to die to return home, Rebecca. I didn't tell him *when* as I knew he wouldn't be able to lie to you. *I'm sorry.*"

"Please, leave me alone. Unless it's work related, I don't want to talk to you."

I heard him sigh outside of Bels'—*my*—office door. Turned out, I got a promotion I didn't want. At Belke's expense.

Phone calls and messages were ignored from anyone and everyone. I didn't answer my door or leave the house and opted for working from home when it became too much. Having a minimal amount of time in the physical office was better for me. Looking in the mirror? *Fucking forget it.*

I knew he was leaving, no wonder he didn't tell me *how.* God, how could I be so *stupid.* I'm sure knowing wouldn't make the grief any easier.

I struggled being at home because I saw *him* everywhere. A fucked-up part of me appreciated being in the comfort of my own home, and where I spent most of my time with him. I could still smell him, even the empty spot next to me in bed. That fucking scent I still couldn't figure out. Now, it was a heartbreaking reminder of when I'd see him again. If ever. *Fuck you, Bels.*

Grief was an interesting thing for me, because while I was all over the place and processing, I went through the motions and the random states of euphoria and longer doses of depression. I stopped taking care of myself and went through phases of overeating junk food and days without any food. I didn't shower regularly, and between working from home, I had my groceries delivered, and weeks turned into months.

Time wasn't fucking real.

A hard knock at my door came one day, and I didn't bother getting up. The person didn't go away until I heard two women shouting how they were going to break it down if I didn't open the door. *Fucking great.*

I wrapped a blanket around myself, like a couch-blanket-gremlin while pausing a streaming app. I opened the door, revealing my two sisters Pen and BJ.

"About time you answered," I heard Penny say as BJ came in with bags of stuff.

"Geez, Becca, you really let everything go. When's the last time you showered or ate anything?" Pen asked while wrinkling her nose. *Not that I cared how I smelled.* I didn't have the energy to fight or argue.

Ignoring her while shutting and locking the door, I left them staring after me while I made my way back towards my permanent spot on the couch.

"Rebecca?" BJ asked out into the silence of the room.

Great, now I have to talk to people.

"You've been ignoring us again, what's going on this time?" Penny asked, and I felt them sit on the couch with me.

"Did you not see the news?" I mumbled, wrapping myself further into the blanket as if that would help me escape *this conversation*. Or the realities I refused to face.

"No, what's going on?" Pen asked while BJ pulled out her phone.

"My boyfriend's dead." The words stung as soon as they left my mouth. They tasted bitter, like my breath probably. Lord knows I hadn't looked at my reflection in who knows when.

"What? Really?" Penny went on as BJ sighed, confirming with a nod to our sister.

"Shot and killed," I went on quietly, holding back the tears I could feel heading right towards my eye sockets.

"I'm sorry, Becs," BJ said sincerely as she patted my leg, and Penny adjusted herself, placing my greasy hair in her lap.

"I'm sorry, too," Pen added as she moved the blanket that was partially over her and began petting my knotted hair.

"What you're seeing is grief, and obviously I'm not doing well. I found love—*me, of all fucking people*—and it was *taken* from me." My words went out into the dimness of the room with only the kitchen light on behind us.

No one said anything for a long time, except for my silent sobs. I had been content with grieving *alone*.

But no, my sisters held me through it. We could bicker or go for extended periods without talking, but that was mostly on my part because I liked being left alone. However, while they held me through my sobbing, the weeks' worth of holding it inside while I processed it, dare I say, I was glad they were there.

In some strange way, it reminded me that *I was still alive.*

They said nothing to me, letting me get it all out, until I complained of a headache.

"Take a shower, and we'll make some food. It will be okay; now that we know, we won't leave you. We already spend so much time apart, let us be here for you," Penny said in a soothing voice that made me close my eyes, thinking of how our mother was growing up when we cried over something serious like heartbreak and bullies.

"Okay," I whispered as they both rubbed my back in soothing motions.

I hadn't showered in...five days? *Longer?*

Once the realization of that hit, I went and turned the water to spicy hot in the shower and stood under it, letting the water fall on me as I stared into space.

Although, due to my grief, I didn't really care what anyone thought, so if I didn't shower when it was just me alone in *my home,* who cared? I knew it was the depression part of grief, but *still.*

I couldn't remember how long I stood under the piping steamy heat, *missing him,* until the tears consumed me again. They subsided the minute I turned the water off later. I ran a brush through my wet hair, avoiding my reflection while putting on comfortable pajamas, and made my way into the living room.

The smell of chicken filled the house, along with vegetables. Knowing how Penny was with health and nutrition, I shouldn't have been surprised.

Penny and BJ were both moving about, so I wandered over to the table and sat there, spacing out.

"It's almost done," BJ mentioned, bringing me a glass of water and two pills for my headache.

"Thank you," I whispered and before too long, I took the meds and downed the glass of water, seeing food being brought over.

Penny sat across from me, while BJ sat on the barstool feet away.

"What are you going to do, Becca?" Penny asked gently.

Maybe that's the part of grief that hurts so much, *the aftermath.* I didn't want to think about an *after Belke.* I didn't want to think at all.

"Find someone to replace me at work and come back home. I mentally can't do this solo shit anymore. I need to remember what it was like to feel *alive.* He's gone, and I need to find meaning again. I'm surrounded by *him* everywhere I go, so being in this city is hard now. I want to come home."

I stared into my plate, eating slowly as my insides were hurting since I hadn't eaten in days. Never thought I'd want to live back at home with our parents, but unfortunately, I had to swallow my independent pride.

"Mom and Dad will love it," Pen said between bites.

"We're here for whatever you need; we can help you move and keep you company. I have contracts that I can work on in Atlanta, so work isn't an issue for me," BJ told us, finishing her plate at the same time Penny did.

"I will have to travel back and forth, so it's not so easy for me, but we'll make it work." I looked up at Penny as she offered a smile and I nodded.

"Thank you both for being sisters I don't deserve... I'm glad you're here." It was honest and I meant every word.

Penny and BJ exhaled in unison as if they knew our complicated dynamics but loved me anyway.

"Don't say that. Yes, we bicker and fight, but if you need us, we're here. When you have more than one sibling, obviously we're bound to annoy each other until the end of time," Penny went on, and BJ gave a half smile at that thought.

"I'm sorry, I'll work on that," I mumbled, eating only half of what was on the plate, not being able to eat anymore.

"We'll get through this together," BJ said, coming over to me, placing her hand on my shoulder. I took in her black hair, shocked on how for once it wasn't a crazy hair color, as she was always doing fun things with her hair.

Penny reached across the table for my hand, squeezing it. "Yes, we will," she said with tears in her eyes, looking at me as my own watered.

Although I was lost in my grief, *along with being traumatized,* I still needed to tie up some loose ends before I left Atlanta.

BECS

YOU ARE
BEAUTIFUL

It was another two weeks before I could convince myself to go into the office. BJ temporarily stayed with me and held me when I cried on occasion at night.

We weren't the closest, not like me and Penny in comparison, but she was also fine with silence like I was, while Pen liked to fill it with words. She was like our mother in that sense.

Donte sent me an email, asking if it were okay if he could come to my office, and I sighed, agreeing.

BJ had recommended me getting prescribed Xanax to dull the anxiety that would creep up as a temporary solution to deal with *life*.

I think the only reason I agreed to the meeting was solely because I took one pill before heading back into work. It was a low dose, so I could still function *somewhat*.

I heard a knock at the door, and saw Donte enter and close the door behind him.

"It's good to see you, Rebecca. I am sorry for months ago...that you had to see that. He asked that you not see his death, and for me to look out for you." He slowly moved towards me before sitting across from me in the green chair.

"I'm only traumatized for the rest of my life," I mumbled, looking away from him, "and I didn't even have to witness it... I don't need you to look out for me. I've been deciding how I want to end things in this place. I'll be putting in my notice. I'm moving back to my hometown, but don't worry, I'll make sure the position gets filled as well as tying up some loose ends."

He crossed his leg, placing his hands on his knee.

"I'll come with you. I'm oath-bound to protect you. He is my brother."

I raised my eyebrow, then recalled what Belke had once told me about what *brothers* meant in his world—not the same thing as what human society deems as brothers. Withholding an eye roll, I realized I didn't need him to babysit me, nor did I want to be around Belke's killer. Fated or not.

I exhaled heavily. Grumbling, I went on, "Not necessary, and I don't like hovering, but do what you must. With that being said, I need a few favors."

He seemed more attentive then, sitting up straighter. "What do you have in mind?"

I ignore his friendly attempts, starting with my list. "Ashlee deserves a promotion, and a few others *a demotion*. They haven't changed in over two years, but I'd like to be the one to fire them if that's okay. I've already worked on gathering the reports that were left and sending them to HR. With our zero-tolerance policy, I will have the most satisfaction being the one to do it."

"Consider it done... Anything else?"

"Yes, I'd like to do another benefit party, appreciating our benefactors and partnerships, along with reprimanding one."

"Is this about Joseph? He did mention you had relations in the past…"

I scoffed. "Of course he'd say that. I suspect he'll harass me at this next party, when he does, *since you're my new protector,* why don't you step in, catch him being who he truly is, and end that partnership? What's that saying about dishes best being served cold?"

I saw him shiver and grin knowingly.

"I knew there was something spot on about you. My brother did well; I hope I'm just as lucky someday. Consider it done, Miss Stone. I'll work on arranging it. Will you post the job listing online and begin the inter-view processes? I trust you on picking a suitable candidate."

"I will work on that this week. When you can, please tell Katherine Saunders to meet me in my office at two p.m. today. I'm feeling *inspired." Through the power of Xanax, of course.*

Donte smirked, standing up. "Will do. Do you know when you're leaving Atlanta?"

I considered it; next month would be six months of Belke being gone. "A month from now."

He nodded, heading towards the door. "Let me know if you need anything, Rebecca."

"Thank you, Donte," I said as we stared at each other in silent understanding that although he was helping me, I wouldn't forgive him so easily for killing Bels—*even if I didn't witness it entirely.*

I couldn't escape the memory of him standing over his body before I blacked out.

He left my office after that, and I took an early lunch, taking a walk around the city.

I realized then that my student loans were paid off,

between bonuses and the promotions. I actually had a savings account. *Who would've thought?*

My parents were thrilled that I was going back home, and I was sure my sisters were ready to get back to a normal life, too. Part of me debated if Donte really meant what he said on looking out for me, but I supposed I'd soon find out.

It was going to be a long month.

BECS

YOU ARE
BEAUTIFUL

THIRTY-FIVE

BECS

A knock came at my office door right on time.

"Come in," I spoke out, and it opened, revealing a nervous looking Katherine. No scowls were on her face. *Yet*.

Until she shut the door.

Katherine wore a pale fancy dress with another pair of heels that would break my neck and too much makeup. Her nails were far too long, *in my opinion*, not sure how she typed on a computer. But what does the girl who *eats food* know about anything?

"Why am I here, *Rebecca?*" She said in a tone that reminded me of just who I was talking to.

"Please, have a seat." I indicated to the green chair in front of the desk, reeling my attitude in check.

Katherine huffed impatiently, flopping down aggressively across from me.

My expression was neutral even when she snapped at me seconds later.

"Whatever is going on and whatever *power* you think you have–"

"Katherine Saunders," I interrupted immediately, my tone flat and professional.

Her mouth was agape as I did my best to not be a bitch right back like she always treated me. The reality was that I didn't have to stoop to her level. *No matter how much I wanted to.* What would it actually solve by doing so? *Bless her heart.*

Gesturing my hand towards the *large* folder stack on my desk, her eyes followed. I couldn't help to notice how she shifted in the chair uncomfortably.

"What is that?" Her tone was quickly changing, no doubt worried about her own ass.

I continued, "You've done the yearly training online, so you know Toom has a zero-tolerance for bullying and harassing co-workers." Katherine tried to open her mouth to speak, but I cut her off. "There have been numerous reports by your coworkers. With being said, you are fired. You have forty-eight hours to gather your things and to complete the exit interview process with HR. Any questions can be directed to HR as well."

Short, simple, and *professional—back pat for me not being a petty betty.*

She jumped up as soon as the door flew open.

"This isn't fucking fair! You're doing this shit on purpose to get back at me!"

I raised my eyebrow as Donte sauntered forward with two members of security.

"Not everything is about you Katherine, but good luck on your future endeavors. I recommend doing a little reflection on how you treat your coworkers."

I nodded to Donte as he indicated his head towards security.

"Come with us, Miss Saunders," one of them stated as she glared angrily at me.

"This is bullshit! These bitches shouldn't be such sensitive babies! Fuck you!"

The two guys grabbed each of her arms as she leaned over the desk as soon as I scooted my desk chair back.

Jesus Christ.

Looked like she didn't need forty-eight hours...

Security dragged her out of the office kicking and screaming as she cursed and fought them.

Rubbing my temples, I sighed heavily.

"One down, one more to go," Donte said aloud to himself more so than to me.

Not surprised on her reaction, but damn, that woman was absolutely *ridiculous.* No blessing of hearts would *ever* fix *that.*

I gave Donte a dulled look as he gave me a look that said he would take care of the rest before shutting my office door.

Naturally, David was next to meet in my office the following day. The rest of the afternoon I spent on writing the job listing for my position. The sooner I left this place the better.

David sat across from me, staring with his jaw clenched.

I had a stack of files on him, too. Same size as Katherine's but different offenses.

"It's interesting that you're on the other side. What did you have to do to get that position anyway, Rebecca?"

I kept my face blank. I was certainly expecting his reactions, unlike Katherine's. "Is it that I'm a woman in a position of power that intimidates you? You just assume I had to go about other means to get a promotion, while you lied the entire time about a position that I was *more than* qualified for, saying it wasn't available. Hmm? Yet, *I've* done nothing wrong."

"I don't owe you anything. *You worked for me.*" His tone was lowered and angry. Leave it to this man to be grumpy about his wrongdoings and blaming someone else.

"This is precisely why we're in this meeting, because you're fired. There have been several reports and investigations on you and your workplace behavior—"

He interrupted me, and I could feel my nerves working overtime, holding back. I didn't take meds today so I could focus on *this fucking conversation.*

Misogynistic prick.

"You aren't my mother, spare the lecture. You've been planning this *with him* from the start. Don't think I didn't notice how he treated you better than anyone else. *You lying bitch.* Good riddance, I say. Zavier Bel is better off dead."

I saw red then. Jumping to my feet, I kept my face in check, despite the volcano erupting within. That fucker was lucky I was on the clock and didn't jump across the desk.

Donte appeared in my doorway then, on high alert.

"You have until the end of the day to get your stuff, and we have your things monitored, so if you even think about covering your tracks on how you've been spending department money, we already know. Now. *Get. Out.*" My tone was firm, authoritative, and boss-like.

He glared, mumbling shit under his breath before angrily pushing out of the chair and leaving saying, "This is fucking bullshit."

Donte made sure he left for good before returning.

I sat back down. *Fucking asshole.*

A knock distracted me.

"You alright?" Donte asked, leaning in the doorway.

"Not really," I grumbled.

"Take the rest of the day off."

I glanced up. "Okay."

"Don't worry about him," he tapped the door frame before walking away from the office down the hallway.

I rolled my eyes. David's last comment triggered me that my hands were shaking and emotions erupting from within.

I spent an hour ranting to BJ and Penny that night as they helped me sell things from my apartment.

They listened and validated me—which certainly helped after that bullshit day.

We were able to sell most of my things, and I got some money for my TV and furniture. I wouldn't need furniture if I moved back home with my parents. It wouldn't be forever, only temporary until I figured shit out. Whatever that shit was, I'd find my way again.

It wasn't fair.

Donte didn't need to babysit me and aside from that, I'd probably never see Bels again. He even said it probably wouldn't happen. The probability wasn't in my favor, and I needed to accept that. No matter what hypothetical, mathematical equations I ran or made-up physics on portals and wormholes, the results remained conclusive. The probability of Belke returning in my lifetime was slim to none.

Thinking about it only hurt me, and it was hard to do when most of our memories were at work and at *my place.*

Only a few more weeks until I was gone.

BECS

$(x-$
$y^2 = z$
$x^2 + 2ax + a^2$
$\frac{\partial}{\partial y} \lim_{\delta \to 0} \frac{\partial x + z}{\partial y - 1}$

$+a)$
$\sin x \cdot e = \cos x + tg y$
$(y-1)^2$
$\sin a =$

YOU ARE
BEAUTIFUL

THIRTY-SIX

BECS

The benefit hosting event was on one of the rooftop spots that beheld a spectacular view of downtown Atlanta in the distance.

I stood near the edge, holding my drink, and admiring the view. The view of the city was one of my favorites, but nothing gave me as much joy as it used to. Seeing the sparkling lights and the city come alive was certainly spectacular though.

I invited both of my sisters to the event as my way of saying, "*Thanks for putting up with me and my bullshit—I love you.*"

Penny was mingling and conversing with Donte. Dare I say, Pen was extra smiley around him. BJ enjoyed the view of the city from nearby, taking photos, *as she typically did.* She even got a good one of me with my drink as I gazed at the city I had called home for many years. But what did *home* even mean to me anymore?

Now, it was a place that brought me pain. Reminders of a tail-wagging demon and the hole in my heart of his missing presence. *That shit was for the birds.*

My choice of attire was a dark blue dress with my hair pulled up. It suited my mood. I had lost more weight from not eating, and I did get a checkup with the doctor, and they were impressed with my weight loss considering my hypothyroidism worked against me *constantly*. Not that I told them about my *loss* and not eating much.

All my doctor knew was that my levels looked good, and I took Xanax as needed for anxiety. It was always a war with my body, and now I was so into my grief, I didn't enjoy *anything*. Who fucking cared about anything? I sure as hell didn't.

Well minus a few things. Such as finding small joys in enacting my revenge on all the people who had wronged me. I got two out of three. *Three will be happening very soon*.

I knew not to mix meds with alcohol, so I didn't take them that day since I knew I'd be drinking.

As I did that, I took in downtown Atlanta from the rooftop, taking the city's image into my memory, because it was all I'd have once I moved from here.

"I heard about your boss, I'm sorry." I gave a side-glance briefly to see that it was Joseph.

"Thanks," I muttered, not really giving a damn about his words or lack of empathy since the last time Bels saved the day... I took a drink at the reminder while ignoring the male presence beside me. *Trying to anyway*.

"As I said last time, you look great. You've looked like you lost weight again, not that I'm complaining, but...are you okay?"

Of course, that bastard isn't complaining. It's all about image with him.

I sighed over his audacity. "How I am is none of your concern. I'd like to drink in peace if you don't mind. Leave me alone. Donte is over there if you need to talk to someone." I waved him off.

I knew Donte was nearby since he was my babysitter now.

He puffed out a breath, clearly getting irritated at my dismissal. "I don't want Donte, *I want you*. Would you stop acting like a complete bitch, and have a civil conversation with me?"

Hold up.

I threw back the rest of the drink and threw the emptied glass into the distance, hearing it smash onto a wall of the building closest to me.

I gripped the edges and snapped my head to the side. "Do you want to try that again? *Are you fucking kidding me?*"

"Rebecca—"

"Do NOT interrupt me. I wasn't good enough when I was more *overweight,* but when you find me alone and enjoying life *without you,* or grief stricken, and whoop-dee-fucking-doo weight loss, *now* I matter to you? Get the fuck over yourself, Joseph. I don't owe you a goddamn thing. *Fuck. You.*"

I heard him curse under his breath as I moved to walk away, and his hand grabbed me firmly on the arm. My air matched his as I met his gaze ten-fold.

"I believe the lady asked you to leave her alone, Joseph." My new savior, Donte to the rescue.

It bothered me and made me feel queasy then. The memory of Belke was coming on too strong from the last party a demon stepped in.

Joseph let me go immediately, and I found my sisters standing close by, scowling.

"Yes, sorry—" Joseph began, but Donte had a polite but murderous look.

"Come with me, *please.*"

Joseph hesitated, looking between me and Donte.

"I won't ask *twice,*" Donte urged, his tone was low and threatening, reminding me of his brother then.

I had to leave immediately.

As Donte guided Joseph away from me, I walked the opposite way, holding my hand up to my two siblings that tried to follow me.

I needed a minute, and the walls felt like they were closing in. *Dammit. Not here.*

It didn't take me long to find the women's restroom and lock the door behind me. Thank fuck, no one else occupied it.

Shaking, I tucked my head towards my knees, hyperventilating.

He's gone and he's never coming back.

Worthless. Not good enough.

Letting out a quick yell of frustration, I hit the door, and stormed out of the stall. I glanced around, saying loudly, "Goddammit Bels! Fuck you for doing this to me! *If you'd only just—*" I stared into the mirror as tears began to stream down my face, then the sobbing started. I leaned my arms on the counter and soon my face into them.

This shit fucking sucks.

I leave next week, then it will be over, and I can be done with this fucking place without being reminded everywhere I turn.

Thank fuck, it's almost over.

But, is it ever *really* over?

Death is permanent, and I was a fool to think otherwise.

BECS

YOU ARE
BEAUTIFUL

I stood in my empty apartment, feeling my heart ache deep within my chest—a cage unto itself. I had so many good memories there. All of them involved Bels.

When I had asked him if he had a birthday, he shook his head, and go figure, *it was on Halloween that I had asked him.*

I remembered looking at him in disbelief, so I told him, "Well, since it's the devil's day according to some folks, let's make it your birthday, although *you're the sweetest demon-devil I know. A mushy one who wags their tail.*"

I had grinned and so did he as his tail tapped my leg in response.

"Let me make you a cake, Bels." I kissed him cheerily on the cheek before moving into the kitchen.

He sat in the barstool watching me, looking positively delighted while I worked.

"Has no one ever made you cake before?" I remembered asking him.

"No. We don't celebrate birthdays—time differences

remember? Birthdays are a human celebration and construct."

I frowned, feeling bothered by how...*sad* it sounded—how lonely.

"Well, time for some new traditions then," I mumbled, icing the cake, and making shapes with the frosting. *I wasn't the best baker, so I tried to stifle my laugh.*

I drew a cat with a long tail and whiskers and a big smile, making the ears look like little kitty horns. It looked cheesy at best, but what mattered was the taste. Strawberries.

I wrote *Happy Birthday Bels* and brought it over to him on the counter.

"Please find humor in the moment and take a bite," I urged on, holding a fork.

Instead of laughing—like I hoped, you know, in playful fun—he got teary-eyed.

"It doesn't need to be a masterpiece for me to love it. It's a thoughtful gesture, and it means a lot that you went through the trouble to make me feel loved and lucky to be alive... *I love you.*"

Still a big mush.

My own eyes misted. "You're welcome," I told him gently, taking a small piece of the cake with the fork and holding it out for him.

He opened his mouth slowly, watching me as I stared at him while leaning across the counter. When he kept my hand in his, he stood up while walking around towards me and pulling me closer.

"That's tasty. You know what would make it *better*?" I leaned into him, looking up into those cherished eyes.

"What?"

"Eating it off of you," he whispered, tugging on my lips.

"It's your birthday, Bels, I'll do whatever you want."

His tail perked up, "*Anything*, you say?"

I coyly stripped until I was nude, tossing my clothes elsewhere, then I grabbed the cake and walked backwards into the bedroom.

"Come and get your cake, and eat it, too, Bels," I teased while he stalked toward me.

"This cake is all mine," he concurred as I sat on the edge of the bed with the cake beside me, grabbing a fistful, leaning back onto the bed. I made sure to do it in a slow manner, smearing it down my abdomen and over breasts.

"Is this what you want?" I asked, breathing out as he moved the cake to the dresser.

"Yes," he got out before his lips and tongue were upon me immediately, lapping me up like the birthday cake dessert I was.

Now, *that* was some sexy shit.

Standing in the doorway of my bedroom, I remembered that cute moment all too well.

On Christmas, he dressed as a sexy demon-Claus, and I ended up joining him in the old cosplay outfit from the convention with the added Santa hat and dressed in red velvet.

Bels seemed *more than happy* with that. After that, we watched Nightmare Before Christmas and kissed under a mistletoe I threw together randomly.

It was so cute. God, we constantly did cute and disgusting things I wouldn't do with anyone else. There was no one else made for me, not like he was. Nothing on earth would compare.

Turning around in the very spot to face the area when he showed me his black feathered wings the first time, and how he stilled at my touch. I thought I had hurt him, but he was restraining himself with how pleasurable it felt.

My demon boyfriend was happy worshipping or binge-watching some rom-com or Adam Sandler movie with me. *So normal for a demon and a human to do.* No one would believe it, that was for damn sure.

One of our last conversations were in the living room on the couch, and I asked him something important, because I needed to know.

"Bels, if you...didn't have to return *home,* what would you want in the future? What would make you the happiest in an ideal situation?"

Okay, maybe two questions.

His arm was drawn around me, considering me thoughtfully, lightly rubbing my hair and holding my hand with his free one.

"This. All of this. I've never known a normal life, and I'd be complacent with having what we have currently for the rest of our lives. Ideally, there wouldn't be a demon rebellion, I would find a way to make you into what I was, or become human permanently, whichever option was easier. It would be *me and you, always.*"

I swooned over his words with how kind and loving they were. He always made me feel so cherished and loved even when I didn't think such a thing was possible with the bullshit I had to deal with in the past before he came around.

"I'd want a tail, too, so I could wag mine just like you," I teased him, squeezing his hand as he smiled.

"*That* would be a sight unto itself. *I like the way you think.*"

I leaned my head against his other arm before he drew me into him, holding me.

"Those sound like ideal living conditions, and I'd be

happy with any and all of those things. I love you, so naturally, I'd want to spend the rest of my life with such happiness," I told him honestly as he kissed my forehead.

I remembered those words, hoping that it wasn't a pipe dream the minute Bels walked into my life, whether I lured him unintentionally or not. It turned out to be the best and worst thing to happen to me. I'm forever changed and never the same.

A knock at my half-opened front door distracted my thoughts and memories of Belke as I stood in the empty living room, nearly trapped by those past ghosts lingering there still.

"You ready? We're loaded and ready to go, BJ turned in the keys," Pen said as I sighed and nodded, following her outside, but not before taking one last look.

Ashlee got promoted into Donte's department, doing something more worthwhile. We hired a front desk person, and I hired an intelligent woman to replace my position as well as someone to replace the accounting position.

Donte had given me approval, and when I was cleaning out my office earlier in the week, he lingered in the doorway.

"Leaving in a few days?" he asked casually, and I understood what he was getting at.

"What did I say about hovering? *You don't need to come with me.* My parents won't let you in the house."

He huffed a laugh. "Maybe so, but I don't break my oaths. Don't worry, I won't hover. You won't even know I'm there."

I gave him a knowing look as he held up his hands in defeat.

"No. Hovering," I insisted again as I handed him my office keys and carried my bag and a small box.

He walked with me to the elevator. "Did you already do the exit interview?"

"An hour ago, and the women hired will be amazing; *of that, I'm sure.*"

"I never had any doubts, Rebecca. I'm sad to see you leave, but I *understand.*"

I exhaled as he went down to the ground floor with me.

"Functioning is hard enough, I can't do it when I *see* him everywhere locked in my memories. They're wonderful memories, but right now, they hurt too much. I need to leave Donte, *for my own human sanity.*"

He patted my head in a way that reminded me of what it'd be like to have an older, protective brother. It annoyed me more than anything, especially since I was still working on forgiving him.

"I miss him, too, you know. I'm happy he found happiness with you, I hope you know that."

"I do now, thanks, Donte. I appreciate all you've done. Especially that prick, Joseph."

He chuckled. "I heard what he said, and I knew Belke would kill me for not doing anything about it. Plus, you're right—what a prick."

I grinned as the elevator pinged, and we strolled out.

It was semi-bittersweet leaving. I managed to text Ashlee goodbye and had lunch with her yesterday. I had also let Figgy know I was moving and that I'd see them at the next convention, *whenever the fuck that was.*

As I watched Atlanta fade from my vision in the passenger seat of my car, while BJ drove, and Penny drove a rental. The backseat and trunk were packed with clothes and cosplays, along with the rental car full of art stuff and fandom shit from conventions.

I wasn't sure what the next chapter held for me, but it felt like I could begin to heal and get my mind right.

Time would tell, wherever in time, Bels was.

His time was worth it to me.

I wouldn't change it for anything, except miss him until the end of my days.

BEES

YOU ARE
BEAUTIFUL

THIRTY-EIGHT

BECS

"I'm so sorry, Rebecca, my sweet daughter. Take all the time you need, you know you always have a place at home. I know you value your independence and solitude, but I—we—are always here for you through all of life's joy and sorrow. I love you, my sweet girl." Hearing that from my mother's lips when I saw her again for the first time in a while made me realize that I'm the worst, and I didn't deserve her. Not with how grieved I still was, and how I truly isolated myself.

I was right where I was meant to be.

Self-pity and wallowing aside, I was happy to be home again. My room still looked as it did when I left for college at eighteen. It held dark blue walls with various artwork and a wrought iron queen bed with pale pink linens. I had a small desk tucked in a corner and a bookshelf next to it, along with a dresser between the two doorways of the shared bathroom, with the closet Penny and I shared. There was some astronomy and Einstein quotes hung up, because obviously he was my inspiration on mathematics and physics.

I had a few pictures of my sisters and I from growing up,

when we'd go through phases of *not* bitching at each other. Typically, when we'd bicker and argue was when others asked too many questions we weren't ready to face or answer. Then, we wouldn't talk for two months, then pick up where we left off...after apologizing. A crazy family cycle, but it was my family. At least I wasn't completely alone.

It was a complicated family dynamic, and my parents weren't the best, but they weren't the worst—everyone makes mistakes, but I think it got better once we all began to leave the house. *Too much estrogen under one roof.*

After a few trips from the car inside, I sat on my bed, feeling nostalgic and *lost*.

I quit my job, *left,* and part of me wondered if I should get a part time job, doing brainless work for extra income. I didn't need to, but I *could.*

So, instead, I helped around the house, and my dad began house projects and upgrades, so I spent the summer of 2023 helping him. It bled into the fall, and my sisters popped in on occasion to check in.

I was at home a year after that. I read all the books, binge-watched all the shows, went to more cosplay conventions, and met up with Figgy and Marissa one month after living back in North Carolina. They were sad to hear about Zavi. But I did my best to have fun—it *wasn't the same though.* My heart wasn't in it as it used to be. I didn't have the heart to go all in for those cosplays, so I stole anime girl vibes from Marissa, doing the school girl, rave bunny, and a gender bend character.

After that first year living at home, *I had to get a job and get out of there.* I was shocked at how long it took for me to get annoyed with living at home. My mother was desperate for my company, and I needed more space.

What helped was me getting a part time job working at the North Carolina Aquarium at Fort Fisher. It was a fun little job, and on weekends I'd head to the beach and read a book there or walk the boardwalk at Carolina Beach.

When my sisters were visiting in summer 2024, we went down to Kure Beach and had a fun time. It was fun during low-tide to go along the rocks as we'd done growing up on the beach a couple miles away. It wasn't recommended, but all the locals did it—we were safe.

Donte thought it'd be best to communicate with *Pen* instead of me directly since I got cranky with his hovering.

We were out on the beach one day when she told me, and I looked at her from where we lay on our towels.

"You can't lie to me, Pen, you know he's not just using that excuse at my expense..."

She glanced at me, tilting her sunglasses down to give me *a look.*

"What do you know, Becs? A lady never tells."

BJ smacked her with her book she was reading, and I grinned.

"Hey!" Pen complained.

"You can't lie to your sisters, Pen, *now spill!"* I echoed the same words she once said to me.

"Ugh," she grumbled, leaning back, flat on her towel, wearing a flattering yellow bikini that looked great on her tanned skin that she spent all summer working on.

BJ and I exchanged knowing stares with a wink, before looking down at our sister who *had it for a certain male.*

"It's *complicated,"* she complained.

"My boyfriend's dead, so don't even go there. *Tell us, Penny!* Before I shout to the entire world your government name!" I shot back.

"You wouldn't dare!"

"Penelope—"

"No!"

BJ and I busted out laughing, hearing Pen sigh.

"I...*might* be in love with the guy," she said looking up at the cloudy sky with her shades covering her eyes with a pouty look.

"Aw!" BJ and I cooed in unison, nudging her playfully.

"I personally blame you for leaving Georgia. He doesn't mind when I ramble endlessly...as I tend to do."

BJ and I nodded in agreement, knowing *exactly* what her rambling entailed.

"Does *he* know that?" BJ asked.

"I'm not sure. We both agreed to keep things...not complicated—go figure."

"You should tell him, Pen," I told her, knowing how precious time was. Hell if I knew, maybe Donte had to leave like Bel at some point, too. *That would suck, but as someone who knew all too well, it wouldn't surprise me. Dimens were unconventional at best.*

"Should I? Do you think?"

"Yes," I said as BJ agreed.

She sighed, sitting up with her arms splayed beside her. "A dip in the ocean, while I strongly consider it. It's been a year. He's been...amazing quite honestly."

"Good thinking, Pen. He deserves to know. If he's not on the same page then throw *him* into the ocean," I told her.

She shot me a smile as BJ added, "We'll even help you do it."

Pen half-laughed, striding toward the rolling waves.

"If Pen found someone, Bees, what about *you*?"

"I'll pass on that question as I have nothing to share... Have you thought about getting back out there yourself, Becs?"

Way to turn it around to me, BJ, thanks.

"Never. I don't care if I look good or not," I shrugged, feeling brave in my fun tankini.

I ended up cutting and dying my hair blonde months prior, and it was super cute. It was a little past my chin in these fun, messy layers.

"Well, just consider it, even if it's just sex."

"I don't mind being single forever. You know most dudes don't know their way around a vag."

She snorted and laughed. "Aren't we a fun bunch," she said after she exhaled heavily.

"I don't know what the future has in store for me, Bees, but we shall certainly see what happens, won't we?"

"Truer words have never been spoken. We shall see, indeed."

BECS

YOU ARE
BEAUTIFUL

THIRTY-NINE

BECS

I was walking alone after lunch one September afternoon in fall of 2024.

Work at the aquarium ended early, so I changed clothes, and Penny happened to text me that if I was feeling stressed to take a walk near the gazebo on Fort Fischer Beach which was a pretty sweet spot. The idea was intriguing enough, and I hadn't been there in a while, so I didn't think anything of it. A walk *did* sound pretty damn good after a busy week at the aquarium.

There was a nice breeze, and it was overcast, so not too many people were nearby that I ended up walking over to the empty gazebo. I leaned on the railing, watching the waves roll in for a while. Strangely, I found peace in that moment in time.

The past year was eye-opening. Time healed, but not all wounds. That rang true for me. Support systems aided in that, but I needed to make the journey on my own. *What a fucking journey it was turning out to be.*

Ocean air and the waves relaxed my spirit as I closed my eyes, inhaling that sweet, salty breeze.

I must've spaced out because I didn't hear anyone until footsteps echoed from *inside* the gazebo.

My eyes popped open, afraid to disturb whoever decided to join me. Part of me hoped it wasn't some pervert, but I didn't turn to find out either. I wanted to enjoy the peace and quiet a little bit longer.

"This is a lovely view," I heard a voice say quietly behind me.

"It is... I'll just be another minute, then I'll give you the space," I said to whoever was behind me.

I heard a light sigh and movement. For a second, I thought the person left, but instead they were leaning beside me.

"Are you sure about that?" I heard them say at the same time I decided to finally *look* after catching a masculine tone.

No, it couldn't be.

I made a noise of pure shock as my heart leaped up into my throat. It wasn't long before the realization hit me like ocean waves, choking out a sob.

"Am I dreaming?" I asked, standing up to meet my match.

The one and only Bels.

"No, and I'm sorry it took me so long," he whispered, pulling me closer immediately. I sobbed into him, clutching him tightly.

"I'm sorry I left you, Becs. It was the worst day of my existence. I've been fighting for you ever since."

My hands reached up to cup his face, making sure he was real. *God, he certainly felt real.*

"I wasn't sure I'd ever see you again, Bels. I had to assume you would be gone *forever*, otherwise I wouldn't have made it to the next day... You did say there was a possibility of it." I wiped my tears on his white shirt where they dripped. Tears were in his human blue and brown eyes as he squeezed me briefly before kissing the top of my head.

"I don't blame you, but I'm so fucking glad to see you alive. When I realized it was nearly two years, *without me*, and that you had to go on so long. I can't explain the pain of knowing that and for the time you suffered. *Please forgive me, because I'll never leave you again.* If you'll have me."

I wiped my face on his shirt, not caring anymore. Leaning back to stare up at him, Belke cupped my face in his hands.

"Do you promise?" I asked, searching for those familiar human eyes.

"Yes. I could never leave my mate, willingly, *ever*. In fact, I have more good news."

"Mate? As in...*soul mate?*"

Untethered emotions remained in those eyes as they watered once more, a few escaping down his perfect cheek. *I don't think I've ever seen such joy on his face like this.*

"The very same. I suspected it but needed clarification. The Elders back home confirmed it, and they also aided with getting me back here to either live out my days until you die, or if you so choose, you can join our world. It's called *the binding of souls*. It involves a sort of blood ritual with sex. Because of who I was and who I am to you, it must take place in the same place we first laid together in my original form. The blood can be a prick on our fingers, or we can pretend to be vampires from the movies."

I snorted a laugh, wiping my tears, finding this shit all too unreal.

"I'm no longer a sex demon, Becs. I've been put into non-sexy duty, like capturing *the bad guys* and bringing them back home."

I blinked up at him with the new information and closed my eyes, more tears streaming down. They were mostly happy tears and the *release of emotions*.

"I think all of that sounds perfect." I had the overwhelming urge to hug him and never let go or out of my sight ever again.

"*Me too.*" He pulled me closer, holding me while leaning his forehead against mine.

"I don't have my apartment anymore is the only thing."

"Don't you worry about that, let me take care of it. Nothing is stopping me or you from making it official, as per *our* customs."

I nodded, feeling his lips brush against my forehead. Opening my eyes, we stared at one another, and his hands dropped.

Then, I remembered *how* he left me.

I'm sure my expression changed because he tilted his head, "What—"

I smacked his chest. "While I'm fucking glad to see you, don't you *ever* do that to me again," I told him seriously, adding on, "Don't hide shit from me. I don't care whether it's to spare me or not. Do you know how long it took for me to even *look* or *speak* to Donte? You ass!"

He blinked at me before he held his hands up in surrender. My burst of anger being directed at him was probably a shock but *come on,* he had to know that shit was not okay!

"I know, dick move. I'm sorry. *There won't be a next time. You* also have guaranteed passage to my world, so I won't have to worry about you being in some other fucking dimension *without me.*"

Not really grasping his words, I huffed a sigh still staring daggers. "You better, *or else.*"

"You know, when you threaten me, *that's some sexy*

shit." My anger began to sizzle out over that comment, knowing that's *my phrase.* My lips curled as he quickly pulled me closer.

"Now, come here and let me hold you a while," he whispered into my ear, and I leaned into him, sniffling away my anger and previous tears.

"Let's go sit in the sand, and enjoy this moment more," I suggested, leading him away from the gazebo hand-in-hand.

After finding a good, lonely spot, I indicated for him to sit. As he did, I climbed into his lap facing him. Wrapping our arms around each other, I kissed him first. A kiss to seal the deal.

I heard him groan, deepening it while cupping my nape.

It still felt unreal, until he kissed me, *touched me.*

"I missed you so fucking much," he breathed out between kisses. A desperate plea, a begging for forgiveness.

"You? Talk about *timing.* It's been over a year for me, you're one to talk," I whined, refusing to let go of him. The knowledge of being joined at each other's hips came to mind. *Back to being gross and wagging tails.*

"Too fucking long, if you ask me." He trailed kisses down my jaw then to my neck.

The minute he moved his hand to grope one of my boobs, he froze.

"What..." He looked down at them and then up at me.

"I lost...more weight than intended. I was in a deep depression of grief after you...*died,"* I said awkwardly, wiping another escaped tear. Belke sighed, nuzzling my bosom.

"You're still perfect, but it makes me worried that you weren't taking proper care of yourself... Also, *where* are *my* perfect voluptuous breasts?"

I snorted. *What a horny beast.*

"Just because they're not 38DDDs, doesn't mean they're gone. *Calm down.* I'm at a 36DD. One cup size... ONE. *And you lose your mind?*" I shook my head at his ridiculousness.

He grunted, still pouting and I couldn't get myself together on how serious he was being.

"I need to see you and confirm they're the same breasts I know and love, and curse them for disappearing on me, *even by a size.*"

"*I literally can NOT with you!*"

He met my gaze, smirking. "I'm here to worship, remember?"

I sighed in defeat, remembering the lost puppy I once knew. "If you want to have sex with me, it's going to have to wait until we go back to Atlanta to *ritual it up.* Better get to it," I told him, meaning every word. This was no time for games and jokes. *He could wait after everything.*

Not even five minutes, and he was being mushy then went to boob-talk. *This guy...*

He laid his head on my chest, looking off into the distance. "Evil woman... I'll make it happen though. Give me... forty-eight hours?"

I ran my hand through his hair, enjoying the dark softness, yet missing his demon form. "Clock is ticking," I joked, and he huffed a sigh.

"I love you, Bels," I told him honestly and caught a glimpse of his humanity staring right back at me before stealing a kiss.

"I love you, *always,* Becs."

Belke

FORTY

BELKE

Over One Year Ago

I stood at the end of the hall of the Elders.

The hall stretched endlessly in reds, golds, and whites decorating the place elegantly. Not a speck of dust in sight. Polished white stone floors led all the way down to the open circular room at the end.

The open room had a half crescent shape of a large raised ledge that reminded me similarly of Earth's courtrooms from watching movies. The colors matched the hallways, and the Elders wore hooded cloaks of varying colors. No faces, horns, or anything was noticeable, so only other Elders knew who they were. It was more than likely for immunity and security of having friends, because it was known that when you have power, *people will use it against you.*

I had just finished asking them about if I had a mate, and the future of what I needed.

The Elders also held secrets, wisdoms, and powers that

people of our world didn't have. *They knew where and when the portals occurred.*

They confirmed as much, along with Rebecca being my mate. I was given options while also respecting *her* decisions. If she agreed to the bonding of soul ritual, they would write her into their books, so that when she died in her world, her soul would be carried over. Her sisters were included in that, too.

They explained the bonding mate ritual along with marriage. Since I couldn't claim my old identity and my forms wouldn't change, I needed to have Donte change it, and to take Rebecca's last name should Rebecca agree to the marriage.

They also told me of my job duties of killing the rebel dimens back on Earth. I couldn't deny the shock of how forthcoming and honest the Elders were.

So, what felt like mere hours was over a year in *her time.*

I cursed to myself as they began to tell me the rest of what needed to be said.

"Great work, Belke. We are most pleased with your work as always. A portal will be opening at the end of the hallway in ten minutes that will take you back to earth, and you'll be in the same spot you died, so try and make sure you aren't seen by too many humans. If you time things right, it will work out. Do be sure to give Donte the following message: *He has a year from now from whence you arrive, Belke. You are to kill him, sending him here. He'll have important questions of his own, like you. He too has a mate. All he needs to do is look within. He already knows the answers to his questions, if only he'd stop avoiding the truths.*"

I bowed politely. "I will relay the message. Thank you

for your guidance and wisdom, along with the freedom to be reunited with my mate."

"It is as fate intends," a white hooded Elder spoke, continuing onward, "We'll see you again soon. We recommend a painless sleep as a way to go and less messy. Don't let anyone destroy your human bodies, for you'll need the vessels when you return."

I nodded, and it took me a minute to figure out what they were talking about, and by then I had stepped through the portal that looked like a doorway into endless dark, yet it was anything but.

Once I found myself in the same spot I died, I quickly took in my surroundings, thankful it was nighttime. I instantly began running far away from the area, until coming to a sidewalk. I stole a random guy's phone, dialing Donte's number while hoping it was still the same.

The guy yelled and ran after me, but I kept running faster until eventually Donte picked up.

"Hello?" he asked.

"It's me, I'm finally back."

"Damn, brother, it's so good to hear from you. Welcome back. It's been over a year."

"A *year?*"

"Yeah, man."

A whole fucking year, Becs was going to strangle me. I hoped she was still alive and doing okay.

"Fuck," I muttered, quickly adding, "Is Rebecca still alive? Is she still in Atlanta?"

"Yes, alive. Changed, but alive. Her grief over your

death changed her, but no, she lives in Wilmington, North Carolina with her parents. She works at the North Carolina Aquarium at Fort Fisher. Do you need me to come get you? I can only do so much until we figure out what to do with your identity."

"I have a plan; I think I can hitch-hike my way over. I'll be in touch, and don't tell anyone. I'll call you when I'm up there, and then I need a favor."

"Will do. I'll be awaiting your call."

I hung up and placed the stranger's phone on the side-walk next to a random store and began running towards a gas station that I knew semi-truck drivers would be. *That would be my best bet.*

Thankfully, I was right and convinced a stranger to take me with them as they drove to Wilmington. I told them I didn't have any money, but if they wrote their contact infor-mation, they would be compensated. Somehow, they agreed and asked no further questions.

Once we made it to a truck stop there, I asked if I could use their cellphone to call my family and they agreed.

I dialed Donte again, walking away from the driver for some privacy.

"It's me, I'm here."

He sighed heavily with relief. "I'm glad to hear it. Where are you and I'll get you."

I looked around until I found the name of the truck stop and rattled it off to him.

"Alright, I'll be there in twenty. Don't move from that spot."

"Can you wire money to this phone? The truck driver did me a solid without any money or identification."

"Of course, see you soon, brother."

"See you."

Seeing $2000 send over, I sighed in relief, heading towards the driver with their phone.

"Thank you, my ride will be here shortly, and they sent money for the trouble."

They nodded as I walked off and waited after using the restroom and splashing water on my face. *I looked the same as the day I died. Christ, I looked worse for wear.*

Before I knew it, Donte showed up in a white SUV. I hugged him immediately after walking towards him when he got out of the car.

"I've missed you, brother, I'm glad to see you." He hugged me in return.

"Me too. I desperately need a shower and some clothes."

"Consider it done, hop in. Then, I'll drop you off at the spot. You still have a few hours until Rebecca gets off work, so it'll be good timing, and she had a long week already, so Penny and I planned a surprise."

I grinned, happy to hear that he and Pen were closer. *"Perfect. Tell me more."* So, he did. The beach and gazebo. Penny had texted Rebecca, hinting at the idea, and Rebecca agreed to take some time to visit the beach and relax for a bit.

Donte spent the rest of the time filling me in on the past year. It pained me to hear about Rebecca's depression and withdrawal and that she lost weight.

"Thank you again," I told him later after catching up, showering at his hotel, and stealing some casual clothes fit for a fall day on the overcast beach. A white shirt and pants.

"What are brothers for? I'm sure you'd do it for me."

"Always, brother," I returned honestly, which reminded me of how I needed to relay the Elders message.

As I did, Donte steadied himself, gripping the steering wheel as he drove me to the designated surprise location.

"*Assholes,*" he mumbled under his breath.

"I highly doubt it; they were generous enough for me, and at least they said you have another year. *Have you found your mate?*"

"I don't know... Maybe? How the hell am I supposed to know?"

I gave him a knowing look. "You can't lie to me, brother. You know—*look within.*"

Donte rolled his eyes, shaking his head at the word usage repeated from the Elders. "Well, I doubt she wants to be tied to me though. We had an interesting beginning of being a fling. We're good now but mentioning the *m-word* might not be it right now. I don't know... One thing at a time."

I clapped his shoulder. "New beginnings for us both, then?" He pulled into a random driveway.

"I suppose. Beach is right there; give it thirty minutes and she'll be here. Good luck," he told me.

"I think *you* need it more than I do, brother. *Go get your girl.* You deserve happiness too, you know. I promise it will be worth it."

"Whatever you say. We'll catch up later. Go on." He moved his head in the direction of the water, urging me out.

I saluted him, getting out and walking towards the sandy beach to an inconspicuous spot that she wouldn't see me. It was there I waited for *my mate* to finally arrive.

BECS
$(x-$
$\dot{y}^2 = z$
$+a)$
$(y-1)^2$
$\frac{\partial x}{\partial y} = \lim_{\alpha \to \infty} \frac{\Delta x + z}{\partial y - 1}$
$e = \cos x + tg y$
$\sin x$
$\sin \alpha =$
YOU ARE
BEAUTIFUL

FORTY-ONE

BECS

I don't know *how* he did it, but he convinced the person in the place to vacate the premises for a full day for maintenance issues—a water line fix to be exact.

I smirked, shaking my head as we looked at the new décor in the place. Whoever lived there was *plain*. Or they didn't have the chance to decorate.

"This is crazy, Bels," I whispered, feeling like a trespasser.

"Actually, it's not the craziest thing I've ever done, but what we're about to do."

I tracked his movements as he strolled into the kitchen, grabbing a knife off the butcher's block. *Oh wow. Serious-Business-Belke over here.*

I wore a coat covering the red dress I wore with sexy red lingerie underneath for some good ole' razzle dazzle. It was to be our first night together, plus whatever else we were about to do. *I wanted him to appreciate my sexy efforts as it had been a while for me.*

"So, explain to me how this works again?" I asked while

I took off the coat, placing it on the counter. I saw his eyes light up at the red dress that was revealing and spicy.

He didn't say anything for a bit, taking me in fully. I felt myself heat up under his lustful gaze. Sex demon no more, but I knew his tendencies weren't eliminated.

The fact that he withheld himself for over forty-eight hours was *impressive. Along with my own horny self.*

"Sex. Blood ritual. Once we're mated, you have time to figure out what's next."

I considered him with a coy expression of my own, shrugging nonchalantly.

"Alright, horny boy, come out and play." I quickly took off the dress, tossing it, revealing my bustier, garter, and the whole works.

I'd never felt so powerful to see his eyes and form change immediately, stalking after me as I did a slow walk into the bedroom.

This poor stranger's bed. Why did they choose pale linens of all things?

Sitting on the bed that happened to be in the same position as my old bed, I leaned on my hands that were spread out beside me, cleverly crossing my legs.

"Remind me what it means to be worshipped, *Bels.*" Somewhere long ago, I remembered similar words at the start of our journey.

I stared at the sexy demon I knew and loved with his wings tucked behind him. Taking *him* in fully, I let my gaze feast on the wondrous beauty of him. Bronze skin, horns arching away from his handsome face, and canines peeking out slightly. His dark hair was longer and more slicked back. Thick powerful thighs, lickable muscles, and that fat cock on display, ready for my tasting. Can't forget his tail that's hanging off to the side or those claws.

Letting loose a light sigh of the happiness, it was indescribable to finally see him as he was, *unchanged*. I couldn't wait to ruffle his feathers.

"You are as handsome and ethereal as always, *my dimen*," I added as he dropped to his hands and knees, crawling toward me with his tail slightly wagging.

I smirked as he came upon me, pausing and still kneeling.

"I'm yours until the end, *and even after that*," he whispered.

I grabbed his chin with my hand. "Good, because we have a lot of time to make up for, and new oaths to be made. I am yours. You are mine. *You and me, always*," I said with all the love and promise in my soul. A soul he had protected and loved despite all odds.

Releasing his chin, he trailed light kisses over my legs, knees, then upward toward my thighs.

"Open for me and let me taste you."

He moved my legs gently, not rushing anything, although just as desperate and horny as I was.

His claws were out, and it reminded me of cat claws the more I watched him inch closer to me. I couldn't help my sly smile. "I told you that you were a *cat*."

Belke looked up from where he was kissing on my thigh and once he realized I was talking about his claws, he took two fingers and ripped my underwear. I gasped as he pulled them off, throwing the shredded flimsy thing elsewhere. Wouldn't *be needing those, I supposed*.

"My claws are sharp, just *like my bite*."

I didn't even feel it, but I realized my thigh was bleeding from where his claw previously was. Once he noticed, he licked it before leaving a hickey. It was strange, yet somehow sexy?

It was oddly turning me on, but it was probably because he was so close to my treasured pussy located inches away from his face.

I huffed a sigh, remembering I was exposed and bare. "She's ready when you are," I indicated as much, pushing my hips upward towards his pretty dimen face.

His eyes darted towards mine before moving in. "Let me see if you're warmed up enough for the task ahead," he murmured, licking me fiercely without a further thought.

I certainly didn't have any thoughts while I twitched slightly over that tantalizing tongue. He was sweet for taking things slow and making it romantic and sensual... *I was beginning to feel more carnal in my pleasure though.* It had been so fucking long.

"Bels, I love you, and I appreciate you for being slow and gentle, but I've been without you for so long, I need you inside me—*soon.* I don't want to play games. I just wanna be fucked—*by you*—with that fat, lovely dimen cock. *Please.*"

He paused, mid-lick, looking up at me and the handsome sight of it made me groan, flopping back on the bed.

"Is that so?" His hands, careful of his claws, were on my thighs, and that desire plated on his face made me hold my breath in anticipation. He looked as if I was taking his favorite treat away. It made me wet as fuck.

"Let's do things *our way. Where's my BCT?*" I was sitting on my elbows as he tilted his head.

"What's a BCT?"

My look was feline, sitting up fully, cupping his head in my hands that were still between my thighs.

"I'll be happy to tell you and show you just what I mean. A BCT is what I call a Belke *Cock*-Tail. My soul mate has a special drink just for me."

The tail in question raised, taking the form of a second cock. *Oh, thank fuck.*

As soon as he registered what I meant, I was already running my hands along his horns.

"You are absolutely precious. One BCT coming right up." He sounded delighted, amused too, and I found myself on my back as he crawled over me, running his hands up my torso.

"These," he said, nearing my breasts, using his claws to rip the fabric until I was exposed and softly sighing at his gentle hands on me, "Are my favorite. I will oblige in your requests after I taste *these cotton candy pillows.*"

I huffed a laugh as a claw went over my nipple, and not long after, his lips were enclosed around it, sucking and licking the blood he drew.

"Open your mouth, Rebecca," he got out gruffly before continuing with his task, doing the same thing with the other breast and a moan slipped out.

Then, my favorite BCT appeared, and I beamed, whispering, *"My favorite,"* before taking it into my mouth.

An idea occurred to me then. "Let me borrow one of those claws," I told him, pausing what I was doing as he groaned and held one up. Part of me wondered if it would hurt him, but I was careful when I took his claw and used it lightly near the tip of his BCT enough to allow a little blood but not to do any damage. He made a noise, realizing what I'd done, but my mouth was on the spot, sucking and licking.

It was interesting, but who said rituals were *normal* by any means? I heard him hold back a moan himself, and I licked him fiercely, closing my eyes.

"You almost done? My vagina is lonely," I pouted, licking him once more over the cut I made.

Another grunt and he had himself positioned at my entrance. "Is *this* what you want, Becs? I'll happily show you what missed *you*."

"Mhm," I got out as I played with his BCT using my tongue.

I heard a delighted noise echo in his throat, his cock easing in, and I paused briefly to release a moan.

"You're right, *I took too long*," he whispered before scratching my tit again, and began again with his toying.

I sighed through my nose, eyes still closed.

"I want us to say what's on our hearts as we share blood, and you ride me into hellish bliss."

I paused, invigorated, feeling sexual energy surge through me, at least that's what I thought it was, since I was hornier than *hell*.

He snuck his tail away and pulled me with him, sitting up. I climbed into his lap and set him inside me again. He stretched his wings so that we were enclosed in them. I had to resist the urge to run my fingers against them until the time was right.

We sighed out in unison, and I caught his blazing look.

"I'll go first, Bels."

He nodded, awaiting me while slowing our pace.

"I never thought I'd see you again in this lifetime, and I swore I wouldn't let you go if I were fortunate enough to be reunited with you. You came into my life, a blazing set of horns and heat. You protected me, defended me, *fucked me*, and loved me like no other. I'm grateful for your sacrifice, and I love you. Never to be parted again, not even in death, or life. It's you and me, and I'm honored to be your mate. Forever bound to you."

On cue, with tears in his eyes, he held a bleeding wrist towards my lips, and I took it, suckling gently. The metallic taste didn't bother me like I thought it would. His blood was darker than I imagined, but I didn't think anything of it. Blood was blood after all, no matter where you're from. *Dimensional being or not.*

"My turn," I heard his words echo as I released his wrist with my hand that held it, and his arms went around me as mine dove into his hair while I moaned loudly at the hard pump he gave me.

"I was determined to make it back to you. I had a feeling you were always meant to be mine, ever since I saw you in this very same spot. Your sexual energy was consuming, and I knew I'd do anything you asked and follow you anywhere. I love you, and I crossed time and space to ensure I'd make it back to you. You've accepted me, and I'll happily be your house-cat-puppy, as you like to say. Never to be parted again, not even in death, or life. *It's you and me, always.* I'm honored to be yours, *your mate.* Forever bound to you."

My own eyes were teary as he skillfully and swiftly took my wrist, slit it, and put it to his mouth, sucking like a vampire would. I breathed out, feeling a tingle spread from head-to-toe. Then, a sense of euphoria washed over me as we increased our pacing, done with our words.

His wrist was still bleeding, so I took it. Then, I felt his BCT tap my butt cheek as if in warning. I nodded towards him, and he entered my ass with it, using self-lubrication that I'd forgotten about.

I gasped out blissfully as we clutched our wrists to each other, and my free hand went to his shoulder as I cried out in bittersweet agony of finally being reunited with him, filling me full of him *in both holes.*

"You complete me in every sense, now let's finish this, my beautiful mate," he whispered in a heartfelt way that made me release his wrist and he did the same, capturing one another's lips instead.

Clutching him close, he deepened his strokes within, and I was nearly weeping in ecstasy. I couldn't tell as it felt like he was within me as I was within him. Such a lasting bond that was forged in the moment. A strange, new sensation that I couldn't describe, but sex with him was soaring to a new and interesting level.

A sweet release was heading towards me fast, and at the same time, I reached my hand to run my hand over his feathers. Fortunately, it was right on queue as we both called out each other's names, coming hard enough to see stars.

We weren't finished though, not by a long shot.

"That's an interesting mate trick," I said while laying on his chest, tracing circles.

"From my information on mates while I was home, after confirming you were *mine*, I asked. I needed to know how it all worked, the ritual of mating aside. Mates, like empathy, can feel what the other feels, see what the other sees, whether it's in dreams or what not. Such as touch and taste —all the senses are *bound*. Like right now, can you feel how your tracing circles on my chest, *on your own?*"

"I can. It's...fascinating, weird too. But positively *cool,*" I told him in wonder, kissing his chest, before feeling the sensation on me as if he were doing it back to me. Even though he certainly wasn't.

"It's a high sensitivity to each other; we literally are *one soul.* Fascinating, indeed. *I told you before, your soul is mine to keep safe."*

My heart panged at his sweet words that I now knew the full meaning to. "My favorite part though?" I asked sitting up, to gaze down upon him, stroking his face lightly with my fingers.

"What's that?" he asked, and I straddled him.

"*This.* The intensity of sex now. It doesn't even compare to the sensations of before, not that before wasn't anything below five-stars. You know, ten-out-of-ten would and will ride again."

He burst out laughing over my antics, and I joined in. After we eased up on the laughter, I set myself on his *dimen* cock where he was already readily waiting for another round.

"You aren't wrong, though. T*his—you—will always be where I want to be."*

I took a deep breath, inhaling his scent, a name coming to mind.

Bels smells like *home. My* home.

"Me too, Bels, me too."

Belke

FORTY-TWO

BELKE

2 years later

"It's been a couple of years, Becs. Do you want... Are you ready to become what I am?"

Her eyes were so bright while she smiled at me.

Off and on, we discussed it every six months, and I talked about what it was like to be a dimensional being, all about Hell, and did my best to explain any questions she had that had come up in the last two years. Slowly, I could see her doubts and hesitations melt away, as if we weren't mated and couldn't feel everything she did. But I knew, I always knew where her head was at. I couldn't willingly move forward until she was 1000% certain on the next steps.

I glanced over at her in our overly sized bed in our apartment.

"Let's do this, Bels. I'm ready to serve you a RCT. *So, you'll know what it's like.*"

I gave her a deep-bellied laugh, reaching for her hand

for a quick squeeze. "I look forward to it. *I'll take one of those at the start.*"

Becca grinned, let her eyes linger on my human form. "Will you be with me?"

To reassure her of any future doubts from now until the end of time, I nodded. "Of course, Becs. You're stuck with me whether you like it or not. No take-backs."

"Good, because I wasn't *asking.*"

I wiggled my eyebrows playfully and held up two needles so she could see every step of the process beforehand. I told her about what the Elders recommended and that they weren't scary; we'd be meeting with them very soon.

"It's like sleeping; I'll be right beside you, every step of the way. I love you, and I'll see you soon," I shot myself with the needle as her breathing hitched before I did the same to her as we agreed upon, because she didn't feel comfortable injecting herself.

"Donte knows, right? I don't want my family to see any of this and have a heart attack."

Scooting closer to her side, I knew we had less than a minute left as I rubbed against her cheek with mine. "No one will know but Donte and whoever else he tells. It will hit soon, let me hold you in death."

"I love you," she whispered as we turned inward to hold each other close. I kissed her forehead gently.

"I love you, Becs. I'll see you soon," I whispered as blackness swallowed me whole to make the journey home with her.

The familiar red, gold, and white decked out hall of the Elders met my gaze as I followed behind my mate. Even in death, she stood confident and ready, so I trailed behind wagging my dimen tail. I was in my natural form, wings, and all.

Once we made it to the room at the end, Rebecca greeted the Elders with a slight bow of respect as they sat in their seats faceless and cloaked in anonymity.

One of the Elders in a gold cloak spoke then. "Welcome, Rebecca Stone. Matehood is treating you well." Becca grinned in response, glancing back at me and reaching for my hand that I took in turn. I moved to stand beside her with a fond smile of my own.

"Before we continue," the Elder spoke again, "Do you wish to return to earth until you're called here again?"

"Yes," she said without hesitation.

I knew she wanted to be near her parents until they passed and to be near her sisters. Earth was all she had ever known, plus we still had a mission of the rebels to complete.

"Very well. We'll let you work alongside Belke, Penelope, and Donte to finish what was started years ago to bring back balance to Earth. We suspect your sister, Bobbie Jean, to be in league with one of the rebels. We need you four to investigate, and for reassurance if she gets killed, she'll be transported *here*. Kill that conspiring rebel once you find him."

Rebecca nodded in agreement. "I suspected as much. We will bring him down, along with whoever is left of the rebels."

"Then, without further ado, welcome to our world," the Elder went on, waving a cloaked arm of some sort towards her, with no visible hand, and before I knew it, she transformed before my very eyes.

Well, fuck me.

The sight was everything I knew it'd be and more.

I sank to the floor, weeping at her feet, before kissing those very same feet.

She looked down at herself, and she mirrored *me* in looks. Except her hair was way longer, but her eyes were the same as mine. I'd never seen a more beautiful being in my entire existence. She was beautiful as a human but seeing her mirror what I was—*it* made me feel unspeakable, yet pleasurable and heart-wrenching emotions. It wasn't bad, but overwhelming at first sight.

It would be my favorite sight and moment when I saw her as who I was for the first time. The lover of my soul.

"Belke," she whispered, hot tears of joy running down her face as her hands ran through my hair in comfort.

"Enjoy your matehood. A portal back to Earth will open in ten minutes at the end of the hall," another Elder in gold spoke as the crescent row of seats of hooded figures stood in unison.

"Thank you, sincerely," I heard her tell them, bowing before the Elders disappeared instantly.

I held her legs as I wept, feeling far more emotional than ever before.

After a minute of it, a tail tapped me while her claws stroked up my horn. I glanced up into those crystal blue eyes. *Now, I know what she experienced every day when I was in my form.*

"Oh, you're in trouble now. *I have a tail to wag.*"

I laughed as she kneeled, taking my face into her hands.

"I love you, Bels." Her sultry tone beckoned my eyes closed at their master, leaning into her hands. "Are these good tears...or?" she asked hesitantly, wiping them once I opened my eyes.

"Blindingly good. I've never seen a more beautiful masterpiece. Now, I know what it feels to be on the other end, gazing at you with your full naked form."

She looked down, realizing as such. Her dimen figure was identical to mine minus the height and more feminine features with large bronze breasts and a blindingly good looking pussy on display. Her wings were a sight, and I was the first to witness all her dimen splendor.

"How do I put clothes on...?" she asked quietly, and I chuckled at the question while admiring that nude dimensional form that was birthed in existence.

"Just think of what you want to wear, *truly visualize it,* and it will appear. It's easy; I can help this first time, and you can always practice later, my love."

"What should I wear?" She narrowed her eyes playfully, helping me stand up with our hands intertwined.

"*Red.*"

She huffed a laugh, and I imagined her in a cute red dress as our forms changed to human with her dressed in red and me as well with pants and a t-shirt to match while we neared the entrance of the portal leading into blackness.

"I will teach you how to be *a sexy demon,* although *you* don't have to try very hard," I teased her, taking her hand as we hovered near the portal, grinning.

"Oh? *Is that so?*" she asked knowingly, and I could almost taste the delicious promises of what awaited us when we walked to the other side.

"Yes. I'm more than anxious to see the RCT in action and while *I* ruffle *your* feathers, for once."

She hollered with laughter, pausing slightly before glancing toward the darkness beside us.

The arch of the doorway turned into a wall when portal

wasn't active for transport. It seemed the Elders knew the timing of them each time.

"Oh, Bels, *you're in for it.*"

I made an *mmm* noise, and she beamed brighter than the start of the universe and the big bang as we knew it billions of years ago.

"Do you know how long *I* waited to have you in that form? The convention years ago doesn't even compare. *You* will always be in for *my worship.*"

"Well, looks like we're both in for some sexy shit," she said with a wicked smile that I matched.

"Always, *you and me,*" I told her as the low hum of the portal indicated it was time to leave.

Rebecca and I stared at one another, holding each other's hands.

"You and me, Bels, with our horns *and* heat."

"*I look forward to that for the rest of my life.*"

Then, we stepped through the portal back to Earth.

FORTY-THREE

DONTE

One year.

That's what my brother had said. One year to tell her I loved her.

It was long past time to tell her I was serious about her, and that it wasn't just a fling for me. Not just a *friend with benefits*.

I spent this entire time avoiding the truth.

The Elders loved to call me out on my shit.

The sun dipped on Carolina Beach as I stood there, watching the rise and fall of the waves.

I made sure Rebecca was safe during the time Belke was in our home world, and I worked in conjunction with others to hunt the rebels down. I found one in Atlanta the other week, and they leaked information of the leader being on the west coast. There was also the L.A. situation, too.

Once Belke made an appearance, my own clock started counting down. My nerves were fizzled with anxiety and the knowledge that *I was running out of time now.*

The past year was an interesting ride.

Once I saw Penelope at the rooftop party before

Rebecca moved, I made the move to talk to her. She was beautiful, motivated, and charming. Her mouth was worse than her sister's, which I found *delightful*.

I always enjoyed a type of strong woman, even better if they had a sassy attitude, and a no-fucks-given honesty. Most people didn't like it, but I was like my brother. *We liked our women with a foul mouth. An inner fire.*

Women didn't have to be soft and pretty and fit the norms of what the older generations thought. *Absolutely not.*

What I loved was their hearts, their minds, and their opinions. *Their bodies, especially.*

Men were okay, but women really did it for me. My dimen had a sexual orientation that didn't discriminate as people did in my earthly human form.

Their soft sighs when you were doing something right, or the way they clutched and moaned when things were really going well.

Don't even get me started on how women are when they're fucked stupid.

I meant the term in a *devious way*.

When *I* fucked a woman stupid, her brain stopped working and she had no words left. *The sex was that good.* That sexual energy exchange fueled me into what I am from my home world. *Hell.*

I was determined to fuck *Penelope* stupid after conversing with her for hours, appreciating her voice and view of the world. I wanted to know more about her and listen to her speak passionately.

I also wanted that energy directed at me, as it rolled off her in waves. A sexual energy that beckoned me closer, calling to me on an irresistible level.

During the party, I dreamed of her mouth around my cock, and her clutching me as she cried out in pleasure.

She would be mine forever if it were the last thing I ever did.

TO BE CONTINUED.

Donte and Penny's story and more about the demon rebellion will occur in book 2, Horns & Flames.

ACKNOWLEDGMENTS

Firstly, thank you to my beta readers and ARC readers for reading and reviewing, along with a few others who helped me make some finishing touches to this book baby! It's because of you that I keep going, and my undying gratitude doesn't feel like it's enough. (Please hold while I scour the universe for a portal to Hell for a cinnamon roll demon.)

Thank you to Colby, for your feedback and for making these covers for the series! You are one of my ride and dies! 🤍

To Amy, who always gives me honest feedback in nice ways to improve something or when something isn't working right.

To Cali, Adam, and Emily for letting me read aloud for feedback as this book is sweeter and less dark than anything I've written, thank you for reminding me that sweeter reads aren't so bad for the repository of this author.

And last, but certainly not least, thank you to YOU, the reader, who picked up this book and made it to this point. I hope you stick around for Penny and Donte's story and BJ's!

I'll see you at the end of the next book! 🤍

ALSO BY R. N. ARCADIA

<u>The Para-Series</u>

Parasite

Para-Psych

<u>Triad Bite Series</u>

Into the Black

Into the Red

Into the Blue

Into the Fire

<u>Standalones</u>

Poa

Lee

The Misfortunes of Tommelise

Granite & Sugar

<u>Horns & Heat Trilogy</u>

Horns & Heat

Horns & Flames

ABOUT THE AUTHOR

R.N. Arcadia is a neurodivergent, day-dreaming Pisces, living in NJ with their family.

When R.N. isn't working or writing, they enjoy traveling, going to the beach, binge-watching/binge-reading whatever series they find themselves engrossed in, while listening to all sorts of music to stay sane.

https://linktr.ee/r.n.arcadia